A WAVE OF MURDER

• • •

The Maui Mystery Series

• • •

Kay Hadashi

D1520068

Kay Hadashi

www.kayhadashi.com

Kay Hadashi

Table of Contents

Prologue

Kala'keilani fell to the ground, wounded. One of the other warriors knelt next to her, while arrows and spears flew all around them.

"Kala, an arrow!"

"Pull it out, Kulu."

He grabbed the arrow shaft and gave it a tug, causing her to wail in pain.

"It's stuck in bone. If I pull too hard, the tip could stay stuck in there forever."

"I'm close to the gods already, Kulu. Just pull it out."

When the shaft came out from her body, the tip was no longer on it. Kala'keilani felt blood pour from the wound with her hand, learning how close she really was to gasping her last few breaths. She would lose the fight with death, but she wasn't giving up on the fight against the invading army from another island. Struggling to her feet, she followed Kulu forward, closer to the archers that were hiding in the forest before them. While he ran easily over the rough terrain, for her it was a limping advance.

"We need to get their chief, and the only way to do that is to get past those archers and spear throwers," she said.

"How can we do that?" Kulu asked.

They were further ahead of any of their village warriors. Both of them were covered with the blood of the dead they had found, warriors from both sides of battle. But it was her own blood that was saturating her simple tapa cloth skirt.

"We can't charge. We must wait until their arrows are gone. Let them think we're dead. Then we attack." She pointed to a clear area in the trees, the only way they could advance without having to slow down. "Don't stop to fight. Just keep running until you find the chief and kill him, Kulu."

"And the same for you, Kala."

"No, I won't make it this time. There is something wrong with my leg. I won't be able to keep up. It's up to you to kill their chief, Kulu. Do this for our village, for our island."

He looked at her wound, now bleeding profusely. He knew her fate. Touching her face lightly with his bloodstained hand, he smiled the way she liked, the reason she loved him so.

"Your name will live forever in the hearts of the villagers as a proud warrior."

"Don't let the others find my body."

"I'll put you in a place worthy of royalty," he said.

An arrow skipped off the rock and hit Kala'keilani in the shoulder. This time she pulled it out herself and snapped it in two.

"Ready, Kulu? Go!"

They jumped from their hiding spot and charged forward. Kala'keilani couldn't keep up, but she fired the last three of her arrows and threw rocks at the faces of the enemy. She was almost through the enemy line when a spear caught her in the chest.

She went down in a heap. Kulu paused his charge.

"Go, Kulu, go," she told him, blood sputtering from her lips. "Save our island."

After touching her face one last time, he charged forward, never stopping until his spear had been rammed through the chest of the enemy chief. Once his gruesome task was done, he took the red-feathered kahili standard that marked the man as ali'i and returned to his own chief.

Later that night, long after the fighting had concluded and the enemy raiders had been killed or paddled off in their canoes, Kulu searched the field of battle. Dozens of warriors littered the taro patches. The ones that had been found alive had their heads bashed in. Others still had arrows and spears protruding from their bodies. It wasn't until far up the slope toward the mountain ridge that he found Kala'keilani, a spear in her chest along with two arrows. Pulling those free, he laid the weapons on her chest, wrapped her body in the tapa cloth she had been wearing, and carried her up into the mountains. As a child he'd seen caves high in the cliffs, nothing more than small openings in the lava. Not even a trail led to one high on a cliff that overlooked the valley below. It would surely be the perfect resting place for the love of his life.

There was no other way to get her body there but to climb down the rocky cliff. As tired as he was, he begged his muscles to obey his orders, to allow him the strength to cling to rocks and notches barely big enough for his fingertips. When his foot finally touched down on solid rock, he lay her body down. Sitting next to his beloved, he chanted her favorite song for a moment.

"I'm sorry, my love, that I was never a better singer for you." He touched her hair, much of it matted to her body by blood. "You were as graceful as the palms in the breeze when you danced the hula. Such beauty and elegance. That is what I'll remember the longest, even to the day I die, my love."

Kulu watched as the clouds tumbled over the pali, driven by the wind. He could not believe he would never again hear her soft voice, see her easy smile, or sense the warmth of her body next to him. His fists clenched with rage; his body shook with fury.

"No," he said, relaxing. "Not today. No anger for your funeral, my love."

Carrying her dead body in his arms, Kulu struggled to make his way across the perilous ledge to the small cave. Getting there, he lay her body down.

"My love, I will miss you forever, until the gods allow us to meet again."

Pushing her body, he tucked it into the small cave. Once Kala'keilani was hidden and out of the weather, Kulu placed the spear and arrows that had slain her next to her body. He covered her with his tapa loin cloth and hid the entrance to the cave with broken branches and stones.

Turning to face the heavens that hung low over the valley, he raised his hands into the air and called out a prayer for her passage into her next life. He added a curse at the end.

"May anyone who disturbs the sacred grave of Kala'keilani suffer a more painful death than what she has suffered!"

Chapter One

The young man tried taking a deep breath but his ribs hurt too much. His jaw didn't feel so good, either. Wondering if it was safe or if his beating would continue if he pushed up from the sand, he looked at the two men who had assaulted him.

"What happened at the library?" the man with fists of stone asked.

"I tried moving the case but it's bolted to the floor. The glass is thick, like it's break-proof. You'll need something heavy to break in."

"And the museum?"

"That case is locked up tight and alarmed. You can see the wires. Maybe if you know something about disarming museum display case alarm systems, you might be able to get that stuff."

The one in charge, the one with the fists, took the beaten man by the neck. "Don't tell us how to do our work." He tossed him back down again.

"You said you found some stuff up in the hills," the partner in crime said. He always seemed to have beer on his breath. "When do we see some of that stuff?"

"I told you I'd have it for you tomorrow."

"You talk a lot, you know that? You said the same thing last week and again yesterday. How many tomorrows do you think you're gonna get from us?" one of the men asked while looking down at him. "What're you doing here at the beach, anyway?"

"Get some summer surf in. The waves are good."

"Seems to me you'd have better things to do than going out surfing right now."

"Like?"

"Like getting your hands on what we want. Namely, the stuff in the mountains you keep telling us about."

"I keep trying to explain why it's taking so long!" said the young man. "I have to cross private property to get to the trailhead, and there's always someone home."

"How hard is it to sneak past a house? Quit being a dope and just go get the stuff."

He sat up, rubbing his jaw. "Every time I go, they catch me. The last time they were talking about calling the cops."

"The cops! Listen to this guy! Nobody calls the cops because of a trespasser."

"Dude, if you want to make any money in this business, you're gonna have to risk getting in a little trouble from time to time. Learn to talk your way out of having the cops called on you."

The one with the fists gave him a nudge with his foot. "Just tell us where the stuff is so we can go get it ourselves."

"Tell you where I find the stuff? Forget it. I know better than to give away business secrets."

"Yeah, well, guess what surfer boy? You wanna say farewell to your teeth?"

"What's that supposed to mean? Are you seriously threatening me?" he asked, still kneeling.

"Dude, we don't threaten, we promise. We'll give you more like you just got a couple minutes ago."

The young man was outnumbered and outmuscled. He had little choice but to tell the two thieves where they could find ancient Hawaiian artifacts. It was proving too difficult to steal things from museums and public displays, so they had turned to finding it in the West Maui Mountains. Maybe it took more effort to hike the trail that led to the pali, but there was less risk of being caught and more stuff to find. Just a cursory cleaning of it, take a few photographs, and put it up for online auction. The gang of thieves was running a tried and true scheme that had already worked on the mainland with Native American

12

Indian artifacts. But instead of doing the work of finding it for themselves, they'd hired the surfer to find 'historical merchandise'. He decided to spill the beans on the cache of artifacts he'd found.

"Go a mile past the big hospital. There's a house on the same side of the highway, all by itself on the slope. You'll have to park down by the highway or across at the resort, then walk up their driveway. Go past their little garden and you'll find a trail through the grass. Follow that for a couple hundred yards to a gate in a pig fence. That's the tricky part, getting past the house, but it's the only access. I suggest waiting until there are no cars parked there."

"Don't tell us what to do. Just the directions, bro."

"You'll have to hike about five miles up into the forest. Once it gets steep and rocky, you'll be above the koa trees. That's where…"

"Dude, do we look like botanists?"

"Huge trees with giant branches. You'll see bottlebrush trees around there also. Past the last one is where you'll take a tiny path to the left for another half mile. It's hard to see but it's there."

"What's there?" Fists asked.

"Caves, not real big and hard to find in all the brush. I just found a new one that looks like it could have some good stuff in it. There's one with a ledge in front of it. You won't be able to climb up, but climbing down from above is the only way. You'll have to crawl in and use a flashlight if you expect to see anything."

"What's in there?"

"Arrows, spearheads, bones. Best to leave the bones behind. I've heard the Hawaiians are really sensitive about bones in graves being disturbed."

"Who says it's a grave?" Fists asked.

"Yeah. It might not even be a Hawaiian in there," Beer Breath said.

"I've heard that's what the Hawaiian did a long time ago. They buried warriors in little lava tube graves, along with the weapons that killed them."

Beer Breath and Fists looked at each other for a moment. "Think it's worth it?"

Fists shrugged. "If there's good stuff, sure. We might even find some other caves up there."

"There are plenty of other caves up there. Trust me," the surfer told them. "Take a backpack with you, and maybe some rope so you can do some climbing."

"Don't tell us what to do. We've been doing this for a lot longer than you have, bro."

Now that they had what they wanted, Beer Breath and Fists started to walk away.

"Hey! I want to be paid!" the surfer shouted at them. Still grimacing from the pain in his ribs, he pushed up to a sitting position.

"Paid? For what? We have to get the stuff ourselves!" Fists said.

"Okay, just pay me half."

"Sure. Come to the house at midnight. If we find anything worthwhile, we'll pay you half."

"Promise?" the beaten surfer asked.

"We don't want any trouble with some punk that might go to the police, so yeah, we'll pay you. We'll also be done with your help. Don't come back asking for more work."

"Or money!" Fists shouted over his shoulder.

The surfer watched as the two men left him behind, driving away in a pickup truck. He wouldn't be getting much money from them for the information he'd just handed over, but it was cash, something that was in short supply. Maybe best was that

14

they no longer wanted him. Right from the start, he'd been looking for a way of getting out of that little gang of thieving punks.

"Yeah, it's time to go get a legit job. No more of this petty thievery stuff. I'm tired of getting beat up."

A big part of his new lifestyle of living on Maui was surfing. Knowing the surf was at its best right then, he collected his board and walked into the water. It wasn't his jaw so much as his sore ribs limiting his ability to paddle into the surf. Trying to push up and stand when the first good wave came along, he found he couldn't do it. Pressing on the side of his chest where he'd been kicked, he figured at least one rib was cracked. But he wasn't going to waste a good afternoon in the sun. He had a minor victory to celebrate, of the promise of getting some hard-earned cash a few hours later, and freedom from his free-fall into a life of crime.

Continuing to paddle out past the surf line to calmer water, he never realized he caught the receding tide. It wasn't easy, but he got his T-shirt and shorts off to work on his overall suntan. Lying prone on the long board, he let the tension wash away. Soon, sleep crept into his quiet mind.

There was a fair amount of ocean traffic between the Hawaiian Islands. Cruise ships made the rounds from port to port; pleasure craft occasionally took water skiers out to the open ocean to test their mettle; small fishing boats looked for the big game fish of deep tropical waters; even cargo ships loaded with containers coming from the US mainland and from Asian shipping ports found their way to island ports. But none of them would've expected a lone surfer dozing on his board to drift so far out to sea.

The surfer never heard the thrumming engine of the cabin cruiser as it sped directly toward him. When the bow of the boat hit the tail of his board, it flipped him high into the air.

Landing with a belly flop, he lifted his head to gasp for a breath. His cheap rental board was shattered to pieces, none of them big enough to use for flotation. All that was left was the leash that hung from his ankle, swirling in the currents of water. When the boat came around again to rescue him, he waved his arm in the air to let them know where he was. Watching the boat return, it didn't seem to see him, only racing forward on a collision course. He tried ducking into the water at the last moment, but it was too late. The hull of the boat rammed into his head and crushed his chest, ending his surf excursion—and his life.

It was Dr. Melanie Kato's last week at work at the hospital before going on maternity leave. As it was, she was cutting things pretty close by doing long surgeries only days before she was due. Putting the final stitches into her patient's chest, she stepped away to allow her assistant to finish the procedure.

"All yours, Harm. Make the scar look pretty," she said to the Physician Assistant she'd known for more than two decades. She'd come to know him when they both worked as Air Force medics on the Korean Peninsula, and later when he married her best friend, Trinh.

Like in so many marriages, a roadblock was slammed into when Harmon Ellis found his fancy with another woman. But now here he was, apologetic and contrite, and trying to win back Trinh's heart. To do that, he had to go through the overly protective Melanie.

'Harm' had quit his job back in San Francisco and had been hired at the larger of the two hospitals on Maui, where Melanie and Trinh worked. That meant hiring into Melanie's busy surgical practice, not an easy task. Not only was she perfectionistic, but she also held high expectations for everyone else when it came to patient care.

The conniving ways of both man and woman must've worked, because Harm was gainfully employed at the hospital, and wedding bells were ringing on Maui. Trinh and Harm's wedding was planned for two weeks later, with the idea that Melanie would have given birth by then. Everybody likes a newborn baby, especially at a wedding. As long as it's quiet.

"How are the wedding plans coming, Harm?" she asked him before stepping away.

"Fine, it sounds like."

"You don't know?"

"I'm barely in the loop. All I know is that I've been told where and when to show up, and what to wear. Trinh's taking care of everything else."

"The last time I talked to her about the wedding, she made it sound like she was overwhelmed with everything. Maybe you can offer to pitch in a little?" Melanie said.

"I'm already paying for it. Every few days, I get another bill in the mail for something, and I never have a clue what it's for. Then she started making noise about having another kid."

"And that's not in the cards for you?"

"If we had one right away, I'd be in my eighties by the time the kid graduated from high school. If I live that long."

Melanie stepped away and removed her surgical gown and gloves. "So, it's up to you to decide? Trinh and the kids don't have a say in it?"

"I should at least get an equal vote in the deal, have some discussion about it. Relationships are difficult enough, even when things are discussed and decided together."

"Unlike the time you…oh, I forgot. We're not supposed to bring that up anymore."

"I came here to be with Trinh," he said curtly.

"Instead of bickering like a couple of old maids in front of our co-workers, let's save it for another time, okay Harm?"

That brought the topic of past infidelities to a close. Sitting on a stool at the desk in the operating room, Melanie checked her phone messages. She hadn't heard from her husband and three-year-old daughter since early that morning, unusual for them. In the past, Josh had often sent naughty text messages, disguised in their own personal text-speak language, just to say hello. However, since the birth of their daughter, the naughtiness seemed to be on hold. Setting the phone down again, she began to write post-op orders for the patient.

"One more week before Baby Kato joins the family, right?" Ainslie, the nurse, asked.

"It can't come soon enough. Between carrying around a bunch of bananas under my shirt, two sacks of rice on my butt, and having watermelons for ankles, I'm ready to deliver this kid. And forget about trying to contain these cantaloupes in a bra. Seriously, I don't know when I turned into a fruit stand."

"You look great. Very motherly."

"And motherly is code for being built like an offensive lineman."

The desk phone rang and Ainslie gave it to Melanie. "Somebody needs to be seen in the ER."

Melanie tried not to whine. "Now?"

Ainslie shrugged when she handed over the phone to Melanie.

"This is Doctor Kato."

"Melanie, Bob Brown here in the ER. I have something you need to see. How soon can you get here?"

"Five minutes." She hung up the phone, sped through writing orders for her patient, and struggled into her white lab coat that no longer spanned her waist. "Harm, get the patient tucked into the ICU and then come find me in the ER. Ainslie, hold off on setting up for the next patient. We might have an emergency to do."

Pregnant women were nothing new on Maui, long known as the 'bedroom community island' of Hawaii. But when six foot tall, nine months pregnant Melanie hurried down the hall to the Emergency Room, people stepped aside to let her pass. By the time she got there, the bouncing in her belly had turned the ache in her back into a strain. When she pushed through the double doors into the large department, she glanced around.

It was easy to find the most critical patient in any emergency room by locating the biggest gathering of nurses and doctors. This time, it wasn't particularly busy, only a pair of nurses coming from behind a privacy curtain that was drawn in an area typically reserved for children. The looks on their faces hinted at what was hidden behind the curtain.

"What's going on?" Melanie asked them. "Is there an emergency or not?"

"You're about a day too late, Doctor Kato."

Confused as to what that meant, she ducked behind the curtain and found Bobby doing an examination on a man quite obviously dead.

"Bobby, why am I here?" she asked, keeping a full step back from the stretcher. As a clinician, Melanie knew death by trauma wasn't contagious, but as a mother, she was too superstitious to take any chances. It was almost as if the baby could sense what she was looking at and gave her a kick. "Or better yet, why is he here and not in the morgue?"

"Melanie, hi. I'm having every drowning victim brought to the ER for the next few months for an article I'm working on."

"Good for you. It's pretty obvious at first glance this victim didn't die by drowning."

Bobby continued to examine the corpse. "My hamster could've told me that."

"Hamster?" she asked, confused.

"Sorry. I don't know why I said that."

Between spasms shooting down one leg, the never-ending headache due to lack of caffeine, and her aching feet, Melanie had a hard time keeping a civil tongue. As horrific as it was, she couldn't stop looking at what was on the stretcher in front of her. "Why am I involved with your mess of a dead body? Are you looking for a co-author for your paper?"

"Maybe. Your name carries a lot of weight in journal articles."

"Not that anybody ever reads them," she muttered. "Once again, why am I looking at your victim, or whatever that is?"

"There's something about this I thought you'd like to see."

"Bobby, after six years of Air Force Search and Rescue and a dozen years of surgery, I've seen pretty much everything there is to see in a dead body. Maybe you haven't noticed, but I'm about to produce a new kid at any moment, and I'm way too superstitious to be bringing my unborn around a dead body if I don't have to. What's so fascinating about this one that you called me in particular?"

"It wasn't a simple drowning."

"That's obvious. If it was, there would still be more to the body than what I'm looking at. And I gotta tell you, it's turning my stomach, okay? So, get to the point."

"According to police and paramedic reports, his body was found by other surfers just off Lahaina. His board leash was tangled in coral, which they figured was why he drowned, that maybe he'd been dunked a little too hard and hit his head, the leash holding his unconscious body below the surface of the water."

"What happened to that guy is more than just hitting his head on coral. I have enough coral scars on my body to know what surf injuries look like. "Sorry, but those injuries aren't the result of a simple surf accident."

"Right. These injuries are different. He suffered high-energy impacts."

"At least. Then the fish got to him, and maybe a small shark, before he ever got snagged in coral." Melanie tasted stomach acid rise and tried not to retch. "There's too much of him missing for me to make a guess."

"Obviously. Crushed skull to the point of being unrecognizable, flail chest with nearly every rib on one side snapped into pieces. Any of his injuries would've been enough to kill him outright, but it was his broken neck that did him in, not drowning."

"How do you know that?"

"I tapped his lungs and there was very little water in them. That means he died suddenly. He never struggled to take a breath after the impact. The theory about the leash holding him underwater just doesn't work. I think his leash got tangled in the coral long after he died."

"You're playing coroner now?" she asked. "Why not leave the post-mortem to be done in the morgue by the coroner? His body is evidence of a possible crime, Bobby."

He seemed to ignore her. "Look at his chest on this side. All the ribs are crushed, which is consistent with the type of lateral cervical fracture he sustained, and his head injury. There was a sudden and massive impact with something, or something with him."

"And once again, that's quite obvious. It's also best left to the coroner to determine what."

"But look here." Bobby uncovered the rest of the man, making Melanie wince at the sight of his mangled and twisted body. "On the other side of his chest is a bruise, along with one on his jaw."

Melanie finally stepped up to the stretcher, standing sideways to it because of the size of her belly. "And he wouldn't have bruises if these were a part of his accident."

"From the color of them, they look like they were several hours old, but less than a day. I got X-rays, and found that his jaw had a non-displaced hairline fracture on the opposite side of his body as the impact. His lethal impact was on the left, but the jaw fracture and bruise on his chest are on the right."

"Sounds like he got beat up by a southpaw and then went surfing."

"That's why I called you. I know you're an avid surfer, and have been through the ringer a time or two. I imagine you've had a broken rib along the way. Would someone go surfing right after they'd had their butt handed to them like this?"

"Surfing takes a fair amount of core strength, and he would've felt that in his ribs. He was pretty dedicated to go surfing after getting punched hard enough to break a jaw. It sounds like he was in a bar fight yesterday. The swell along Lahaina yesterday was the best it's been in months."

"You keep track of surf reports?" he asked, as he picked up the man's hands to examine the skin on his knuckles.

"I have an app on my phone that gives daily surf reports for the island. How do his knuckles look?" she asked.

"His hands are okay. He didn't fight back."

"Or he was held by someone. But I don't see why being beat up right before going surfing is so interesting? Unless you're thinking he killed himself? He got in trouble, got beat up for it, and thinking there was no way out, he paddled out to the shipping channels to wait for something to run him over? That doesn't make sense. Was his board found?"

"The paramedics that brought him in didn't mention that," Bobby said. "Why?"

"If he was going to kill himself, he could've waited for a shark to find him. If that was the case, his board would have big chomps taken out of it." Melanie continued to keep stomach acid down. "Of all the ways for someone to kill himself, that seems least likely. Seriously, who wants to be eaten by a shark?"

"See? Not so simple as you thought."

"If I was on a little island out in the middle of the ocean and I was in enough trouble to get beat up for it, I'd go to the airport. No reason to risk trouble a second time in the same place."

"I just don't think he committed suicide," Bobby said.

"First, you need to figure out how he got the massive blunt trauma," she said. "And once again, that's the job of the coroner, not an ER doc."

"I'm still trying to figure that out. Look at the shape of this bruise on his chest. Does that look like anything in particular to you?"

She leaned down to look closely at the side of his chest that was relatively uninjured. The dark mark had a well-defined edge, a half circle about the size of a baseball. "Toe of a work boot?"

"That's exactly what I thought," he said. "And the bruise on his jaw is consistent with knuckles on a fist."

"Bar fight, plain and simple." Melanie stood up straight again, trying to keep the look of impatience from her face. "Did you draw labs for blood alcohol or a tox screen?"

"Can't really generate lab charges on a victim brought in DOA. I'd have to pay out of my own pocket."

"Why are you spending so much time on this, Bobby? You said your paper is on drowning, but this is massive trauma. I say, give it a rest and find something better to do with your time, such as curing the common sunburn."

"Aloe."

Melanie sighed. "And again, what does this have to do with me?"

"I thought since you're our chest and vascular surgeon here at West Maui Med, you'd be interested. And since you're mayor of the island, you'd probably get involved in this, no matter how it shakes out."

She flung open the curtain to leave. "I'm missing lunch to look at a dead guy, Bobby. Thanks for that."

"Wait for a sec. I need to talk to his family, but I hate making those calls."

"And you expect me to? Leave it for the police or the coroner. As it is, they've probably already gone to his home."

"Apparently the police haven't positively ID'd him yet. Something about his prints not being in the usual database, whatever that means."

Melanie made a quick call to Ainslie to get the next case started. "Still not our problem, Bobby. Let the police take care of figuring out who he was and contacting the next of kin. Getting involved in something like this when it doesn't concern us is asking for trouble. I'd be glad for your company while eating lunch, as long as you don't talk about dead people."

Being a bachelor, he didn't have much to offer when it came to talking about the only real news in Melanie's life right then, that of her due date in a week. After poking at a salad and picking apart a muffin, she got a call from Ainslie just as she was finishing her meal.

"If you hear any more about your new friend, let me know." Melanie pushed her empty food tray onto a cart. "Bobby, you're new here and right out of training. I know you want to get involved in an interesting case, but I strongly suggest leaving it alone. Just let the coroner manage things with the police. That's something they don't like, is having hospital docs interfere with their investigations."

***

Melanie got her headlight tightened to her head and put on her loupes, along with a surgical mask. She did her scrub-up for her last surgery before going on maternity leave. All she had left were rounds and half a day in the clinic the next day. Then it would be a week of sitting on the couch at home waiting for the baby to come. Somehow, she knew it wouldn't be as simple as that. As Maui's mayor, she had those duties to contend with, along with an energetic toddler daughter and a nervous husband. He wasn't much more than a toddler himself most days.

The last case went more quickly than expected. She was tossing down the last few knots in the slender blue suture that she had used to repair the patient's aorta when Harmon brought up the emergency call.

"What was in the ER?" he asked.

"Nothing. One of our new ER docs is working on a paper about drowning victims and wanted to show me something unusual on a corpse."

"Why isn't the coroner handling it?" Harmon asked.

"That what I asked. The injuries weren't consistent with drowning, though. From what I saw, he had the crap beat out of him, and then got clobbered by a boat while out surfing. Probably rammed by a container ship that never even saw him. Just left him behind without knowing they'd run someone over in the water."

"That's awful," Harmon said.

"Then the fish found him and turned his body into an all-you-can-eat buffet."

"Eww," muttered Ainslie.

"No kidding," Melanie said. "But the odd thing was there were two different sets of injuries. Harm, you remember back in San Francisco, when you were still working as a paramedic and I was in my residency, you guys brought in the scab laborer who'd been kicked and beat up by those union dockworkers?"

"I remember him. Black eyes, split lip, half a dozen broken ribs. Happened on Christmas Eve, right? What a way to spend the holiday."

"Remember the bruises on his chest where he'd been kicked? They were all half circles, the size and shape of half a baseball, matching the toe of a steel-toed work boot perfectly.

Well, the victim in the ER today had the exact same mark on his chest, right over a broken rib. Plus, the classic fist print on his jaw."

"And you think that had something to do with his death?" Harmon asked.

"Bobby does, and I hope he leaves it alone."

As the nurses began a final count of sponges, Melanie started closing the patient's abdomen.

"You know, you look miserable," Harmon said. "Let me close while you write orders. You can meet us in the ICU in a few minutes."

"Yeah, like I feel like walking somewhere." She handed over the suture driver and forceps to him. "Right now, a trip to the bathroom would be like sitting on Cloud Nine."

She broke scrub, tossing the surgical gown and gloves away. After returning from a mad dash to the OR locker room, she sat on a stool and let her long legs sprawl while writing orders. "Harm, once I'm done in the clinic tomorrow, Doctor Wellman will follow my patients."

"I'll lend him a hand whenever I can."

"I know. I doubt he'll need anything. These patients today have been pretty straightforward."

"Only taking a month off to be with the baby?" Ainslie asked.

"Not much choice. Anyway, my mother-in-law is coming to help," Melanie said with a sigh. "Again,"

"Supposed to be another girl, right?"

"Yep, and the last one. If Josh wants another kid, he'll have to form one out of dust from the Garden of Eden. Or wherever Jewish babies come from."

"I thought you were Buddhist?" Ainslie asked.

"I am. So will be the kids. But Josh is part Jew, part something else with a long name. There's also a Catholic hiding in there somewhere. Between his family and mine, our kids are little United Nations." Melanie rubbed her aching forehead. "I don't know what that means."

"Well, once you're done in the ICU, you have to come back here to the OR," Ainslie said.

"More walking?" Melanie thought all day something was at play, and could tell by the sparkle in the nurses' eyes something was cooking. "Why?"

"We have something for you."

"For the baby," the scrub nurse added.

"You guys already gave me a baby shower."

"We were sworn to secrecy but we have something cute for the baby."

"Swearing nurses to secrecy is futile," Harmon said, laughing.

"I'll try to act surprised," Melanie said. "What is it?"

"A little onesie with pictures of tropical flowers all over it and a package of diapers."

"Onesies and diapers I can use. The giant box of stuff I got from my in-laws the other day I'm not so sure about." Before she could go on, her phone rang with a call from Josh. She went out in the hall to take it. "Where have you guys been? I've been sending texts all day."

"Been all over. Mostly at the beach. There was a big deal at Lahaina today. There were cops, and…"

"The death at the beach? Already heard about it. Saw the guy, as a matter of fact. No news there. What's for dinner, anyway?"

"Can we go out?"

"If going out means sitting on the couch, yes."

"Come on, please?" he begged.

"To?" She had a pretty good idea of where he wanted to go.

"The Island Breeze?"

"Our own restaurant?" she asked. "The place we bought from Aki, who bought it from my mom, the same place I worked at while in high school? On all of Maui, you can't think of anywhere more interesting than that?"

"We like it there!"

"But once a week?"

"We need to keep an eye on things, Melanie. Otherwise, the cooks and waitresses will start to slack off."

"Buddy, you keep your eyes off the waitresses, and that new hostess you insisted on hiring. Seriously, it's a physical impossibility for anyone to get any perkier than her."

"And looking at the numbers for last month, her perkiness is bringing in more business."

"We're running a restaurant, not a brothel, Josh." A pang of something hit her, maybe latent pregnancy nausea, maybe hunger over the idea of having a fresh meal. "How's Tay? You've been putting sunscreen on her?"

"And her hat, and she's been drinking water faster than she can whiz it out. I've never met a kid who has to go potty so much as her."

Melanie hurried to the locker room. "Another topic besides peeing, please."

Just as she was sitting in a bathroom stall, her daughter came on the phone. "Hi Momma! Having fun today?"

"Fantastically great fun, as always, Sweetie. I'll tell you all about it at dinner tonight. Put your daddy back on the phone again."

"When will you be out from work?" he asked.

"Give me two hours to tuck someone into the ICU and then waddle through rounds before you pick me up outside the ER entrance."

Two hours later, at least according to her way of telling time while pregnant, Melanie breezed through the ER. Bobby was still there, tapping a pencil on the desk at the nurses' station.

"Would you rather have it busy?" she asked him.

"An appendectomy patient every two hours would be nice. Or a sprained ankle. Even a mild heart attack, something easily managed, just to make the time pass. Sitting around like this makes me nervous."

Melanie chuckled. "And to think you left behind gangster drive-bys and freeway trauma on the mainland to work with us here at West Maui! The most exciting thing we want is an uncomplicated gall bladder or a coral gash."

"Even looking at some kid's tonsils would be more fun than this. Hey, I heard a little more from the police about that vic you saw earlier."

As a doctor, there was nothing she could do about the poor man that had perished in the ocean just down the road from them. As a superstitious woman pregnant from one end of her body to the other, she tried hard to not have interest. But as mayor, she knew she would have to deal with the unusual death of a newcomer to the island. She looked at her watch and noticed the two hours she'd promised Josh had turned into a pregnant three. "And?"

"They ID'd him and called next of kin. His mother is flying in from Arizona later tonight. She wants to see him before they do the autopsy."

That's when Melanie was certain she was going to be involved. "I suppose she's bringing a lawyer with her, ready to sue the county for negligence?"

"All I know is she gets here first thing in the morning and is insisting on seeing him then."

"That victim was something a mother shouldn't see." Melanie rubbed her forehead. She had a clear line of sight out the double door entrance and saw Josh's car parked in the second row back. "Thanks for the heads-up. But once again…"

"Don't get involved?" he asked.

"Right."

Thérèse skipped along next to Melanie, who waddled down the walkway to the restaurant while holding Josh's hand. It was all fun and games until the girl caught a toe and took a fall. Scrambling to her feet rear end first, she kept going as though nothing happened.

"You okay, little one?" Melanie asked, checking the girl's hands for scratches.

"I okay, Momma. Jus' a ghost fall me down."

"A ghost?" Josh asked.

The girl nodded, her pigtails bouncing. "Lady ghost."

"Is this a new game I haven't heard about?" Josh asked.

"Not that I know of."

Not far from their restaurant was the hair salon Melanie normally patronized but hadn't in several months. Another superstition, she tried to avoid the place since becoming pregnant. It was where Thérèse had been born during a tropical storm, and even though she denied it to her husband, Melanie was superstitious about it. When the door opened and her friend Lailanie came out, she couldn't avoid her. The two families had dinner together only the week before, but that wouldn't have satisfied Lailanie's insatiable appetite for gossip.

"Hey, lady. We haven't seen you here in a while."

"Just trying to avoid a repeat of last time she was pregnant," Josh said, tugging at Melanie's hand to keep going.

"Are you going to the county council meeting tonight?" Lailanie asked. "I have a couple things I'd like to bring up."

"Cancelled for this week, probably due to lack of interest," Melanie said.

"Or they're tired of bickering over nothing," Josh added.

"Daddy, what's bibbering?" Thérèse asked.

"Daddy'll explain later." Melanie touched her hair that was gathered in a short ponytail. "I've been too busy to come in, but right after the baby comes, I promise."

"Momma's gonna have a baby," Thérèse said.

"She sure is, and any minute, too!" the hairdresser said, laughing. "Are you sure I can't talk you into something? I'd love to have the company."

"After what happened last time she was in that condition?" asked Josh. "Are you nuts?"

Melanie and Lailanie both laughed.

"What's so funny?" Thérèse asked.

"Nothing, little one," Melanie said. She looked at Lailanie and almost wished she could risk going in, even if just to sit in air conditioning and have a long gossip session. She had an unexpected free evening and didn't want to open the 'care package' that had been sent from Wyoming by Josh's parents. Being doted over was much more appealing than trying to act interested in what would surely turn out to be a box of junk. "Wish I could, but we have our usual dinner plans at our usual table in the usual restaurant."

They watched a young couple dressed like wealthy tourists come out and walk away, hand in hand. When they were out of earshot, Lailanie said, "Oh, yeah. Got to keep an eye on the place, otherwise the help makes off with the profits."

It was Josh's turn to laugh. "There are profits?"

The hairdresser held Melanie behind while Josh and Thérèse went in the restaurant. "Just come by to chat for a while after dinner. It's been dead quiet all day and I'm here until closing this evening. No reason for Josh to be so protective, just because I need some fresh chitchat."

The tic in Melanie's eye hit for a moment. "As much as Josh is overly protective, I'm a little concerned about going in right now."

"Yes, good ol' superstitious Melanie Kato. If it's any help, I'll cross myself and say three Hail Marys before I start."

"What did she want?" Josh asked suspiciously once they were seated at what had become their personal table whenever they went in.

Melanie hid behind her menu. "Just asking about the baby."

"More like looking for gossip."

"Yeah, so? What's wrong with woman gossiping about each other?" Melanie said from behind her menu. "Not talking about you."

"You're not going in there, not right now. We got lucky the last time. Let's not press that luck, okay?"

"Lightning doesn't strike in the same place twice, Josh."

"No, but hurricanes do. And one is due here next week, exactly on your due date."

"It was a tropical storm." Melanie put down her menu. "Clear skies out there today. Anyway, I'm just going in for a while to keep Lai company until she closes this evening. It'll be nice to talk about something besides hospital or pregnancy stuff."

"She's looking for something to gossip about."

"And again, so what?"

"I don't trust her," Josh said, shifting nervously.

"Be real careful about that, buddy boy. Lai's one of my best friends."

"Can I come?" Thérèse asked.

"It's big girl stuff to talk about, Sweetie. But you and I get to spend a whole month together, starting tomorrow after I get home from work."

"Yay!" The girl's face curled into a frown. "How long is a monf?"

"Four weeks. Just you and me and Daddy, and pretty soon, a brand new baby."

"Actually, I'll be teaching five days a week this quarter. They just added another class to my schedule this year," he said.

Melanie glared over the top of her menu. For some reason, she was still determined to keep their spats hidden from their daughter. "I was hoping you'd have more time at home, not less, at least for this quarter."

"We'll have the nanny five days a week instead of just three. It'll work."

"Except we don't have a new nanny yet. The other one quit because..." She looked at her daughter for a moment, innocently playing with her napkin. "...it got a little too weird."

"If you ask me, the nanny was the weird one, not us. She wasn't so trustworthy, either."

A plate of fresh vegetables was brought for Thérèse when Josh's meal and Melanie's salad were brought to the table. She shared her dressing with the girl, for something to dunk carrot sticks and broccoli florets into. Just as she was fixing her salad the way she liked it, Melanie's phone rang.

She had five ringtones altogether. One was for Josh, one for Trinh, one for the hospital, one for official mayoral duties, and one for everyone else. This one was from someone looking for Melanie Kato, Mayor of Maui County.

"Yes, sorry to disturb you, Doctor," the man said with a heavy local accent. "My name is Keanu Kalemakani. I'm assisting in the police investigation concerning some stolen Hawaiian artifacts."

"Hi, Keanu. What can I do for you?"

"It sounds like the county council meeting has been cancelled for this evening?"

"That's the message I got earlier today, yes. Why?"

"Well, I think we might need to hold it anyway."

There went her evening off. "For?"

"Like I said, I've been investigating the theft of stolen Hawaiian artifacts from the local museum. Something else was stolen from the library, and today one of the police crime techs searched an online auction site that deals in historical artifacts. It appears those items are available for public bidding. This is something that needs to be discussed, and maybe a task force set up to prevent any further thefts or trafficking."

The theft of Hawaiian historical items was a serious offense, a felony, as serious as the theft or removal of Native American Indian artifacts from tribal lands. There were few remaining artifacts to begin with, as the Hawaiians had been simple in tool making and had no real concept of private ownership. When the missionaries came to the islands, they often burned items they believed were used in religious ceremonies. What few things remained were considered cultural treasures.

"I see. Yes, we should get something started. I'm eating my dinner right now, but I can be in Wailuku at seven o'clock, the usual time."

"What?" Josh asked, after she ended the call.

"Council meeting is back on."

She called Trinh, her Vice Mayor, best friend, and next-door neighbor, to let her know the usual Thursday meeting would be held after all.

"Can't it wait until tomorrow? Harmon and I are doing last-minute plans for the wedding, Mel."

"I wish it could wait." Suspecting something else was going on right then at Trinh's house, maybe practicing for their honeymoon with Harmon, Melanie explained what the meeting was about.

"Sure. I have nothing else better to do than go to town this evening. Me and the kids can skip dinner, just so I can go play junior politician to a cranky lady mayor."

"I'm not that bad, am I?" Melanie asked.

"Your crankiness increases exponentially with your level of pregnancy. You didn't know that?"

"Been a little detached lately. Maybe Josh mentioned something. Tell you what? I'll stay up with you later tonight to work on your wedding dress."

"When was the last time you sewed a dress? Mel, you're a wonder at suturing aortas and hearts, but you suck at sewing clothes. Sorry."

"Yeah, I kinda do." Melanie tried remembering why she was on the phone but got lost in her thoughts. "Why'd I call you again?"

"Hello? Earth to Space Cadet Kato! The county council meeting in town this evening. What time am I picking you up?"

"We're at the Island Breeze and judging by the look on his face, Josh looks like he'd rather I leave right now."

"I'll come get you. Just make sure you use the bathroom before we leave. Honestly, I've never seen anyone go to the bathroom as much as you do."

After the call, Melanie called Lailanie, cancelling her gossip session until another day.

"You're having the meeting anyway?" Lailanie asked.

"Unfortunately. What did you want to bring up?" Melanie asked.

"I want to talk about traffic. Maybe it's time for some speed traps again, just like a few months ago."

"But Lai, you got caught in one of those traps, remember?"

"Yeah, and it worked. I drive a lot slower now. The traffic along this side of the island is nuts, Melanie. Something needs to be done."

"How late will you be?" Josh asked once Melanie put her phone away.

"Probably won't be as long as usual, maybe just an hour. There's no old business to discuss, just something new."

"Which is?" he asked while walking her out to the parking lot to wait for Trinh.

"I don't know much about it. It sounds like there've been some thefts of historical artifacts on Maui and they're turning up in online auctions."

"That's too bad. I can see why the police want to discuss it."

"The detective is part Hawaiian, about as much Hawaiian blood in him as you'll find in anybody in the islands. He's taking it personally, but I would too if someone was stealing part of my heritage and selling it to the highest bidder. Lai wants to talk about traffic."

"Maybe she should learn to mind her own business?" he said.

"Traffic is everyone's business, since we're starting to have more accidents lately."

"I bet you anything there's more to it than that."

"Yeah, and you know what?" Melanie stopped her rebuttal when Trinh pulled up. She struggled to bend down low enough to kiss her daughter. "Be a good girl, okay?"

"Mel, you look like you're gonna explode," Trinh said as she drove along the highway into Central Maui.

"I feel like it. I wasn't so miserable with Tay, and I'm having trouble with my back."

"Still? That's been going on for a while. You stand all awkward in the OR," Trinh said. She was an operating room nurse that often worked with Melanie.

"Sort of hard to reach the patient, and standing sideways makes me bend in odd positions for too long. That's aggravating something in my back that's turning into sciatica, which is the last thing I need right now."

"Same side was where you got shot in the rump?"

"Yeah." Melanie squirmed to find a better position so sit. "I haven't been able to do my physical therapy or yoga for months."

Instead of discussing Trinh's upcoming wedding, they talked about Melanie's pregnancy, due date, and her plans for being induced when that day came.

"No surprises this time?" Trinh asked, just as she was pulling into the small parking lot behind the city hall and county building in town. "Takes some of the fun out of giving birth."

"For once, a Kato woman is going to give birth in an organized manner, and not in some mad dash to the finish line."

Trinh laughed. "As if that's going to happen."

During the meeting, Melanie, Trinh, and two other council members listened intently to Detective Nate Nakatani as he read from his notes, filling in for the other detective.

"From the museum, the feather kahili has been missing since two days ago, and two shark tooth battle axes were stolen last night. The library was the first place to be hit, losing the spear that has been in its glass case for so long. All said items are already receiving bids at an online auction site."

"That spear had been there since I was a kid," Melanie said. "They just broke the case? Did they take anything else?"

"Both times, they disabled the building alarm, jimmied the lock at the back door, and broke the case with a heavy implement, probably a baseball bat or tire iron. Took nothing else from either place. They knew what they were doing though, by disabling the alarm systems."

"You said they've been found online?" Melanie asked. Her stomach was grumbling for food, not getting much of her salad earlier. She tried to drown it by swigging from a bottle of water. "You're sure they're the same items that were stolen?"

"Yes. Our crime techs were able to match official museum digital photos with what's displayed at the website, finding several markers that indicate a perfect match."

"We can't just buy them and have them returned?" Trinh asked. "I know it only allows the crooks to profit, but those things belong here, not in someone's home who will never appreciate them the way local Maui people do."

"Actually, we discussed that, but the bids are already high, too high for us to compete with. It seems Hawaiian artifacts are hot stuff to collectors these days."

"What site?" Melanie asked.

"Artifacts Empire dot com," he said.

She jotted a few notes. "Okay, I heard something about a task force?"

"I'd like to bring someone over from Honolulu who's experienced in this sort of thing. I hope you don't mind, but I gave HPD a call earlier today and asked around. They have someone available," Detective Nakatani said.

"Isn't Honolulu Police Department where you got your start?" she asked.

"Yeah. Me and the missus decided to bring the kids here to raise. Only been here a few months."

"Glad to have you. How long do you think your investigation will take?"

"Hopefully just a few days. Talking to that HPD detective, he can bring some fakes with him, something they used in a sting a while back when they heard rumors that the Bishop Museum might get broken into. That's what I want to do, is set up a sting, by putting the fakes in display cases, aim a dozen hidden security cameras at them, and wait outside."

"You think it'll work?" Trinh asked. "They won't have moved on to another island? How do we know they'll hit the same place a second time?"

"That's how a sting works, by setting it up to make it seem like easy pickings at the same place, too easy to pass up. But yes, eventually they'll likely move on to a different island."

"Do we have money in the budget for an extra officer?" Melanie asked. It didn't really matter much, since she had a secret sugar daddy for budget overrides. She wasn't telling the police department that, though.

"For a few days. If it lasts longer than that, we'd have some serious shuffling to do. Even that leaves us one officer fewer to provide security the next time we have a major sporting event come to the island."

"What's your precinct commander think of the idea?"

Nakatani shifted his weight nervously. "I haven't actually talked to him yet. I still don't know my way around the precinct."

"You want me to talk to him? I know him quite well."

"I'll talk to him first thing in the morning, but he might be calling you about the cost overruns," he said.

"Actually, for something like this, he probably wouldn't mind getting a call tonight. He's that way. But whatever happens, please give me an update every evening on the investigation. These artifacts are too important to Maui, and to Hawaii, to let go."

When Nakatani sat down ending part of the meeting, Lailanie popped up like bread from a toaster.

"Mrs. Esposito, welcome back to the county council meeting. How may we help you?" Melanie asked her friend as formally as she could. She tried to smile but put more energy into tapping her pen on her legal pad.

"There are too many speeders on the highway from Kahului to Lahaina. I think we need more police along that road. More tickets would slow people down."

"As we just discussed a moment ago, the department is already stretched thin," Melanie said.

"If the police wrote enough tickets, wouldn't that pay the salary of an extra officer to patrol along that road?"

Melanie could feel Trinh's eyes burn into her, along with the other two council members. Even Nakatani looked up for her answer.

"The budget is an issue, but it's also about finding qualified applicants to join the MPD. I'd love to park a patrol officer at each end of the road and let them write tickets all day long, but we just don't have enough officers. The council is always open to suggestions on how to attract more officers from neighboring islands, or even from the mainland, to live and work here. That's what Detective Nakatani has done. Moved his family from Oahu to here. But if we take from them, that leaves a hole in their department. With increased crime and heavier traffic, we just can't keep up. And with our high cost of living and low wages, it's hard to attract people from the mainland. As it is, MPD is starting an important investigation with only two detectives, and one is on temporary loan from Honolulu. In fact, a couple of the detectives are working overtime as patrol officers. I'm afraid if they put in too many hours, they risk exhaustion, which is never good in high-stress occupations. But like I said, if the public has suggestions on how to attract and retain qualified police officers, we'd like to hear them."

Detective Nakatani seemed satisfied with Melanie's response, even if it was canned.

"What can we do?" Lailanie asked.

"Drive safely." Melanie looked around at the few people who had shown up for the weekly meeting. "Any other business?"

When she saw everybody looking at phones or picking at their nails, she adjourned the meeting.

Trinh scooped up her papers and tucked them away on her briefcase. Melanie did the same but was stuck in her chair, unable to push back from the table. That only allowed Lailanie a chance to come in for an attack.

"Lai, there really isn't more I can tell you. If I had more officers, I'd put an extra one on patrol on the west side of the island, and another on the east, overlapping them in Central Maui. But MPD just doesn't have the personnel for it."

"It's okay. I got the answer the first time. I was wondering if I should put you on my schedule for tomorrow?"

"Oh, yeah, in the afternoon, I guess. I'll call in the morning to let you know a good time."

Lailanie looked at Trinh in the way she had that didn't allow someone to escape easily. "What about you, Trinh? Am I doing your hair for the wedding?"

Melanie looked at her friend for the answer, also curious. Trinh had had good luck and some bad in Lailanie's salon over the years.

"The last I heard, the wedding was off."

That stunned Melanie. "Huh?"

"Oh, well, maybe you should come in anyway, and bring the pregnant lady with you," Lai said.

"What do you mean, the wedding is off?" Melanie asked as Trinh drove them home.

"Harmon said he was troubled about something. Personally, I think he has cold feet."

"He didn't the first time you guys got married. What's the problem now? Is he…"

"He denies he's seeing anyone else."

"What do you think it is?" Melanie asked.

"What's the saying? Why buy the chicken when he can get the eggs for free?"

"Not sure that's how it goes, but I get the idea," Melanie said. "So, keep your eggs to yourself for a while. See if that makes him pay a little closer attention to the ring on your finger."

Trinh held up her left hand and wiggled five bare fingers. "Gave it back."

"Wow, it really is off. Sorry."

"Not your fault."

Melanie tried shifting her position but couldn't push hard enough with her legs to get much movement in her rump. Even with that little effort, she got a jolt down her leg. "Maybe it is. I kinda got into him for a moment at work today. He said something about you wanting another baby, and that seems to have put him off his oats."

"You think I should?" Trinh asked.

"Have a baby? No."

"Why not?"

"Because you just asked if *you* should have another, not if *we* should have one. Harm said just about the same thing, almost wanting to hold a vote on it. Maybe I'm old-fashioned, but don't you think it should be a team effort? That both of you should want one?"

"This coming from the lady whose kids both came as surprises," Trinh said. "By the way, did you get the onesies from the nurses at work?"

"And enough diapers for twins. Remind me to send a thank you note."

"You do realize your delivery room is going to turn into a party once they hear you're in labor."

"I get that idea. Don't they have anything better to do than gossip about me?" Melanie asked, watching as their shared driveway loomed.

"Not really. Think about it. You're one of the busiest surgeons at the hospital, you're our mayor, and you're on your second kid since you started working there. Plus, you're the second generation of Kato to work at West Maui Med. The place would be boring without you, Mel."

"Great. What happens when I stop producing kids for them to chat about?"

"You'll have to go back to dyeing your hair weird colors."

As soon as Melanie was home from the meeting, she went to Thérèse's bedroom. She expected her to be asleep already, snoring away. Instead, she was playing with her stuffed green dinosaur toy. She sat on the edge of the bed.

"Why are you still awake, Sweetie?"

"I dunno."

"Maybe because you're playing with your new friend? What's his name again?"

"Mister Crumpet."

Melanie took the toy for a closer examination. "Hello, Mister Crumpet. My name is Melanie. Why aren't you and Thérèse sleeping now?"

"Mister Crumpet is worried about stuff."

"Like what kind of stuff?"

"You and little sister. Daddy. Auntie Trinh and Unca Harmon. Peeschool."

Melanie smiled, trying not to laugh at her daughter's clumsy pronunciations. "*Preschool*, not peeschool. It means the school you go to before starting regular school."

"I no gotta go pee there?"

"Only if you have to and you ask the teacher first. Why are you worried about little sister? She's not even born yet."

"I seen other babies. She gonna be so small. What if something happens to her?"

"That's why she has me and Daddy to take care of her. And Auntie." Melanie hated the idea of laying a guilt trip on her daughter at such an early age, but didn't know how else to make Thérèse feel included. "And you. You'll be really important to her. You'll be a good big sister, right?"

"I don't know. I never been a sister before."

"Well, most of the time it'll be really easy. Daddy and I will help you. Why are you worried about Daddy?"

"Cuz he's always worried about stuff."

"Well, you let him worry about his stuff. He's pretty smart and knows what to do." She gave Mr. Crumpet back and pulled the blanket up to her daughter's chin. "Why are you worried about me?"

The girl shrugged.

It was a struggle to get into the right position on the girl's single bed, but Melanie lay down next to Thérèse. "Come on, you can tell me."

"No wanna hurt your feelings."

"Oh, I see. You better tell me anyway. We can't keep secrets from each other."

"Cuz you're different now," the girl whispered.

"Different how?"

"So big."

"Because I'm pregnant. I've got baby Sofia inside of me. When she comes out, I'll be back to normal. I promise."

"You no like baby Sofia?"

"What? Why do you think that?" Melanie asked.

"Not so happy these days. Maybe you'll leave her behind someplace."

"Don't think things like that. I like her just as much as I like you and Daddy. Nobody is going to leave her behind. Not ever, okay?"

The girl nodded her head while yawning. She had bad breath and Melanie knew why. She felt the girl's neck under her jaw.

"Now, what I want to know is how you got Mister Crumpet off the shelf? You're not able to reach that high. Did you use magic?"

"Maybe."

"What's our promise about you using your magic?"

"Not supposed to," the girl said, yawning again.

"And it's a secret from everyone else, right?"

Thérèse nodded.

"So, no more magic, or there's trouble. Promise me, little one."

"I promise."

The girl was soon asleep, leaving Melanie to find a way off the bed without jostling it around too much. Turning lights off as she went through the house, she found her husband in the bedroom.

"Tay needs her tonsils out," Melanie said while Josh unbuttoned her blouse in back.

"Or a soundproof room. That's why she's snoring so much?"

"Her nodes are swollen and her bad breath means her tonsils are ripe."

"I can take her to the pediatrician tomorrow," Josh said, now unzipping Melanie's skirt in back.

"Thanks. Maybe there will be time to have them taken out before she starts preschool." She sat on the bed knock-kneed and breathing hard, just from undressing. "I need to stalk with Trinh this evening for a while. Can you survive without me? Or are you worried we might gossip about you?"

"Funny," he said sarcastically.

"Actually, it's not. She needs an ear to talk to."

"I'll muddle through without you somehow. It sounds like she's having some anxiety over the dress," he said.

"If we get as far as getting the dress on her. The wedding might be off again."

"No surprise there. That's how many times they've called it off?" he asked.

Melanie began changing her clothes in slow motion. "Four in as many months. Even Tay is picking up on a vibe between them."

"But you're going to help her work on the dress anyway?"

"Love springs eternal, or whatever crap the greeting card companies are feeding us these days. Sorry. Extra grouchy today."

"I don't know why. You're only forty-seven months pregnant, you do surgery inside people's chests, and you're mayor of three islands and the state's second most populated county."

Melanie pulled an old pregnancy T-shirt over her head, trying to adjust the fit over her belly. "Don't remind me."

"I've never understood all the nerves over a wedding dress."

"All brides are anxious over their wedding dress, even if they're marrying the same guy for the second time. It's the only time we'll ever wear it, and of any moment of our lives, we want to look our best. But how'd you know she's anxious about the dress?"

"Oh, just from helping her with it earlier. She's lost a lot of weight."

Melanie turned around to look at Josh. "Just exactly how do you know she's lost weight?"

"Like I said, from helping with her dress."

"Helping how? When was this?"

"Today, while you were at work." He stopped talking, a look of panic spreading over his face.

Melanie cocked her head. "Just exactly what did the two of you do while I was at work?"

"She, well, wanted my opinion on the dress, and needed those things, what are they called? Tucks made here and there."

"You made tucks in her dress with pins? Where at?"

"Over at her house."

"Where was Tay when tucking and pinning were going on?"

"Thérèse came with me but napped."

"I meant what part of the dress?"

"Oh, uh, around the waist, I guess. And I think the other part is called the bodice."

She walked over to stand right in front of Josh, who was perched on the edge of their bed. She stuck a finger in his face. "You stay away from Trinh's waist, her bodice, and every other part of her, understand?"

She left her side of their adjoined homes and went around to Trinh's front door. After greeting the two younger kids and getting an update on the eldest's news from being to college in Honolulu, they got started on looking at the dress spread over Trinh's bed.

"You doing okay, Mel?"

"Yeah. Just have a lot of things on my mind. Why?"

"You're breathing hard, like you just got through swimming a race."

"I think it's just the baby pressing on my diaphragm."

"But you've already dropped," Trinh said.

"Maybe there's a basketball player in there. I'm collecting so much water lately, I think I've gained twenty pounds of it in just the last couple of weeks."

Trinh took a look at Melanie's ankles. "You're really puffy. Your face, too."

"Just what I wanted to hear."

"Take a diuretic. I think I have some in the bathroom cabinet."

"Forget it. It'll drain when it's supposed to."

Trinh sighed. "Good ol' Melanie Kato. You can prescribe the stuff for your patients but won't take it for yourself. At least go see your doctor."

"I see my OB tomorrow afternoon. I'll do what she tells me." Melanie eased down onto the bed, trying to recline, but only flopped onto her side. With Trinh's help, she was able to sit up again. "Trinh, can you do me a favor and not ask Josh for his help with your wedding stuff?"

"I thought something was up when I heard my name mentioned through the wall, sorta loudly. Is he okay?"

"Not bleeding, anyway."

"He mentioned about helping me with my dress today?"

"Of course he did. Getting info out of him is easy. I wish he wouldn't tell me half the things he does. But until I stop looking like the before picture for diuretics, and you looking like you're ready to swim in the Olympics, could you keep your distance from him, please?"

"So touchy. Just like last time."

Melanie rolled over onto her back, letting Trinh stuff a pillow behind one side of her rump to prop her up a little. "I can guarantee this is the last time I'm doing this pregnancy business."

"Not gonna try one more time? Try for a boy?"

"Forget it. Girls are all Kato women are able to produce. There hasn't been a boy since my grandfather was born."

"Yeah, well, nature has ways of changing people's minds." Trinh set aside the fabric for her dress. "Speaking of changing minds, you think I'm doing the right thing?"

"Marrying Harm?" Melanie asked, not surprised with the question. They were covering old ground. "Or calling it off?"

"What's the point, you know? Not really sure if I love him. Sure, he's the father of my children, and I get the hots for him sometimes, but I just don't have the same feelings for him I did a long time ago."

"So, don't get married."

"But the kids are getting a kick out of seeing their mom and dad get married."

"Get married, then."

Trinh flopped down on the bed next to Melanie. "Think he'll do the same thing again?"

"Cheat on you? Maybe."

"That doesn't help, Mel."

"Well, maybe he won't. How the heck am I supposed to know?"

"Okay, that's it. I'm cancelling the wedding completely. Nothing wrong with just being friends with benefits, right?"

Melanie gave her friend a thumbs-up. "Right. Friends with bennies every Saturday afternoon, and sometimes again in the evening."

"You know about Saturdays?"

"Thin walls, Trinh. We can hear you guys fooling around as easily as you can hear me bitch at Josh."

"Really?"

"Honestly, I don't know what makes you giggle so much."

"I do not!" cried Trinh. "Can we please discuss the meal selections?"

"I thought you were cancelling?"

"Changed my mind again."

"Okay, one chicken, one fish, and one vegetarian selection. Saffron on the chicken, ginger on the fish, and raspberry vinaigrette on the salad for us vegetarians."

"How do you know what goes on chicken and fish?" Trinh asked.

"Believe it or not, I listen to you nurses talking in the OR. It's always broiled saffron chicken, seared ahi with ginger, and ras vinaigrette."

"You make it sound boring. Maybe I should just serve Spam with rice."

"You could do that."

"Are you even listening to me?" asked Trinh, beginning to make notes.

"Yeah. Why would a guy go surfing right after getting the crap beat out of him?"

"Huh?"

"A guy was brought in today that was beat up, then went out surfing, only to get hit by a boat or whatever. No water in his lungs. Dead instantly from a massive head injury. Found him submerged in the reefs at Lahaina, his board leash caught up in the coral, but no board."

"His lungs were empty but he was submerged? That means he was dead before he got wound up."

"Right. Probably dead instantly when he was struck before drifting for a while, maybe as long as a day before he was found. Fish had been nibbling at him for a while."

"Poor guy. Why was he brought to the hospital?" Trinh asked.

"That new ER doc, Bobby Brown, is doing an article on ocean drownings. He was all jacked about this victim, trying to figure out what happened even before the autopsy is performed."

"That would be a rotten job to have."

"No kidding," Melanie said, yawning. "The victim's mother is coming and wants the coroner to hold off doing the autopsy until after she sees his body. He can't look much worse than what I saw of him today."

"Well, forget about chicken or fish for the reception," Trinh said, scratching those off her list.

"Sorry. Are you going to try on the dress?"

Trinh stripped to her undies and stepped into her dress. "I think some of these tucks Josh…some of these tucks are a little too tight. What do you think?"

"It's nice. You can't gain any weight before the wedding, though, or you might have a wardrobe malfunction."

Trinh tried looking at her back. "Malfunction where?"

"Pretty much everywhere."

"That's what I get for trying to repurpose my first one."

"Why not just use one of my mom's dresses? She was shorter than you, but you're skinny enough to fit into them."

"You think she'd mind?" Trinh asked.

"She's been dead for more than twenty years. I doubt she'd mind. Anyway, she was your mom for a while, too. Stepmom, anyway."

"What about that one she wore when she married my dad?"

"Yes, the wedding in Spain. That didn't really look like a wedding dress. What about the one she wore to marry my dad?" Melanie asked.

"The wedding at the California hacienda, or the one in the White House?"

They both laughed and said in unison, "The White House wedding!"

"Seriously, that one was a pale peach color, super pretty. I tried putting it on once but there was no way I could ever fit my figure into that dress. You and Mom just never had hips or boobs. Pearls and an updo and you'd totally rock that dress."

"I still can't believe my stepmom was married to the President, and then married my dad, a grocer."

"Add up all five of her marriages and she barely had one complete marriage. Such a weird family," Melanie muttered, now looking at one of Trinh's bridal magazines. She stalled at one picture in particular.

"Five? She was married to your dad twice and then my dad."

"There was another that didn't last very long when she was super young that nobody is supposed to know about, and one other in between the two times she was married to my dad, also something nobody is supposed to know about. I'll tell you about those some other time. She was totally fickle, but when she was married, it was the real thing and with all her heart. That much I know." She handed the magazine to Trinh. "Look at that."

"Pretty dress, but I don't have the time to have something like that made. Wait, is that…"

"Yep. A long time before I ever came along. I still find old pictures of her and Auntie Amy in fashion magazines sometimes. Just recycled pictures of older styles that have become popular again. I wouldn't have recognized her except for her dimple."

"Your mom was so pretty."

Melanie took the magazine back to look at the picture again. "Yeah, Mom was something else. But hey, I need to go home pretty soon."

"Tomorrow is your last day, right?"

Melanie helped Trinh out of her wedding gown. "Half day in the clinic, then I'm free for four weeks. Tay and Josh have all these plans for us, but I'm planning on staying home with the baby the whole time."

"You've decided on Sofia for her name?"

"Sofia Kailani Junko Kato-Strong."

"Another United Nations kid," Trinh said, just as Melanie was leaving to make the short walk around the house to her own back door.

Josh was on the couch in the living room watching TV, with all the lights on. Melanie went around the room turning most of them off.

"Feeling frisky?" he asked when she settled on the couch next to him.

"Saving money on the light bill."

"Oh, so you're not feeling in the mood?"

"I can barely move, Josh. What could you possibly expect?"

"I remember last time we made it work."

"Because we were trying to induce. We'd heard some old wives' tale about nookie bringing on labor. But right now, I'm trying to hold off one more week, then I'm letting my OB induce, and that's after I've been admitted to the hospital and have my epidural put in, not a moment sooner."

"Not that you're an old wife, but that trick didn't work last time, right?"

"No, nookie didn't work. Neither did eating raw tomatoes with a spoon, going for a counter-clockwise walk on a moonlit night, pretending to sneeze while pinching my nose closed, or any of the dozen other crackpot ideas we tried. It took a storm to get Tay out of me."

"See? That means we're okay if we fool around a little."

"You're serious?" she asked. "It's been months."

"No reason to get rusty."

"Okay, buddy, you're on." She tried sitting up but couldn't. "Just help me into the bedroom and I'll make all your dreams come true."

Just as he was getting her upright, a news item came on the TV.

"Hey, they showed this a little while ago. It's about what your county council meeting was about tonight, right? People stealing Hawaiian artifacts?"

Melanie turned up the volume while Josh took his glass to the kitchen. The report was on the local Maui news channel, one not always reliable when sourcing their news stories, or with hiring their reporters. She listened carefully anyway.

"The Maui Police Department is barely able to keep up with the spate of recent thefts from local cultural institutions. While Hawaii's heritage is stolen and sold on the black market for pennies, the police and City Hall stand by doing nothing," said the newscaster, Jenna Harkins.

"What?" Melanie said back to the screen as though it was two-way. "Police and City Hall had a strategy meeting about it this evening, you…"

"Hey, not so loud," Josh said. He used the remote to flick off the TV. Tossing that down, he took Melanie's hands and helped her up.

"What does she mean by that? The oldest theft is just three days old. We're already setting up a task force. We have help coming from Honolulu, an expert in the theft of museum artifacts."

Josh led her down the hall to their bedroom by the hand. "Yes, I know, but let's not wake the kid over it."

***

Melanie's heart wasn't into what Josh had on his mind, and convinced him to knock it off with the threat of a broken knuckle. Once he was asleep, she got up again. Trying to keep her bathrobe around her, she went to the laptop computer on the small desk and logged onto the internet.

"What was that site name again? Artifacts Empire dot com, something like that."

She waited for the results to come up, eventually learning it was a new site dedicated to marketing 'items of historical significance'. Typing in a few search terms, the stolen kahili came up.

New listing! Red feathers, wooden handle, authentic, Maui region. Bidding now open to all collectors.

"Yeah, that must be it," she mumbled. She looked at the numerous bids, which were anywhere from ten dollars to five thousand. "Ten dollars? This is a piece of Maui's history, Mister Relic Collector, or whatever your real name might be.

Spend your ten dollars on a bottle opener made in the Philippines."

It took only five minutes to open an auction bidder's account at their site. Going back to the sacred kahili that had been stolen from the local Maui museum, she made a bid offer that she hoped wouldn't be refused. Wondering how long it would take before learning if her bid was accepted, she looked for the other items that had been stolen, the matching shark tooth clubs and the spear. The bids were fewer and much lower for those items than for the kahili standard. Doubling what had already been bid, she went back to check on the feather kahili.

It had a large red *SOLD!* sign across it. She hoped it was her bid that had got the attention of whoever the seller was.

"Now they have to ship it to me, but I don't want it to come here. And if I'm lucky, I might even be able to figure out who the seller is, or at least where they are." Checking on the other items, they were still available, with more bids coming in, creeping closer to hers, something of a bidding war starting. She got a pop-up request to fill out her personal background and shipping details. "I need to have this stuff shipped someplace secure. Maybe Auntie's house?"

She started to type in her cousin's address in Orange County but stopped.

"No, better idea."

She typed in an address that had been her personal address for two years when she was a kid, and still had some pull there now, at her father's old hacienda, what had been known as the Casa Blanca. Now, it was his Presidential Library, and just putting down the street address, the shipper wouldn't know that.

"Hopefully, they won't do a reverse address look-up to try and figure out who the property owner is. But the buyer is going to be Aiko Murata." She finished typing, paid with her

PayPal account, and waited for acceptance. She requested and paid for express delivery and insurance. It took barely ten minutes for the entire transaction to complete, with an expected arrival date only three days later. "Look at that. I'm a trafficker in priceless relics stolen from a museum."

On Friday morning, when Melanie was done in her clinic, she had just enough time to make rounds before her OB appointment. Finding Harmon, they made rounds together.

"A week from today, right?" he asked as they went down a corridor.

Melanie checked her watch. "A week from right about now. I'm scheduled for noon on Friday."

"How are you feeling about it?"

"You know, for the most part, I enjoy being pregnant. Except for the morning sickness that goes on forever, and all these symptoms toward the end. I don't remember it being so bad with Thérèse."

"Trinh said you're retaining a lot more water than usual. I have to agree with her," Harmon said. "You look puffy."

"Thanks. That's a real boost to my ego." Instead of going into the ICU, she took him to the family waiting area, which happened to be empty right then. "Harm, Trinh's concerned that you might fool around behind her back again."

"Nothing like cutting to the chase."

"Are you? Because she's seriously thinking of cancelling the wedding altogether."

"And how is this your business?"

"She's my best friend. You better believe her welfare and happiness is my business. You have to admit, your track record isn't so good."

"That happened several years ago, and barely anything happened."

"The barely part isn't as important as the happened part, Harm."

"Is there anything I can say or do that will convince the two of you that I'm serious about her? Apart from giving up my life in San Francisco and moving here to be with her?"

"Well, you need to let her know in no uncertain terms that it won't happen again." Having got that out of her system, Melanie turned on her toe to resume rounds but stopped when she saw the local daily newspaper on an end table. Picking it up, the headline told the story:

Local Museum Artifacts Sold for Profit

"Really? How can they say something like that?"

"Like what?" Harmon asked, looking over her shoulder.

"Oh, we had an emergency county council session last night about the thefts of historical artifacts from the museum and library. The TV news reported something just like this, implying there's some sort of conspiracy by the county to sell off things to make money." She tossed down the newspaper. "Just bad investigative reporting."

Once they were done making rounds and Melanie handed over the reins to her practice to Harmon and Dr. Wellman, she went to her obstetrician's office a few minutes early. Being in her early forties, she was the oldest woman in the waiting room, twice as old as a couple of them. One of the gals was full-term, as big as Melanie, while others were at various stages in their pregnancies. She watched as one young woman came out from the exam area and another was led in.

"You're due pretty soon?" an oversized Filipina said.

"Next Friday."

"I'm on Thursday. I can't wait."

"I know what you mean," one of the others said. She was barely in her second trimester. "I hate being pregnant. Everything is swollen, my clothes don't fit right, and my boyfriend doesn't come near me anymore. I can't wait to get this over with."

"I kinda like it," the Filipina said. "Never felt so much like this before."

"Like what?" the grumpy one asked.

"A woman."

Finally, it was Melanie's turn. Needing help to get up onto the exam bench after changing into the peek-a-boo gown, she kept the paper sheet pulled up to her chin, waiting.

Five minutes later, Dr. Chapman came in. "Melanie, how in the world did you gain eighteen pounds since your last visit?"

"Eating a lot, no exercise, and I think some of it might be water."

Dr. Chapman threw back the sheet to look at Melanie's legs. "You've got water weight all the way to your knees."

"I've been wearing Josh's sneakers lately. None of my shoes fit anymore."

Chapman listened to Melanie's chest for a moment before doing the gynecologic exam. "What's all that business I keep seeing on the news about the museum being broken into and the police don't care?"

"Maybe it's time for me to hold a press conference about it. They do care. They have a dedicated team working on it, doing a complete and thorough investigation. It's that...ugh."

"What?" Dr. Chapman asked.

"That Jenna Harkins. She's been dogging me ever since I took office. She is such a little..."

"Okay, well, your pregnancy is perfect. We're still scheduled for next Friday."

"You make it sound like there's a but," Melanie said.

"But your legs are water balloons and your lungs sound like Niagara Falls. You're a cardiothoracic surgeon. You didn't notice anything?"

Melanie blushed. "I've been figuring it would all drain off after I delivered."

"Well, I'm not waiting. You need a diuretic, and today."

Melanie sighed. "Looks like I'm spending the afternoon walking back and forth from the living room couch to the bathroom."

"No, I'm sending you to the outpatient treatment center. You're getting IV Lasix, a catheter, and I want the nurses to monitor your vitals and fetal heart tones for the rest of the afternoon."

"What? No, I can take the pills at home."

"Melanie, you're very close to being admitted to maternity, at least for the night."

"I'm that bad?"

"Your blood pressure is almost twice normal, your heart rate is skyrocketing, and I'm a little concerned that if too much water drains off your circulatory system too fast, you'll go into shock. I might be an obstetrician, but I still remember a thing or two about cardiodynamic shock. No, you need to be monitored. Now, do you want to spend the afternoon in outpatient, or stay overnight in maternity?"

"Nice trick, Petra. I'll have to remember it for my stubborn patients."

Dr. Chapman had one of the nurses bring a wheelchair. "I thought you'd see it my way."

"I had plans for this afternoon," Melanie complained, settling down into the chair for the ride out of the department.

"This is why I wanted you to take the last month off, but you took only a week. If you weren't ordinarily so athletic, you'd probably be in crisis right now. Those long days of standing in surgery didn't help you any."

The browbeating continued until they got to the outpatient treatment center of the hospital. She was helped up onto an extra-wide stretcher, Chapman supervising the positioning, applying a fetal heart tone monitor belt around her waist, and writing orders. She gave Melanie one last warning to behave herself, with an 'or else' tone to it.

"Your monitor is hooked up to telemetry, so I'll be able to monitor you from my office. If I see any signs of fetal distress, or if you start getting shocky, I'm inducing you today."

"Yes, Ma'am."

"Don't give me that ma'am nonsense. If we were still in the service, you'd outrank me by now. You want me to call Josh?" Chapman asked before leaving.

Melanie got her phone from the nurse that was stowing her clothes. "He's not expecting to pick me up for a couple more hours. I'll call once everything here is settled."

The usual vital sign monitors were applied--blood pressure cuff, EKG leads, oxygen sensor on her finger--before the IV was started. She scanned the monitor readings, now seeing how out of whack her body really was.

"Okay, here comes the Lasix," the nurse said. "It won't take long for this to take effect."

"How far is the bathroom?"

"You won't have to worry about that. Doctor Chapman ordered a catheter for you."

For the second time in an hour, Melanie's cheeks flashed red. It was hard enough for her to be examined by a doctor she'd known for years, but having a stranger doing a personal procedure was almost too much.

"Okay, did you survive?" the nurse asked once the job was done. She hung the collection bag on the side of the stretcher.

"Barely."

The nurse began jotting notes in the chart. "Wow, the Lasix is already working."

Feeling a little demoralized by not having more control over what was happening, Melanie made a call. "Lai? I have to cancel my appointment again."

"You okay? You sound down. Where are you?"

"I'm still at work. I just need to get some rest. I'll be there in a couple of days."

Melanie called Josh next, a call she really didn't want to make.

"Why are you in the treatment center?" he asked after she explained twice what was going on.

She used a corner of the blanket to blot her eyes. "Can you just bring Tay in for a few minutes? You'll figure it out when you get here, okay?"

"We're at the pediatrician's office. I think we're next."

"You got her in that quick?"

"Toss around the Kato name and they push you to the front of the line," he said.

"I wish you wouldn't have done that. She's not that sick. You should've made an appointment for her." While she'd been talking, her monitor lines and IV tubing had gotten tangled in her arms. "Look, things are a mess here right now. Just come in when you can."

While she waited, she got the newspaper from the nurse, still curious about the headlines she'd seen earlier. There wasn't much in the lead article, nothing more than what she'd been told the evening before by the detective. What caught her eye was another article at the bottom of page three, a filler item about a drowning. Only two paragraphs long, it was about the man who had been found the morning before, and the author of the article guessed it was a shark attack.

"Shark? He was run down by a boat while out surfing. He'd been nibbled on, but that was long after he was dead. Where do these journalists get their news? If they're serious about wanting to know what's going on, why don't they just come to county council meetings?"

An hour later, Josh and Thérèse came into the outpatient center, the girl leading the way. Once she spotted her mother, she made a beeline straight for her.

"Momma, you getting a nap?" she said, while climbing up onto the stretcher. She needed a push from her father.

"Getting some rest, anyway. What're you and daddy doing?"

"We came here to see you!"

"I'm glad you did. I see you brought Mister Chowder with you."

"Mister Crumpet. Momma, what's all this stuff?" Thérèse asked, examining the IV in Melanie's wrist.

"Oh, just some important things I have to wear for the rest of the day."

"Yeah, what's going on? You said something about Lasix? Isn't that for racehorses?" Josh asked.

"It has a few other uses, too. For me, I've collected so much fluid in my tissues and it's interfering with my circulation and breathing, so they're draining off the excess. Probably from working a little too much, standing too long in the OR, and too much salty food lately."

"But you're always so healthy. You're vegetarian and you were an athlete. You still swim and surf whenever you get the chance. Now I have to worry about you having a heart attack?"

"I'm not having a heart attack. Pregnancy does weird things to a woman's body. You know that. Nature wants us to sit down and take life easy for a few months, but with my schedule, I don't always get enough rest or eat right. Sorry, buddy. I'm not the Wonder Woman you thought you married. But a few hours of rest and some meds to drain off the excess fluid and I'll be back to normal. Whatever normal is at nine months pregnant."

"I don't understand. Where does all that fluid drain to?"

"You have a science PhD, have been married to a doctor for five years, and you don't know how Lasix works?"

"PhD in birds, not medicine."

"It works in the kidneys, making them draw the extra fluid out of the blood. That fluid turns into urine and goes to the bladder. After a while, my vital signs will reflect that loss in volume, which will make my heart pump more efficiently. Also, my lungs will be dryer, making it easier for me to breathe. The fetal monitor is there just as a precaution, or maybe to bill me for something extra. I'm never quite sure with gynecologists."

"How do you go to the bathroom with all this stuff on you?" he asked. Thérèse was cuddled up next to Melanie, playing with her dinosaur.

"That's being taken care of."

"I don't understand."

Melanie tried not to roll her eyes. "It's going into a bag. Look at the other side of the stretcher."

Josh looked. "Wow. I'm no expert, but that looks like a lot."

"That's the second bag. The nurse has already emptied it once. After the third one, they'll probably let me go."

"How do they know how much to drain off?"

"That's up to the Lasix and my vital signs. The drug keeps working until the blood is mostly back to normal. By then, my blood pressure and heart rate should be, also."

Thérèse was asleep by then and Melanie draped part of her blanket over the girl. The nurse came to empty the bag again.

"It's not too much stress that's making your vital signs be out of whack?" he asked.

"Let's see. Mother of an active three-year-old and pregnant with another child, cardiothoracic and vascular surgeon at one of Hawaii's busiest hospitals, mayor of one of the world's most popular tourist destinations, and my mother-in-law is coming for an extended visit. Yes, maybe there's some stress involved."

"You're coming home later?" Josh asked.

"Unless I can escape to the airport, that's the idea."

"By dinnertime?"

"I hope so. I can have Trinh pick me up. Can you boil some noodles, no salt, make a salad, no salt, and steam some vegetables, no salt? Make a bucket of rice, too."

Josh said he'd have everything ready for her to have a large, saltless meal, and to get rest. It was another four hours until Dr. Chapman was satisfied with the results, and with Melanie's vital signs. Just as the IV and catheter were being taken out, Trinh arrived to take Melanie home.

"I thought you were in bad shape," Trinh said with a scolding tone helping her into the car. "And don't try and deny it."

"I won't."

"Hey, I heard some news about the theft of the artifacts."

"From the media or the police?"

"Well, first I heard from the librarian, and then the police. I took the kids to the library today for one last summer book to read. While I was there, the head librarian asked me what was new in the investigation, as if I knew anything about it. I didn't want to admit I knew nothing, so I pumped her for information. It turns out the police have been there every day looking for clues, or whatever. Apparently, there was only one set of fingerprints on the case that held that old spear. Now they're searching through all kinds of agencies to see if they can get a fingerprint match with a known criminal."

"Only one set of fingerprints?" Melanie asked. "It seems like there should be a lot more than that in a library."

"That's what I said. The librarian explained the night housekeeper cleans all the display cases so they're pristine, vacuums everything, dusts the counters and desks, so the place is spotless when they open the next morning."

"I want that guy to come clean my house. But that means the burglar broke in sometime after the night housekeeper cleaned the place and before the morning librarian opened up."

"Right," said Trinh. "When I talked to the police, they said the library doesn't have security cameras inside, but they're tracking down security camera feed in the neighborhood, for a car or someone walking along carrying something late at night."

"Any word on anything else that was taken from the museum?"

"Same as what they told us last night. The police have already found the battle-axes and kahili at an online auction site; at least they think it's the same stuff, but they don't have the funds to buy it. I guess there was some high bidder last night trying to get it, which threw the bidding into overdrive. The bad news is that the kahili is already gone. Somebody bought that as soon as it was available for bidding."

"I might know something about that, but you have to keep quiet. Deal?"

"If you promise to get rest, and go for a walk twice a day, and then put your feet up, yeah, sure."

"I bought the kahili."

"No way."

"I was on that site last night for a while, and when I saw the bidding going up in a hurry, I made a bid too good for the seller to pass up. Then when I tried the same trick on the other stuff, it didn't work. That's why those clubs and the spear are so expensive now."

"But you can still go back and try again, with a super high bid, right? If it gets the stuff back, why not? Isn't that the point, to get the stuff back?" Trinh asked. "Seriously, you have enough money to build a new museum and stock it with all the Hawaiian stuff we can find."

"I can't bail out Maui whenever there's a problem like this. Somewhere along the way, Maui needs to figure out how to prevent some of this bad stuff from happening. County finances suck, the police department is under-staffed, our little power grid barely keeps up with demand, and the schools operate on a shoestring. I wish I could help but I can't be a sugar momma every time some financial crisis comes along."

"You've already done too much," Trinh said.

"We. You've donated a big chunk of your money and time to this island. Not like it's ever coming back to us. Where are we going, anyway?"

"If you're feeling okay, I thought we could go for a drive and talk some of these county things over. I'm not entirely sure how many friends we have on the county council."

"You get that feeling also?" asked Melanie. "I do think we can trust the police department, certainly the department commander. Nakatani seems okay. I've always had a funny feeling about a couple of them on the council, though."

"The ones there last night were a little too friendly with your old friends, Jemmison and Tanikawa."

"Not my friends," Melanie hissed. "Anyway, they're in state prison on Oahu where they belong. What do you think we should do about the rest of the artifacts?"

"I vote we bid high on what's still available, just so we can get it back here where it belongs. Then we launch an investigation into how it got stolen, not just by whom. Is it whom or who?"

"I don't know. Talk to Josh about grammar. But an investigation uses a detective, or at least an officer, something the department is in short supply of these days."

"Why not hire a private detective? We can write a check to the county from one of your puppet organizations, make it look like grant money, and get to the bottom of it," Trinh offered.

"My dad's companies aren't puppet companies. But I like the idea," Melanie said, pressing on the imaginary brake pedal when Trinh entered a fast food drive-thru for something to drink.

"The library and the county museum both being hit only one day apart, and in the same way, stinks of an inside job. I think somebody working for the county is involved, somebody with keys."

"You're thinking the night janitor had something to do with it?" Melanie asked.

"Makes sense. Seems peculiar that the whole place got spotlessly cleaned right before someone broke in and left fingerprints on the case. Something doesn't add up with that. And wouldn't the janitor have keys to all the county buildings so he could get in and clean them?"

Melanie took a sip of her lemonade. "I have no idea how many janitors we have working for the county."

"I'll look into it," Trinh said, getting her SUV up to speed on the highway again.

Melanie began making notes on a napkin for Trinh to look at later. "If you're going snooping, try to see if any of them are related to county council members, or even Jemmison or Tanikawa."

"Where did you have that kahili shipped? Not to your house, right?" Trinh asked.

"I had it sent to Dad's library, care of Aiko Murata. But I didn't use the name of the library, just the street address. Even if they do figure out it's his Presidential Library, they might think the place just wants something representative of every state. Since the kahili represented the ali'i chieftain of each island, it would be the perfect thing for display in a Presidential Library."

"That's a good idea. Who's Aiko Murata?"

"An old alias Mom used a million years ago. I'll tell you about it some other time."

"You have a weird family, Melanie Kato."

"You're a part of it."

"Only because my dad married into it by marrying your mom."

"He never knew what he was getting himself into," Melanie said.

Trinh turned the car toward home. "What do we tell the rest of the council about buying back the stolen stuff?"

"We tell them nothing about our part of it, and for now, not even the police. If the council is innocent, they won't care about how or why it was stolen, only expecting us to keep buying it. If they're somehow complicit in those things being stolen, the culprits will never be caught. And if the police know we're buying it, they'll think we had something to do with it and focus their investigation on us, maybe even toss us in an interrogation room for a while. Personally, I've had enough of that."

Melanie's phone rang with a ringtone that meant hospital business.

"Doctor Kato? This is Doctor Benson, the pathologist at West Maui Med. How are you?"

Melanie wasn't sure of how to respond. Had he somehow heard about her being a patient there that afternoon? Or did he have some delayed results from a surgery she'd done earlier in the week? Either way, there was an ominous tone to the call. "I'm fine. Can I help you with something?"

"I'm here in my office and have Mrs. Adelaide Winston waiting for me. She's the mother of…"

Melanie rubbed her forehead. "Of Kenny Winston. Yes, the police have been expecting her arrival sometime today. She wants to see her son before you do his autopsy. Is there an issue?"

"I hope not. There's a police detective named Nakatani here also. We'd like you to be here for when the mother views the body."

"Is this call on speaker?" she asked.

"It is. Detective Nakatani is here with me, but the mother is in another room."

"Why do you want me to be there? I wasn't his care provider. In fact, he was long dead before he ever made it to the hospital. Frankly, I'm still not sure why he was brought to West Maui Med and not taken straight to the county morgue in town."

"Neither are we. But since he's on our turf, we have to deal with him, and with the mother."

"Doctor Kato, this is Detective Nakatani. I was sent by my station commander to be with Mrs. Winston when she views her son's body. We still think there are suspicious circumstances concerning his death, enough to keep the investigation open for a while."

"From my preliminary external exam, it's obvious to me he didn't drown, nor arc there signs he killed himself," the pathologist said. Being the same specialty in medicine, pathologists also doubled as coroners in hospitals.

"That's why the police are opening the investigation into his death," Nakatani said.

"Not because his grieving mother is here to take him home, and will most likely demand an investigation? And if we don't do one, she'll hire outside docs, private investigators, and lawyers instead?"

"Predictive models would indicate that, yes," said the detective.

"Don't give me that nonsense, Detective Nakatani. Maui County is stuck with a dead man and his heartbroken mother, and now we're trying to cover our butts, hoping we don't get sued by trying to sweep it all under the rug."

Trinh touched Melanie's arm, motioning for her to relax. In turn, Melanie waved to be taken back to the hospital.

"Doctor Kato, this might very well be an accidental death, but to determine that, a thorough investigation needs to be done," Benson, the coroner said. "I need to work with the police if we want to find out what happened to this poor boy."

Melanie felt put in her place. "I know. Hopefully, it was accidental. I hate the idea of someone being murdered on Maui."

"None of us like it, Doctor," one of them said, she wasn't sure which.

"Are you going to be here or should we proceed without you?" the other asked.

"Yes, I'll be there in just a few minutes. I'll be there as mayor representing the county, I'll be there as a physician willing to answer questions about his death, but most of all, I'll be there as a mother talking to another mother who has lost her child."

She rammed her finger on the *End Call* button and swore.

"The police think it was murder?" Trinh asked.

"They think it's suspicious. Frankly, so do I. Now I get to go meet with the kid's mother. Do you mind waiting for me?" Melanie asked.

"I have nothing better to do than gripe at the kids when I get home. Want me to come in with you?" Trinh offered. She parked at the rear of the hospital.

"Maybe you should. I look okay? Like a mayor should look?"

"You look ten months pregnant, and way better than you did yesterday, but yes, you look mayoral. Better than our last five mayors put together."

"You'll have to pull me out of your car. My back is killing me and one leg is going numb from sitting too much."

Trinh pulled Melanie out by the hands. "What'd you do to your back? Is this something else to worry about?"

"Next time you see Harm, ask him about a hard landing in a helicopter we had once. I think it's related to that. Just a bad disc that's beginning to hate me, and right now is not a good time for that. Or maybe sciatica, like you said. All I know is that it hurts."

"What does?" Trinh asked.

"Everything."

When they went in the rear entrance to the pathology department and the small hospital morgue, Melanie saw a lady sitting alone in the waiting area. She looked a decade or so older, and had the dark suntan Arizonans were famous for. She went straight to her.

"Mrs. Winston?"

The woman stopped picking at her cuff and looked up. Her eyes were red but dry, and she forced a polite smile. "Yes?"

"My name is Melanie Kato. I'm the mayor of Maui County, and this is Trinh Park, my Vice Mayor. I was asked to come in and visit with you."

Mrs. Winston stood, reaching almost a foot shorter than Melanie, and was as petite as a middle-aged woman could be. They shook hands and shared greetings. Melanie noticed the woman glance at her belly a couple of times but never said anything. She sent Trinh to find Benson and Nakatani.

Melanie kept the woman's hand in hers. "Ma'am, I'm terribly sorry about what has happened to your son. I cannot imagine how heartbroken you must be."

"Thank you. For some reason, they don't want me to see him."

"Maybe we should sit down." Melanie pointed the woman to a short sofa in the waiting area. "It might be best that way. I saw your son when he was first brought to the hospital yesterday morning. Unfortunately, they need a positive ID from someone who knows him."

"They call the mayor for something like that?"

"Not usually, Ma'am. I'm also a doctor here at the hospital, and the emergency room physician on duty at the time asked me to come take a look when he was brought in."

"I still don't understand why I can't see Kenny."

"He'd been in the water for quite a while, maybe as long as a full day." Melanie paused to think of how to proceed. How could she tell a mother her son had been crushed by a boat and then battered around by the tides, before being partially eaten by fish? "The tide had moved him about quite a bit. At this point, I doubt he'd look like your son and would appear more like a stranger."

Mrs. Winston stood. "I'd still like to see him."

"Yes, Ma'am." Melanie tried standing but couldn't get her feet working with the rest of her. Rescuing her was Trinh, just coming back with Benson and Nakatani.

They went as a group to the cooler room where half a dozen stainless steel drawers were in one wall. Along another wall was a stretcher with a body covered by a sheet. Melanie was just behind Mrs. Winston and noticed her stall for a moment.

"We don't have to do this, Ma'am."

"No, I want to. I need to know if it was my son."

Dr. Benson, the pathologist, uncovered the head end of the body, exposing the young man's ashen face. Mrs. Winston took a cautious step forward, still a few feet back. Melanie went with her.

"Kenny?" the woman said, barely breathing the words. She closed the distance and touched his face, immediately pulling her hand back. "You're so cold."

Clenching her teeth, Melanie had to do something. All she could think to do was put her arm around the shoulders of Mrs. Winston. She waited for the woman to touch her son once again before turning away from him. Melanie led her back to the waiting area.

"I'm very sorry to ask, Mrs. Winston, but that was your son, right?" the detective asked.

She nodded while drying her eyes.

Trinh brought a cup of tea for the woman, who clutched it in her hands, maybe warming them after the cold touch of death she'd got from her son.

"His body...wasn't right."

"We think he had gone out surfing and was hit by a boat," said Detective Nakatani, who had joined them. "We've already been searching small boat marinas for damaged craft and have been asking the public for information about the accident."

They talked for a few minutes about what might've happened to her son, how long he'd been in the water, and the types of injuries he'd suffered. Melanie sensed the woman was breaking down, so she called an end to the meeting.

The small group went out to the parking lot. It was a balmy evening, with steady tradewinds, exactly why people lived in the tropics. Mrs. Winston just stood still, looking out at the cars parked there. "I don't know what to do."

"When the time comes, we'll help you make arrangements to take Kenny home," started Melanie.

"No, I don't have a room. Not even a car. I had a taxi bring me here from the airport."

Melanie and Trinh looked at each other and silently shrugged.

"I have a guest room you could use," Melanie offered. "It's not much, but it might be better than staying alone tonight in a hotel room."

Mrs. Winston continued to gaze out at seemingly nothing. "I should find a room. Or maybe I should just go home now."

"Rooms are awfully expensive, especially at this time of year. I'd enjoy it if you stayed with my family and me. And I'm pretty sure there are no more flights to the mainland tonight."

The woman looked at Melanie with the eyes of a hurt puppy. "Yes, I'm far away from home here, aren't I?"

They got the woman buckled into the back seat of Trinh's car and left for the quick ride home. As soon as they were on their way, Melanie called Josh.

"Hey, are you coming home yet?" he asked.

"Yes, and bringing a guest with me."

"Trinh?"

"No, a new friend from the mainland. You'll meet her in just a few minutes."

She ended the call and sent him a text.

Be nice to her. She just lost her son.

Getting her phone out again, she sent another text.

Put clean clothes on T.

Chapter Six

Melanie led Mrs. Winston up the steps to the back door of her house. She could smell several scents of food even before going inside. One was spicy from peppers, something else had too much ginger, and garlic dominated all of it. It was going to be another one of Josh's adventures in vegetarian cooking, and on a night when they had a guest.

"One thing you need to know is that we're vegetarians here at home, Mrs. Winston. I hope you don't mind."

"How can I complain when you've made me a guest in your home?"

"Yes, well, the house might be a bit messy. We have a very busy three-year-old running the show around here."

"Momma!" was shouted from the other end of the house, followed by the squeaking of a tricycle coming down the hallway.

"See what I mean?" Melanie said. She put her foot out in the middle of the floor to stop the trike after Thérèse made the turn into the kitchen. "Mrs. Winston, this is my husband, Josh, and our daughter, Thérèse."

Josh gave a little salute from where he was at the stove. Thérèse made a show of sticking out her hand. "Hello. My name is Thérèse Kato-Strong."

The woman smiled for the first time that Melanie had noticed.

"Well, my name is Adelaide Winston, but you should call me Addie."

Thérèse glanced quickly at her mother.

"Maybe Aunt Addie would be better," Melanie said before leaving the kitchen.

"Addie like numbers?" the girl asked.

"Well, maybe. Do you know how to add?" their visitor asked.

When a number game started, Melanie went down the hall to her bedroom, Josh following her. He closed the door behind him.

"Who's she? We're bringing home strays now?"

As usual, she turned her back to Josh so he could zip open her blouse and skirt. "Be nice. Yesterday she found out her son died in the ocean and came to take his body home. She just got here this afternoon and doesn't have a place to stay. I'm not letting her stay in a hotel room that will only rake her over the coals in last minute booking fees. She can stay in the spare room."

"You just got out of the hospital. You're supposed to be resting."

"It's not like we're going to be mud wrestling."

"Tomorrow is your first day off in how long? You're starting your first vacation in more than a year. Don't you know what time off is?" he asked.

Melanie began coating her belly stretch marks with hand lotion. "Time off from the hospital but not from the county. This is important, Josh. She's having to deal with a tragedy on an island I'm responsible for, in a number of ways."

"But…"

"Don't you have overly seasoned food burning on the stove?"

Melanie desperately wanted to crawl onto the bed and stay there until the next Friday, her scheduled due date, but having a guest in the house, she put on an XXX-L T-shirt and baggy shorts and went back to the kitchen.

Thérèse and Mrs. Winston were already at the kitchen table, and Josh was setting bowls of food in the middle. Melanie took her position at the end with the most space.

"I hope there's something you can eat, Mrs. Winston," Melanie said, filling a small rice bowl for Thérèse, putting steamed vegetables on top.

"It's all very interesting." She picked up the chopsticks that had been put out for her and gave them a long look.

"Tay, maybe you could get Aunt Addie a fork."

The girl hopped down from her chair and went to a drawer, returning with a spoon and fork for their guest. She ate slowly, only picking at the food, steering rice around her plate.

"I could cook some potatoes, if you like?" Melanie offered.

"This is fine. I was just thinking about Kenny. On the ride to the hospital from the airport, I watched the scenery, thinking how Kenny had seen the same sights. I was even thinking of coming for a visit to see him this winter. Now, I suppose it's pointless, without Kenny here."

"Who's Kenny?" Thérèse asked.

"Maybe during this dinner, we can be quiet and let our guest talk?" Josh said to Thérèse, putting her rice bowl back in front of her.

"No, it's okay. Kenny is my son."

"Old kind son like Daddy, or young kind son like Wilson?"

"Please pardon my daughter's inventive grammar. Wilson is Trinh's son, a few years older than Thérèse," Melanie quickly explained.

"He's in between them," the woman said, her tentative smile beginning to crack.

"Where is he? He no want to eat with us?" Thérèse asked, waving her chopsticks in the air.

Josh sprang from his chair and lifted Thérèse from hers. "Okay, you know the rule. No playing at the dinner table, and Mommy and Mrs. Winston want to talk."

Melanie listened to her daughter gripe all the way down the hall until her bedroom door was closed. Apparently, Josh stayed with her to keep her occupied with playing games.

"Sorry," Melanie said quietly.

"She's a little cutie."

"Sometimes. Other times she's a little precocious. And inquisitive."

"I don't mind," Mrs. Winston said. "Such a clever way for her to get around the house in a little tricycle."

"Maybe this wasn't such a good idea having you stay with us? You might've wanted to be alone."

"Actually, being around people might be the perfect thing right now, even if we're all strangers. I don't think I could face being alone. That long flight to get here was horrible, just sitting there with nothing to do but think about Kenny." She dug through her purse to find her billfold. From there she pulled out three snapshots. "This is Kenny and his father when he was just a boy. Ken senior left us for Heaven about ten years ago. This one is from when he was running on the high school track team. And this was taken here on Maui, just a few weeks ago. I suppose this is the last picture of him that I'll have."

She clung to that picture the longest before handing it over to Melanie.

Kenny looked athletic, with bright blue eyes, an angular chiseled face, and blond hair that would be the envy of any college cheerleader. "He was very good-looking. In what part of the island did he live?"

"A place called Kihei. I think it's where the kids like to live. He was never terribly outgoing as a kid, never had many friends. I think that's why he came here, to start over socially, sort of reinvent himself. Do you know that place? You must, if you're the mayor here."

"Kihei is quite pleasant. I'm sure he was happy living there."

"The police say his…he was found near Lahaina. Am I saying that right?"

"Yes, it's just down the road from here a few miles. We could go there tomorrow, if you'd like to…" Melanie was lost. She had no idea of how to treat the woman. Most of the time when her patients passed away and she had to break the bad news to families, she left the aftermath of emotions to social workers to sort out. "…if you'd like to go see where he was found."

"I'd like that."

Even though the woman looked finished with her meal, Melanie kept eating, if in slow motion. "What did Kenny do for work?"

"Oh, he didn't really have a career, just odd jobs. He went to college for a couple of years before deciding that wasn't right for him. That's when he came here. Every time he called home, he made Maui sound like heaven on earth. He'd made so many new friends, and when I pried hard enough, he said he was dating a few girls. Nothing special he always said, but I guess that's how kids are these days."

"People seem to make friends pretty easily here. There are so many outdoors things to do…" Melanie stopped talking. It wasn't the right time to sound like a Chamber of Commerce advertisement.

"He'd been saving his money to buy a surfboard. He sure was excited when he called to tell me all about the first wave he rode. I guess a lot of people here surf."

"It's very popular. Kihei would be the perfect place to learn."

Kay Hadashi

"It sounds like you know how?" Mrs. Winston asked.

"I suppose it's my passion also. I don't have much chance to anymore, being busy at the hospital and now that my family is growing. Did Kenny work in Kihei?"

"He made it sound like he worked all over the island. He waited tables in Kihei, worked on a little farm in some place called 'Upcountry', and did odd job types of labor with some new friends. He was hoping that would lead to something bigger, or at least more money. I think for him, the worst thing in the world would've been if he came home again because he had to, not because he wanted to. But he never asked me for money, not once."

"What kinds of odd jobs did his friends do?" Melanie asked.

"That's what the police asked when I talked with them this afternoon. They asked if I knew any of their names, where they lived, if they lived with him, if they take drugs. Honestly, I never thought to ask Kenny. I was just hoping he'd bring one of his girlfriends home to Arizona, get back into school, and then who knows what?"

"Well, a lot of people fall in love with Maui when they first come here and decide to stay. It isn't long before they discover how expensive it is, and how hard it is to find a good job. Most people end up going home again, but they always have good memories of the place."

Another faux pas. Mrs. Winston would be taking her son's body back home with a heavy heart, not with fond memories of Maui.

"You're certain I'm not in the way, Doctor? Or should I call you Mayor? I'm still a little confused about that."

"I'd like it if you called me Melanie. And you can stay for as long as you want. But I have to warn you, one week from now, there's going to be a fourth member of the family, and I

84

might just put you to work changing diapers if you're still here."

"No, Kenny and I will be home by then."

Melanie took the woman to the guest room, found towels for her to use in the spare bathroom, and had Josh change the linens on the bed while Mrs. Winston showered. Making a quick call next door, she had Trinh bring some of her oldest daughter's clothes over, the only things in the house that might fit the petite woman, even if they were for a younger generation. Once their guest closed herself into her room for the night, Melanie and Josh went back to finish their cold meals.

"Tay's okay?"

"I tried explaining how we had to be extra nice and not ask too many personal questions, but I'm not sure she understood," Josh said.

"There's no such thing as too personal to her. Did she go to bed already?"

He shook his head. "I think she's teaching us a lesson by going on a hunger strike. She said she never wants to eat dinner with us again if she can't eat with the guests."

"Fine with me," Melanie said, finishing her rice.

Melanie heard her daughter's bedroom door open, followed by footsteps slowly coming down the hall.

"Where's Auntie?" someone said from the doorway into the kitchen. Thérèse was half hiding behind the door.

"Gone beddy. Are you done eating dinner?"

"Are there still vegebles?"

"Carrots, green beans, and peas."

"Are they friendly?" she asked, stepping out from the protection behind the door.

Melanie didn't look up at her daughter. "Friendlier than me, right now."

The girl stood at the table rather than sit to finish her meal. "Daddy, what's in the big box?"

"I keep forgetting about that," Josh said. "Your grandmother sent things to us. I think they're for the baby."

"Birfday present?"

"I guess it is, yes. Maybe we should open it after dinner?"

"Is it okay with Momma?" the girl asked, looking directly at her father.

Melanie set her rice bowl down, maybe a little too vigorously. "Thérèse, I'm not mad at you. And yes, we can open the box together, okay?"

Instead of the usual 'Yay!' the girl normally offered, she only hurried through eating her meal. Once they were done eating, Melanie made a chore of taking the bowl and plates to the sink, making the girl help.

"How long are we going to be mad at each other?" she asked the girl.

"Forever."

"That's a long time."

"It is?" Thérèse asked.

"Yep. Super long time. Maybe we should stop being mad at each other now?"

The girl put her fingertip on her chin, giving it great thought. "Okay."

"Do I get a hug?" Melanie asked.

Thérèse reached up, and Melanie picked her up. Something snapped in her back, and after a quick clutch, she put her daughter down again.

"Okay, little one. You take out the first thing on top," Melanie said, once Josh had the box open on the living room floor.

"What's this thing?" the girl asked, looking at embroidered white fabric that was yellow with age.

"It's a baby bonnet," her father said.

Melanie snagged a sheet of paper from inside the box, a list of everything inside.

"It's your great-grandmother's baby bonnet, Josh." She took the bonnet from Thérèse, who was close to putting it on her own head. "How nice."

"Got a big blankie in here," the girl said, pulling something else out.

"Oh good. Your grandmother's old blanket. It even smells…used. Leave it alone, Sweetie."

"Got some books, too."

Melanie read the titles. "Caring for Your Baby and Modern Child Rearing." She looked inside. "Oh, look. Published in the 1930s."

"Good taste never goes out of style," Josh muttered.

"Josh, what is all this stuff? Why are we getting your family heirlooms?"

"Probably because my brother didn't want them. Mom has to unload it on someone."

"We're already limited on storage space around here, and even if this blanket held up while being cleaned, who would use it? The tropics, remember? And am I really supposed to put a grungy old bonnet on Sofia's head?"

"Maybe we could say we tried laundering them and they disintegrated?" he offered.

Melanie kept taking things from Thérèse as she pulled them out of the box. "And the antique books?"

"Spontaneous combustion?"

"I'm sorry, Josh. I know this is all very special and heartwarming, but are we really supposed to be the caretakers of old moth-eaten stuff from a hundred years ago?"

Using the tips of his fingers, he looked at the bonnet. "This stuff belongs in a museum."

"Hey, you're on to something. We could donate it all to a museum as examples of early island missionary household items. We could even put your mother's family name on it as the donor. That way it would have a place to go and not here."

"Momma, what's this thing?"

Melanie took the thing and gave it a long look. "I'm not sure. Some sort of little toy."

"Hey! My old pacifier," Josh said.

Melanie winced. "This thing was your pacifier?"

"And a whole bunch of other Carpenters from my Mom's side of the family. I think that goes with the baby bonnet and blanket."

"Actually, it goes in the trash where it belongs, and nowhere near my children."

***

Josh did the driving the next morning when Melanie took Mrs. Winston to Lahaina. The beach where Kenny's body was found was not far from the old whaling town popular with visitors. Melanie had been there countless times in her life, and the Puamana Beach area was one of her family's favorite weekend picnic spots. It was as peaceful as always, no indication that a death had occurred just offshore.

While Josh took Thérèse to her favorite area for exploring tiny tide pools, Melanie went with Mrs. Winston for a stroll on the beach.

"Ma'am, this area is called Puamana Beach. As you can see, it's mostly vacation rentals along one side and a narrow beach in the other direction. It's a nice place to bring small children since the surf is never very rough."

"No need to be so formal, Doctor. Please call me Addie."

"If you call me Melanie."

Addie kept walking in the soft yellow sand, almost lost in her own little world. She seemed to be paying closer attention to the ocean than to the beach. The only waves were a hundred yards out and barely turning over, the water lapping at the beach the same as it would in a lake. The morning was already warm, the sun bright. A steady breeze fluttered their clothes. At one point, she stopped and gazed out at the giant blue ocean.

"I wonder…"

Melanie knew what the woman wanted to ask, but waited, allowing the woman to have some personal space.

"Such a beautiful place. I wasn't expecting it to look like this. I hear so much about people coming to Maui for vacations and honeymoons. Honestly, I was expecting something like Newport Beach in LA."

"It's very special here."

"You grew up here?" Addie asked, aiming her face into the sun, closing her eyes against the breeze.

"I grew up in the same house where we live. This is a beach my mom and I often came to. We still do. I learned to surf just down the road a few miles."

"You're very lucky."

"I am. I'm hoping I can bring that same sense of good fortune to my daughters, and their children someday. But we all must find our own way in life. Who knows? They might leave the nest and never come back."

The subtle smile that had formed on Addie's face sank when she opened her eyes and looked out at the ocean again. "I wonder where it happened?"

"I spoke with the investigating detective this morning. You can see the edge of the coral reef not far out. Apparently, it was high tide when he was found. His surfboard leash was tangled in some of the coral, which held him underwater."

"That means he drowned, right?"

"It seems he died very quickly, most likely from the trauma of whatever hit him." Melanie took a few steps to stand next to

Addie. "From what I've heard, it seems very complicated. That's why they have a detective investigating his death so closely and the coroner doing his autopsy."

"Complicated how? When I spoke to the police yesterday, they almost made it sound like there was some sort of foul play?"

"There are some odd things. First, his board wasn't with him, just the leash trailing from his ankle. That leash is pretty strong and is meant to keep the surfer and the board together. The other suspicious things were his injuries. They were much more consistent with blunt force than drowning."

Addie hugged herself. "I don't know what that means."

"There was no water in his lungs, which is how people drown. But his broken ribs and injured head mean he was struck by something large, probably a boat."

"This seems too shallow for a boat."

"Right. We think he paddled out to a second surf line that would've had bigger waves. He might even have been caught in an outgoing tide that drew him further from shore than he realized. That happens occasionally with inexperienced surfers and swimmers. Most likely, a boat came along and struck him."

"Wouldn't they have stopped to help?"

"They might not have seen him, thinking they struck something floating in the water, and kept going. Or just afraid of owning up to what they did. The police have a team going from marina to marina, checking for damage on boats."

"Does that mean he went quickly? If he was struck hard enough but didn't drown, he would've died instantly, right?"

"That's what makes the most sense to me," Melanie said. She considered backing off, if the woman had had enough for one morning. Instead, she pushed her luck to potentially have a visitor break down right in front of her. Being on the beach on a sunny day seemed like the only decent place to bring up so much bad news. "There's something else about his injuries we haven't told you or the media."

"What's that?"

"It seems he had been in a fight not long before going out surfing. He had some bruising on his face and a minor fracture to his jaw, which weren't suffered while he was in the water."

"How can you possibly know that?" Addie asked.

"A bruise wouldn't form after death, and the location was such that it was typical of a fist hitting someone. He also had a single broken rib on the opposite side of his other injuries."

"Kenny was beat up?"

"It appears so, and not long before he went surfing."

"If he wasn't still attached to his surfboard, how do we know he even went surfing?" Addie asked.

"His pickup truck was found in the parking area back there, the tie down straps in the back as if they'd been used. Plus, the police didn't find a board at his apartment. They don't know what kind he used or what it looked like. Would you happen to have a picture of him with his board?"

Addie got out her phone and hit a few buttons. "He sent me pictures on my phone but I can never remember how to find them." She gave the phone to Melanie to use.

It took only a moment for Melanie to find the saved pictures. They weren't in folders, only saved individually. As she clicked from one image to the next going backward in time, almost everything was of Kenny or some scene on Maui. She found a few pictures of him at a restaurant maybe where he worked, and a couple of him working in a vegetable patch, probably the upcountry job he had. The pictures were either selfies, or of him posing with other young men, also dressed in casual wear or swimsuits. Very few of the images had women in them. Melanie was picking up on a vibe Kenny's mother apparently hadn't. Then she found a picture of him posing with a surfboard.

"White tanker with a blue stripe," she muttered. She swiped her finger to enlarge the image. There was a sticker near the nose, the logo of a local surf school in Lahaina that catered to tourists. "Gonzo's Surf School."

"What's that mean?"

"Surf schools use boards called tankers. They're extra-long and wide for maximum flotation, making it really easy to learn how to surf, even in tiny waves. Gonzo's is right here in Lahaina."

"Maybe they know something?" Addie asked.

"I doubt it. But I wonder if they've been looking for their rental board that was never returned? They don't use the best boards, but it seems to me they'd be looking for it by now." When Addie wasn't watching, Melanie assembled the pictures in a folder and secretly emailed them to herself. She gave the phone back after giving the mother a quick tutorial on how to find the images. "You have very nice pictures of Kenny there."

"I want to get them printed for a scrapbook." The woman scrolled, looking at them quickly before putting the phone away again. "Can we go to his apartment?"

Melanie stepped away to call Detective Nakatani to see if it had been released from evidence collection yet.

"Yeah, sure you can take the mother. We found nothing suspicious there at all. We still have his phone and a few things we took into evidence. Not that he had much. But Doc, there's something you do need to know about that kid."

"I have a pretty good idea what it is."

"You already know about the fingerprints?" he asked.

She was expecting something else. "What fingerprints?"

"The fingerprints on the broken display case at the library are his."

Melanie took a few more steps away from Addie. "You mean the missing artifacts? Trinh mentioned something about there being only one set."

"Exactly. Perfect match between the Winston body in the morgue and the prints on the case that was broken into. And no other prints anywhere else."

Melanie mumbled a swear word she rarely used.

"That's what I said, but it's a fantastic lead. When we discovered that, we went back to his apartment looking for evidence related to the artifacts, turning it into a burglary investigation rather than possible homicide."

Melanie glanced at the woman, who seemed lost in thought. "But there's nothing about this kid that makes me believe he'd do something like that."

"You're probably right. We ran his prints for wants and warrants. Nothing current but he has a record in Arizona and California. Shoplifting, petty theft, underage drinking, a drunk driving arrest in California that didn't stick because he blew below the legal limit. On the surface, he was responsible, but scratch the surface a little and he's no Boy Scout."

"And now he's dead," Melanie said, sighing at the end. "Can I take his mother to his apartment? Is it okay if she takes a few things as mementoes?"

"Whatever is there needs to stay there for a while, at least until we finish the investigation. Then she can have whatever she wants. But like I said, there isn't much. The building manager is Akani. She'll let you in. But with the matter of the museum thefts, let me investigate a while longer before we tell anyone about it."

"Okay with me, and you can be the one to tell the mother her son was a thief, when the time comes." After the call, she went back to Addie. "Good news. The police said we can go to Kenny's apartment."

"Is it far?"

"About twenty minutes. We can have some lunch in Kihei, if you're feeling up to it?"

"Still not terribly hungry."

As they walked back toward the small parking area, Melanie waved for Josh and Thérèse to come. The girl bolted, running as fast as she could through the soft sand. Just as she was about to ram into Melanie headfirst, she caught a foot in the sand and tumbled into a landing.

"Poor thing," Addie said, bending down to rescue the girl from the sand.

"Our daughter is a little on the awkward side," Josh said.

"You okay, little one?" Melanie asked, looking down at her daughter. She had long since grown out of crying, usually laughing at her own natural clumsiness.

"I okay."

"Well, let's get some of that sand dusted off you," Addie said, taking over at being motherly.

"Where we go now, Momma?"

"For another drive to Kihei."

"Go to the beach?"

"You and Daddy are going to the beach while Aunt Addie and I go to a building."

"Kama-or…Karma-o…Kama…Number one, two, or three beach?"

"Kamaole Three. You and Daddy can look for coconuts for a while."

"These Hawaiian names sure are hard to pronounce," Addie said, more to Thérèse.

The girl nodded, her pigtails bouncing. "That one always mix me up."

"Even for residents, we have a hard time pronouncing some of the names of places," Josh said, getting his SUV up to speed on the highway.

Melanie sat in the front this time while Addie sat in the back with Thérèse as they drove along the coastal highway to another part of the island. When the woman started to play a game with the girl, it gave Melanie and Josh a chance to talk.

"Kenny's apartment?" he asked.

"Yep."

"Which building?"

"The Polynesian Surf, right next to Kam Three."

"Isn't that place mostly for…"

"Yep."

Josh turned off the A/C and opened the front windows, allowing the wind to blow through. "Does she know?" he whispered.

"Nope. And we're leaving it that way."

"Okay."

To keep her hair from blowing around, Melanie put it into a ponytail.

"I thought you had an appointment with Lailanie today?" he asked.

"Things change. We're going to Kihei instead, which is better for all of us."

"Did you have something else to do today, Melanie?" Addie asked from the backseat. "I appreciate you driving me around like this, but I think it's a bit much for you to do."

"Nothing that can't wait. I haven't been to Kihei in a while. I'd like the change of scenery."

"She had a hair appointment," Josh said, looking at Addie in his rearview mirror. "It's how she induces labor. She goes in to get her hair done and comes out with a baby."

"I got borned in a hurricane in a haircut place," Thérèse said, still playing the game with Addie.

"Say it right, Sweetie."

The girl rolled her eyes and sighed. She stopped playing the game to concentrate. Once she had it figured out, she spoke slowly and nodded with each word. "I was born in a hair salon while there was a hurricane outside."

"That sounds very exciting. I'd like to hear that story someday," Addie said.

"I'd like to forget it," Melanie said. "This time, I'm leaving nothing to chance. I'm being induced at twelve noon at the hospital, surrounded by doctors and nurses, and not by hairstylists and my mother-in-law."

She called Lailanie and cancelled her appointment again.

"That's three times in two days you've cancelled on me," the stylist said. "Everything okay?"

"Fine. Just doing some errands. What about tomorrow?"

"Tomorrow is Sunday. Church, remember? Is Josh bringing Thérèse?"

"You and Tay going to church tomorrow?" Melanie asked Josh.

"It might be a while before we have the chance, so yes."

Melanie made an appointment for Monday with Lailanie, and then called the apartment building manager to let her know they were going to be there in a few minutes.

"Which church do you go to?" Addie asked.

"Well, that's a good question," Melanie answered. "Occasionally on Saturdays, Josh and Thérèse go to the synagogue in town, and on Sundays they go to the Catholic Church here in Kihei."

"But I'm not Catholic," Josh added. "We don't have an Episcopalian Church on this part of the island, so I attend the competition's church."

"Why the synagogue?"

"My father is Jewish and Mother is Episcopalian."

"You don't go with them, Melanie?"

"I'm Buddhist, which I got from my mother. My father was Catholic, so it makes sense for our daughter to go to Mass occasionally."

"Doesn't that make it complicated for your daughter?" Addie asked.

"Not really. One day a week she's Jewish, one day she's Catholic, and five days a week she's Buddhist. When she's old enough, she can pick out what she wants for herself," Melanie explained.

"What do you think you are, Thérèse?" Addie asked the girl.

"A girl."

Addie laughed. "I suppose you really are the All-American girl." She took a breath. "We're Catholic, not that Kenny ever showed much interest in the church."

"If you'd like to come with us tomorrow, we'd like to have you," Josh offered.

"Really?"

"Sure! We're rather informal, though. Not so many suits and neckties like on the mainland."

Melanie looked back at Addie, who was now looking out the car window, deep in contemplation. She gave Josh's hand a squeeze and a smile.

"That reminds me," Josh said. "You'll be okay by yourself while I pick up my mother on Thursday?"

"You're taking Tay?"

"It would be a nice way of welcoming Mom if she came to the airport with me."

"Great. I'll nap while you're gone."

"She wants to come sooner," Josh said.

"She'll be here soon enough." Melanie shifted in her seat to look back at Addie. "Sorry. Just some family dynamics to sort out. My mother-in-law is coming from Wyoming, set to arrive the day before I'm due, which is a month too soon, as far as I'm concerned."

"I bet if it was up to her, she would've been here by now."

"If it was up to her, she would've been here nine months ago, supervising every little moment of my pregnancy. She's rather, mmm, enthusiastic about family things."

"As a mother-in-law should be."

Knowing she was treading very close to another faux pas, Melanie let the topic fade away. A few minutes later, Josh parked at the beach parking lot, taking Thérèse by the hand to where middle-age sunbathers were perched on chaise lounges.

"Nice looking building," Melanie said as they walked to the front entrance of a mixed-use condo/apartment/retail complex.

"You don't have to come with me," Addie said.

"It's not a problem. All they'll do is look for coconuts and give them thorough inspections. For some reason my daughter is fascinated by coconuts. Calls them tree eggs. But these resort areas tend to keep them knocked out of the trees so they don't fall on sunbathers. Must be the only place in the world where a coconut injury shows up in the emergency room."

Another faux pas.

"Do you get many drownings?" Addie asked. "Or surf accidents?"

They were in the shaded interior now, the breeze blowing through as natural air-conditioning. "Too many drownings, unfortunately. And one or two surf accidents a month. Usually nothing serious."

Saving Melanie from anything further was their arrival at the manager's door. She knocked.

After footsteps came to the door, it didn't open. "Yeah?"

"This is Melanie Kato. I'm looking for Akani. I called a few minutes ago."

When the door opened a crack, a part-Asian, part-Polynesian face peeked out. "You wanna see rooms?"

"We're here to see Kenny Winston's apartment."

"Kenny gone died."

"Hi. I'm Kenny's mother. May I go to his apartment?"

The girl opened the door. "Sorry. Yeah, I can take you. Let me get the keys."

As they waited at the elevator, two men came out, walking off holding hands.

"You look familiar," Akani said, her eyes going back and forth from Melanie's face to her belly, back to her face. The elevator door slid closed. "Have we met?"

"I'm the mayor."

"Oh."

The three of them watched as the light for the second floor illuminated, not yet their stop.

"Mayor of Maui?" Akani asked.

"Yep."

The light for the third floor illuminated, still not their floor.

"For how long?"

"Almost a year."

They got to the fourth floor, not yet ready to stop.

"They let preggie kind girls be mayor?"

"They made an exception for me."

The fifth floor came and went in slow motion.

"What's your name again?"

"Kato. Melanie Kato."

Sixth floor.

"I'll try and remember."

"Yes, please do. And tell all your friends, too."

The seventh floor.

"Not gonna have that baby around here, are ya?"

"I was thinking of having it at the hospital."

"Should be better that way."

Finally, the eighth floor and the elevator door opened. Melanie bolted for freedom as quick as she could.

"Were you a friend of Kenny?" Addie asked, as the three of them went down the hall.

"On the first of the month, when he paid his rent, just like everybody else here."

The young woman let them in the apartment.

Being second to go in, the place was smaller than what Melanie had been expecting, only an efficiency studio. It was also a mess. Furniture was overturned, drawers hung open, personal things strewn all over the floor. The bed mattress had been taken aside and cut open in several places.

"Addie, I'm sorry. The police told me they were done with searching the place, but I wasn't expecting this."

Addie looked completely stunned. "Neither was I."

They walked through the mess, picking up things here and there, looking at them before setting them down again.

"He was better housekeeper than this," Akani said. She also seemed surprised at the disorder.

While they picked through the clutter, Melanie went out to the hall to make a call.

"Detective Nakatani, why didn't you tell me you left Kenny's place in such a mess? I have his mother here with me."

"A mess?"

"There's stuff everywhere and half of it is broken."

"I don't understand. I was there last evening when they finished searching. It was fairly neat and tidy. Not immaculate, but tidy."

"It's a mess now. Do you suppose someone could've been inside since then?" she asked.

"Exactly what I was thinking. You know, I'm not far from there. I'll be there in a few minutes."

Melanie stood in the middle of the small apartment, snapping pictures with her phone camera while Mrs. Winston picked through the junk that had been a part of her son's life only a few days before. Akani left before the detective got there a few minutes later. He nodded to Melanie before going to Addie, greeting her warmly.

"This isn't how we left it last night," he said. "The door was locked just now when the manager opened it?"

"She used two keys to open the door," Melanie said. "She looked like she was surprised also before she left."

"Why would somebody do this to Kenny's things?" Addie asked, looking at the bread toaster than had been roughly pulled apart.

The detective uprighted a chair for her to sit, before setting up another for Melanie to use. She waved it off to make another call out in the hallway.

"Maybe we should have a long talk," the detective said to Addie, just as Melanie left them.

Once she had some privacy, Melanie called Josh. "Where are you?"

"All the way to Kamaole Two, still looking for free-range coconuts. How are you feeling?"

"I'm fine. I need to put my feet up pretty soon, though."

"Want me to take you home?" he offered.

"Once we're done here in Kihei. I plan on napping for the rest of the afternoon, and if you're nice to me, I'll let you rub my feet and ankles."

"Ooh, that's sexy."

"And that's all you're getting for a while. Just keep going to Kamaole One. We might be a while here in the apartment. Get Tay a shave ice at the food truck that's parked down there. She likes…"

"Rainbow flavored. We've been living on rainbow shave ice all summer."

"That's what the two of you do every day while I'm at work? Get snacks at the beach?"

"Pretty much."

"I want to be three years old again," she muttered.

"You mean being mayor while having a busy surgical practice, while pregnant, isn't your fantasy life?"

"Hardly. And you're responsible for one of those. Remember that when I eventually have my nervous breakdown."

"If you can, try to schedule the breakdown for after the delivery. It would be easier for everyone involved."

"I'll take it under advisement," Melanie said.

"How's it going in the apartment?" he asked.

"Somebody ransacked the place. Really made a mess looking for something."

"Looking for what?"

"I don't know, but there's a lot more to this Kenny Winston than meets the eye."

"Like what? What could a gay surfer dude from Arizona have to hide?" Josh asked.

"First, we don't know he was gay, so don't bring that up again. Second, he's not so squeaky clean as his mother makes him out to be."

"How so?"

"They're still looking into his past, and anything else I say might be a part of their investigation," Melanie said.

"I'm your husband. Who am I going to tell?"

"I'll tell you when I can."

"Yes, that's right, by the book Mayor Melanie Kato. You'll never get anywhere in politics if you insist on being honest, Melanie."

"The only place I want to go in politics is out, thank you very much." She saw Addie and Detective Nakatani come out of the apartment, the cop locking the door carefully with the keys the manager left behind. Addie had a shopping bag in her hand. "It looks like we're done. I'll meet you at the restaurant next door to here, the Surfside Grill."

The detective excused himself to go talk with the apartment manager. While he took the stairs down, the two women took the elevator again.

"Did he let you keep something?" Melanie asked, wondering what was in the bag.

"The silliest thing. Kenny kept the letters I wrote him. Why would I want these? I wrote them. But that was about all there was that still connected us."

"Maybe you can put them with the ones he sent you? Make a little book out of them?"

"He never wrote to me. He always called."

"Well, I think it was nice that he kept them. Only a good son would do something like that," Melanie said, hoping it would sound encouraging.

"That detective told me a few things about Kenny."

"Oh?"

"I guess he had a police record at home. Maybe that's why he came here, to hide out. Did you know that?" Addie asked.

"I heard something about it just a little while ago. But I doubt he was hiding out. From the sounds of it, he answered to whatever problems he had at home before coming here."

"He never said a word to me about all that."

"It's all in the past now, Addie."

"Everything about my son is in the past."

The mood that was setting in was plummeting out of control. At least until they saw Thérèse waiting outside the restaurant with Josh.

"Momma! Aunt Addie!" Instead of taking her mother's hand, the girl took Addie's hand as they were led to a table along a set of windows with a view of the beach. Climbing up onto her chair, she knelt on her shins and knees to sit. "Can you push me in, please, Auntie?"

Addie nudged the girl's chair closer to the table. "You certainly are a polite little girl."

"Sometimes," Melanie said, looking over the top of her menu at her daughter. When she caught the kid's attention, she faked a glare, her silent message to be quiet. The last thing she wanted was a conversation spiraling out of control about Kenny.

Conversation came hard now that Kenny's secret life of crime had been revealed.

"I still think you should put your letters to him in a notebook, and maybe make some notes about your memories of his life," Melanie said, unable to keep quiet any longer.

"It was the funniest thing. When I was there in his apartment, all I wanted to do was clean and go shopping to stock the refrigerator. He had almost no food in there at all."

"Maybe he ate out?" Josh offered.

"He made it sound like he barely had the money to pay rent. I doubt he could afford to eat in restaurants. And he hated fast food. He was very meticulous about what he ate."

"We're vegerarians," Thérèse said, beginning to eat her finger food salad. "But Daddy eats hamburgers sometimes when Momma's not with us. He always say, 'Don't tell your mother'."

Melanie shot Josh a dart. "That's okay, Sweetie. I already know. I can smell it on his breath when you guys come home from church."

"You don't eat any meat? You're so big and strong for being a true vegetarian," Addie said.

"She packs away the rice and noodles," Josh said. "And if something can be made from soy, that too."

Melanie gave Josh an insincere smile, the one that meant, 'We'll talk later.'

The next morning, Melanie could hear Josh trying to control Thérèse while Addie fussed over something in the living room, getting ready to go to church. Finally deciding to wear dark sneakers instead of pumps, something that still fit her feet if she loosened the laces completely, she had to hurry.

"Wait for me," she said, trying to hurry out to the living room before they left without her.

"Momma coming with us?" Thérèse asked, with a confused look to her.

"Yeah, what're you doing all dressed up?" Josh asked.

"I thought I'd go with you for a change." Melanie tugged here and there at the last maternity dress that fit and looked good enough for a trip to church. "Not that this can be considered dressed up."

"You look lovely," said Addie. She was wearing something from Trinh's daughter's closet, a little too colorful for a lady in mourning.

"Are Trinh and the kids going?"

"Everybody, Momma. Even you."

"Maybe I'll ride with her and Wilson and Scarlet can ride with you and Addie, Josh. I have some mayor stuff to talk with her about."

As soon as they had everybody loaded into cars, with Thérèse bookended by Scarlet and Wilson in the back seat of Josh's car, and Addie in the front, they took off with Trinh leading the way.

Even with the car seat all the way back, Melanie still worked the imaginary brake pedal while Trinh hurtled along the highway, outpacing Josh.

"What mayor stuff did you want to talk about, Mel?"

"Not really anything. I just can't take another depressing car ride with Mrs. Winston."

"She just lost her son. How do you expect her to behave?"

"I know. But this was supposed to be a week off from stress while I wait for Sofia to come, not to show a grieving mother around the island."

"You're the one who invited her to stay with you, which by the way is insanely kind. Nobody else would do that."

"That's what Josh said. But Thérèse sure has taken to her."

"And Addie to her," Trinh said. "Whenever she sees Thérèse, her face lights up. It's like for a few minutes, she forgets all about her troubles."

"My daughter, the social worker."

"Has she said when she's going home?" Trinh asked.

"Not yet. She needs to wait for the coroner and the police to release the body. The coroner never did his autopsy until last evening. He's supposed to call me later with his findings. Then I'm supposed to reconnoiter with Detective Nakatani."

"Reconnoiter?"

"I don't know what I'm talking about. This mayor thing is just about the stupidest thing I've ever done in my life."

"You've never done anything stupid, Mel."

"That the rest of the world knows about. But can you do me a favor? Just cover for my mayor stuff for a few days, at least until I get a grieving mother home with her son and this kid out of me."

"You take care of the Winstons while I handle everything else. Believe it or not, Maui should be able to muddle along without your help for a few days. But hey, why are you going to church today?"

"Just thinking about Dad a lot lately. I also called Father Vincent and told him about Mrs. Winston. He's going to have a special prayer for her son. Where's Harm? He doesn't come with you and the kids?"

"They have cases to do at the hospital."

"Anything good?" Melanie asked. It would've been her usual weekend to be on call for emergency surgeries.

"Nothing for you. You're a lady of leisure for the next four weeks."

Melanie pressed on the brake pedal again. "Riding in a car with you is leisure?"

Lailanie and her husband Duane were talking to others outside the church's front door when Melanie and Trinh got there. Duane was an old teammate of Melanie when they were in the Air Force together many years before, both working in Search and Rescue. Duane smiled from ear to ear, while Lailanie called their two smallest kids over from where they were playing.

"Hey, Zito." Melanie leaned in to give him a one-armed hug.

"Howzit, Dog?" he said. They still used their old military call names with each other.

He was swatted by his wife. "How many times do I have to tell you, don't call her that!"

Duane ignored his wife. "What brings Melanie Kato to church? Was there a death in the family I didn't hear about?"

Again, he was swatted. "Duane! Quiet."

Melanie quickly explained about Addie, who was just coming up the walk to the front steps, being led by Thérèse who had a tight grip on her hand.

"Just a semi-official visit today. I need to make sure the competition is playing fair with people's souls."

At the end of the service, Father Vincent sought out Addie for a chat. When he promised to bring her home later in the afternoon, Melanie wasted no time at all in getting Thérèse corraled and in the car for their trip home. Trinh went off in one direction with her kids while Lailanie and Duane took their brood home.

"Momma, can we have lunch in a westerant?"

"Anywhere but not hamburgers."

"Aki's?"

"What's it called now?"

"Island Beegs?" the girl offered.

"Close enough," Josh said.

Twenty minutes later, they were shown to a table in their own restaurant. As soon as she sat, Melanie's phone rang with a call from the coroner.

She went back outside to take the call. "Doctor Benson, what have you learned about Kenny Winston?"

"Manner of death was blunt force trauma to the chest. And if that hadn't done it, blunt trauma to his head would've. He also had cervical fractures that were consistent with rapid demise."

"So, he died three times over," Melanie muttered.

"Four times. If any one of those injuries hadn't killed him outright, he would've drowned."

"I'm glad he went so quickly."

"I doubt he felt any pain at all. Whatever hit him was large, heavy, and carried a tremendous amount of energy with it to do the damage that was done to that poor boy. The police are now conducting the case as a homicide."

"Anything else you can tell me about him?"

"Small patches of hair were missing from his scalp, which might help the police. If they can find matching hairs on a hull of a speedboat or cabin cruiser, that makes it the murder weapon. Or would at least imply manslaughter."

"There wouldn't happen to be the name of the boat in his wounds, would there?" she asked.

"No, but there was a discernible imprint on his skin. It would've been the leading edge of whatever hit him."

"In what shape?" she asked.

"I've made a rubber cast of it. Once that's set up, I'll know better."

"Anything about his condition before the injury?" she asked.

"As in a tox screen? Nothing. No alcohol, no drugs, not even the usual trace amount of THC that I'd expect in his demographic."

"What about his other injuries, the broken rib on the opposite side and his jaw?" she asked.

"The mandible fracture is consistent with being punched, most likely by someone left-handed. The bruise on his chest over the rib fracture matches a boot toe, just like you said, a steel-toe work boot. There's even a distinct line where the sole of the boot meets the upper. It's invisible to the naked eye, but I was able to find it on a cross section of the tissue."

"All we have to do is find a left-handed man on the island that wears steel-toe work boots instead of rubber slippers, and we have someone to interrogate. I have no idea about what, though. Have you told Detective Nakatani about that?"

"Just got off the phone with him. He was the one who suggested I call you."

"Great. Anything else?" she asked.

"When are you due?"

"Scheduled for Friday at noon." She stretched the kinks from her backache, which no longer brought relief. "But honestly, I'm ready right now."

After offering wishes of good luck and congratulations, he let her go. Just as she was going back into the restaurant, her phone rang with a call from Nakatani.

"Detective, I just heard from Doctor Benson about his autopsy findings. Do you have anything to add?"

"Not much. I was hoping for a lead, but got more of a dead end."

"What about the skin imprint?" she asked.

"Probably an edge of something on the hull of a boat. I talked to an old guy at one of the marinas, about what kind of boat would do the damage to a human body that was done to Winston. He said it would have to be a small boat going at high speed, like a cabin cruiser or speedboat. Sailboats go slower and their skippers watch the water for what lies ahead. A container ship's cushion of water would've pushed him out of the way before swamping him. I also checked on ocean liner schedules, and there were none in the channel between islands on the day or night before Winston was found in Lahaina."

"What about that bruise in the shape of a steel-toed boot?"

"There could be something there, but I can't go through the closets of every man on the island."

"Any idea why he got beat up? And why would he go surfing not long after?"

"I honestly don't know why people surf at all. But no, it doesn't make sense. If I had just suffered a broken rib, I'd go home and park on the couch for a day or two. Those really smart."

"Tell me about it. Did you find anything in his apartment the other day? Contraband, drugs, historical artifacts?"

"Nothing. I doubt whoever turned the place since then found anything either."

"Any idea when you'll release his body to be shipped home? His mother will be wondering. She can't stay here forever."

"Give me a few more days to try and figure out what happened, and why."

"Well, from Thursday through next week, I'm out of commission. You'll have to talk to Mrs. Winston directly about her son, and to Trinh about mayoral issues. Right now, my lunch is waiting, followed by a long nap and paying someone to rub my feet. Interested?"

"As delightful as that sounds, I think I'm too busy right now, writing speeding tickets along the highway."

Melanie laughed and asked to be told about any developments before going back to where Josh and Thérèse were already eating.

"Anything exciting?" he asked.

"Not much different than what I expected."

"Which is nothing you can tell me about, right?"

"Right." Melanie barely ate. "Can we go home now?"

As they drove up the gravel driveway to their house just across the highway from where they ate lunch, Father Vincent was just coming down.

"Everything okay with her?" Melanie asked through open car windows.

"She just needs some rest and to mourn."

"I hate to ask, but are there any parishioners Addie could stay with?"

"I could ask around. She's thinking of having him buried here, once the police are done with him."

"Well, until this happened to him, he seemed to have a better life here than back home."

Melanie waved and thanked the priest.

"Auntie Addie isn't staying with us anymore?" Thérèse asked, once Josh got the car going up the slope again.

"She can't stay with us forever, Sweetie."

"Why not?"

"She has to go home. She lives in Arizona."

"How far is that?"

"Far, far away. On the other side of the ocean."

"Can we go there?" the girl asked once they were going in the back door of the house.

"We live here and she lives there. Now, go to your room and take off your Sunday dress, please. I'll be there in a few minutes. Maybe we can take a nap together?"

Thérèse trotted down the hall, stumbled once, and got up again, instantly running.

Melanie peeked into the living room. "I wonder where Addie is?"

Josh looked down the hall. "Her door is closed. She might be resting."

"That sounds like a great idea." Still in the kitchen, she backed up to Josh so he could unzip her dress in back. "I'll be in Tay's room, if the world needs me."

When she went past Addie's door, Melanie heard crying inside. Now not just tired, but deflated, she wondered what to do. Letting her woman's instinct kick in, she knocked on the door.

"Addie, would you like some lemonade? We were just going to make a batch."

"No, thank you."

Melanie barely heard the reply. But when she heard footsteps cross the floor in the room, she waited until the door opened.

"Can you sit with me?" the woman asked.

"Of course."

Before they sat, they shared a long hug.

"I'm sorry about keeping you so busy these last couple of days," Addie said. She looked almost like a child, sitting cross-legged on the bed, with her letters to her son spread in front of her.

Melanie had taken the rocker in the corner. "I think I would've been involved anyway. I'm afraid I haven't been much good to you, though. Maybe you needed to rest and spend time alone instead of having us drive you all over."

"No, I wanted to see those places, even if it didn't answer any questions."

"I heard from the police and from the coroner. It's just as we thought. It appears your son was beat up before his accident. You don't have any idea of who might've done that to him?"

Addie shook her head. "Not at all. He mentioned names of his friends a few times but I never wrote anything down. Every time we talked, I asked him to send me letters, and he always promised, but never did. Kenny just didn't seem to be in any trouble here." She sorted through a few of her letters to him before tossing them down in frustration. "Do they know what happened? How he died?"

Here was a tough answer. Should Melanie tell the woman that any of three different injuries would've killed Kenny, his trauma had been so brutal? Would the knowledge that he died instantly and likely without pain be any comfort to her?

"The police have stepped up their investigation, now considering it a possible homicide."

"Homicide? Someone killed him?" Addie asked.

"That's what they're trying to determine. It might be a case of simple manslaughter. Just like we talked about yesterday, he was likely on a surfboard and hit by a boat traveling at a high rate of speed. He would've died instantly. The impact probably broke up his board and he drifted back to shore with the next tide. Eventually, his board leash got tangled in some coral at low tide, which was in the middle of the night, which was a good thing. Otherwise, we might never have found him. I know that all sounds so cruel right now, but I don't want to hide anything from you."

Addie talked about her son, him growing up without a father at home for most of his life, how he'd been a loner during school. "But when he discovered Maui, it was as if he had a whole new lease on life. He was happy, unconditionally happy for the first time. I wanted so much for him to come home, but I also was afraid he'd fall into his doldrums again. I just had to leave him alone to figure out what was best. Now, I'm sitting here wondering if it would've been better for him to come home and be unhappy? At least that way he'd be alive. I'd still have my Kenny."

Melanie had nothing to say. She'd wrestled with enough deaths of loved ones in her life, but never a child, or even a sibling.

"I guess I could take the philosophical approach and say it was better he died happy than lived unhappily."

While the woman went on about her son, Melanie thought of Thérèse, and how she would feel if she ever lost her. As high-maintenance and energetic as she was, she was the biggest part of her life.

When the woman finally stopped, Melanie said, "Addie, I need to get some rest."

She needed help to get out of the rocker, and once she was upright, she went straight to Thérèse's room.

"Hey, little one. Are you and Mister Clunky playing?"

"Mister Crumpet. We were just talking."

Melanie fell more than lay down on the girl's bed. "What about?"

"Mister Crumpet is waiting for our brother to come home."

"Well, I hate to disappoint Mister Crumpet and you, but you're getting a sister."

"For real?"

"Yep. For real."

"No can change her to a boy?"

"Nope, sorry. What's wrong with a girl?"

"That would be three girls and only one boy at home." Thérèse held up her fingers to count with. "Number One is you. Number Two is me. And Number Three is baby Sofia. But there's only Daddy on the boy list."

"Doesn't seem fair, does it? But you know what? I think he can handle it."

Melanie held her breath when Thérèse yawned.

"Guess what? You're having your tonsils taken out on Wednesday."

"That's what Daddy said. I no need them no more?"

"Nope."

"What about yours?"

"I still got mine."

"What about Daddy?"

"Pretty sure he still has his, too."

The girl began to pout. "Why you guys taking mine away from me?"

"Because yours are sort of broken. You know all those sore throats and colds you get? Well, we can solve that by taking out your tonsils. That's good, right?"

"Guess so."

"Plus, you'll sleep better."

"Sleep better?" the girl asked.

"Big secret: you snore a lot."

"I do? I never hear it."

"Because you're asleep when you're snoring. And we're doing it this week because I'm off from work and you start preschool soon. Daddy and I want you in tip-top condition when you start school, okay?"

The girl nodded. "I have a question."

"What is it?"

"At church today, the two men next to me were holding hands, just like you and Daddy hold hands sometimes."

"So?"

"I was wondering…"

"Wondering what?"

"Are they in love?"

Here came yet another puzzle for Melanie to work out with her daughter. "I don't know. But there are many different kinds of love. There's the kind Daddy and I have for each other, and the kind you and I have for each other, and you and Daddy, right?"

"Uh-huh."

"And when Sofia gets here, you'll grow up together and love each other as sisters, right?"

"Just like you and Auntie Trinh?"

"Yep, just like us. But that's not a romantic love where people have babies, but a sisterly love. I know it's very difficult to understand, even for adults."

"Brothers, too?"

"I think so, but they don't show it the same way as sisters usually do."

"Those men at church, they gonna have a baby?"

"Men can't have babies, Sweetie, just women."

"Oh, yeah, I forgot. But they're in love?"

"If they're holding hands, then yes, I suppose they are."

"Anybody can fall in love?" the girl asked.

"You sure ask hard questions, but I think so. I've only been in love with Daddy, so I'm not much of an expert on it."

"Auntie Trinh loves Unca Harmon?"

"Yep."

"Unca Harmon loves Auntie Trinh?"

"Yep."

"Wow, everybody loves someone. What about Aunt Addie?"

"I don't know. She doesn't have a husband, though."

"That's too bad."

"Sure is."

"Maybe we should find one for her?" Thérèse asked.

"Maybe a better idea would be to leave her love life alone, okay?"

Thérèse yawned again, her eyes half-closed. "Will somebody love me someday?"

"Daddy and I already do. So does Trinh and a whole bunch of other people."

By then the girl was asleep. Melanie cuddled her close as best she could and was soon asleep in the warm room.

***

When Melanie woke, Thérèse was already up from her nap and playing in the living room with Josh. Going to her home office, merely a corner of the master bedroom with a desk, computer, and lamp, Melanie logged onto the internet and found the auction site she'd been watching for the last few days. The items she'd been following had tripled in bid price since she had last looked.

"Okay, that's it. I don't know who wants these things or why, but they're not getting them. I'm going to make it impossible for anyone else to bid higher than me."

Tripling the highest bid, she offered that for the shark's tooth clubs and the Hawaiian spear. Before closing the site, she filled out the personal bio of her as a bidder, making up an alternate version of her mother had she still been alive, once again using the name Aiko Murata.

"Good enough. Let's see how long it takes to get accepted," she said, closing the computer.

Monday morning started with peace and quiet, the way days off should. Melanie could smell coffee and heard the quiet chitchat of three voices come from the kitchen. She was reluctant to get up and leave the tranquility and comfort of bed, but when her usual caffeine headache started to sweep through her, there was no delaying that first cup of green tea, her temporary pregnancy replacement for strong coffee.

Putting on Josh's largest T-shirt, which stretched tight over her belly, and a pair of shorts, the formality of the last two days of having a guest in her home was gone. Shuffling down the hall, she bundled her messy hair into a ponytail and secured that with a band.

"Good morning," she mumbled, going straight to the cabinet with the tea. She packed loose-leaf tea into a strainer and dropped it into her favorite mug, and soaked it with hot water.

"Momma!"

Melanie winced from her daughter's sudden outburst of excitement.

"Good morning, Melanie," Addie said.

Josh joined her at the stove, rubbing her shoulders. "You're tight. Maybe you should get a massage today."

"Or just go in and have this baby. I mean, really. Can four days really make that much difference?"

"Patience has never been one of your virtues. Just wait. In the meantime, there's toast, oatmeal, eggs, and juice."

"Just some juice."

She plunked in her chair at the table and immediately pushed Thérèse's bowl of oatmeal to in front of her. "Eat some more, little one."

"Must be nice that you don't have to go in to the hospital today, Melanie," Addie said.

"I'd be more excited about it if I had the energy."

"You do look a little like you went on a bender last night," Josh said.

"Thanks, buddy. Exactly what a pregnant girl needs to hear."

"You were in the blender last night, Momma?" Thérèse asked.

"No, Daddy said bender. It means…never mind what it means." Melanie tried forcing a smile to Addie. "Sorry about the informality around here at breakfast."

"You mean you're an ordinary woman raising a happy family?"

"Yes, well, usually I'm a little more energetic than this, and more cheerful. It's just that I'm done with this pregnancy, even if my OB and the kid aren't. Right now, it feels like I have an entire basketball team inside me, and they're all playing defense against my bladder."

"Maybe you gonna have two babies, Momma? One of each!"

"Twins would be exciting," Addie said.

"They run in the family. Mom was a twin, and her sister had twin daughters. But to break the cycle of all girls, Thérèse is firmly convinced I'm having a boy, not a girl. But every ultrasound I've had indicates otherwise."

"I tried my best to make a male heir to the throne," Josh said.

"You making the baby on the potty throne, Momma?" Thérèse asked.

"No, a different kind of throne than the potty throne," Josh said, pulling the girl's chair back. "It's time for your Hebrew lesson. We didn't go to temple the other day, so now we have to make up for it with an extra-long lesson. Can you recite the alphabet?"

The girl hopped down from her chair to follow her father to another room.

"Alef, bet, gimel, dalet…"

"She's so smart, but Hebrew?" Addie asked, once father and daughter were gone from the kitchen.

"I don't know why. She's learning Hawaiian, Japanese, and Spanish, also. I don't know how she keeps them straight in her mind. When we started, it seemed like a good idea. Now, it would be a shame to quit."

"She's a three-year-old ambassador to the United Nations."

"Pretty much. How are you feeling today, Addie?"

"I've been better. Still coming to terms with it all. It's almost as if he should call me any moment, but I know he never will. I just wish I knew what I was supposed to do."

"Nobody ever knows," Melanie said quietly. "When my mother died, I didn't know what to do or how to feel. I was in the Air Force then, and fortunately stayed busy enough so it all didn't hit me at once. That was twenty years ago, and I'm still trying to figure it all out."

"What did you do in the Air Force?" Addie asked.

"Combat Search and Rescue."

"Oh, my. You must've seen…"

"Unfortunately. Death is one of those horrible things that happen to people. We're all supposed to live a long and healthy life, but sometimes terrible tricks are played on us, tricks that are hard to endure. Children are supposed to outlive their parents."

"You've lost your father also?"

Melanie nodded. "Dad died a few years ago. We all expected Dad's passing, but when Mom went, it was such a shock. I had a hard time coping with the idea I'd never see her again."

"Josh said she was a doctor at the hospital?"

"A long time ago, when it first opened. It was pretty small then. She was their first neurosurgeon."

"What did your father do for work?" Addie asked.

Melanie pushed away her bowl of cold oats and gave the woman a long look. It was a question she'd never figured out how to answer. "He was even busier than me. He was a lawyer, had several businesses, and did some diplomacy work as a politician."

"Diplomacy work?"

"One of his roles as a politician was Ambassador to Chile for a few years. That makes me half Japanese, half Chilean, and is why Thérèse is learning so many languages."

"That sounds exciting. Did you enjoy living in Chile?"

"That was before I was born. Mom met him sometime after then when he needed surgery. I've read her diary a few times, and in a lot of ways, theirs was a match made in Heaven. But in other ways, maybe not so much. Their relationship was what you could call complicated."

"Aren't they all?" Addie asked.

"Maybe theirs was a bit more than most. Anyway, you don't want to hear about them. Do you have plans for today? I'm sure Josh would be glad to take you anywhere you need to go."

"I really should find a room in a hotel. Is there an inexpensive one nearby?"

"On Maui? Nothing is inexpensive here. We really do like having you stay here with us. Thérèse is quite taken with you."

"She's a doll. I don't get much chance to be around kids her age anymore."

"I keep forgetting to ask what you do for a living? Do you need to be back to work soon?" Melanie asked.

"I just do a lot of volunteer work. My husband did quite well for himself, and when he passed away, he left a substantial insurance policy for us. With just me rambling around that big house, it seems like such a waste. I've been thinking about downsizing. Maybe now will be a good time."

"Well, you're welcome to stay here for as long as you need to. And I'll let Josh know he's your taxi for the rest of the day." Melanie struggled up from her chair. "Now, I need to bathe this enormous body of mine and find something to wear that might still fit around my belly." She stopped to look at Addie. "When you were pregnant with Kenny, did you feel like Noah's ark?"

Addie smiled. "I felt like an aircraft carrier for as big as I was and as busy as he was inside me. Just enjoy it as much as you can because someday it ends."

Melanie started walking again. "I hope so."

By the time she was out from her shower and dressed, Josh was gone, Thérèse and Addie with him. A note was left indicating their itinerary for the day, and the first stop was at a beach before going to the mall. Melanie plunked down on the couch to make a call.

"Lailanie, I'm on your schedule for today at noon, right?"

"Yes. Have you decided what you want done?"

"You know what? I'd rather have a massage. Is someone there today?"

"I have someone new. Just come in anytime. I can't pressure you into doing something frivolous?"

Melanie felt stomach acid rise when the baby kicked. "Looking for way to get rid of some pressure, Lai."

"I'm keeping you on the schedule for noon, Melanie. I'm not letting you back out."

Melanie knew better than to cross swords with a hairstylist, since she had more to lose in that deal. Able to drop in any time for her massage and needing only a few minutes to walk there, she made another call.

"Detective Nakatani, you sound like you're at the beach. Do you have time to talk?"

"I'm at Pohaku Park, but not because I want to be. Official police business."

"Don't you ever take a day off?"

"I wish I had today off. Another body has been discovered, in roughly the same condition as the Winston kid. And I mean rough in every sense of the word."

Melanie swore. "What happened? Who was it?"

"This one washed up onto the beach sometime during the night. Haven't ID'd him yet, but same deal as with the Winston kid, with the surfboard leash on one leg. There was even a piece of the board attached."

"Don't tell me. White with a blue stripe? Thick like it was a rental board?"

"That's right. Just like you said about the Gonzo boards. But when I go back to talk to them this time, they won't be able to wiggle out so easily as before. When I spoke to them Friday, they denied they were missing any boards, even showed them to me. But they had twenty-eight of them then. I'll see how many they claim to have today. That's my next stop after here. Unfortunately, the media has heard about this and I'm dealing with half a dozen newspaper and TV reporters."

Melanie sat up. "You know what? That's my job to talk to them about these things. Can you send a patrol car to pick me up? My house is only a few minutes from there."

"I can manage them, if they all show up at the same time and leave once I'm done. But there are reporters coming in from Honolulu now, old pals I was hoping never to see again when I moved here."

Melanie chuckled. "Yes, we all have old pals we'd like to get rid of. Just send someone to get me. It's time for an official statement from me about this anyway."

"My precinct commander Hernandez should be here shortly. I'll hold off on any more statements until the two of you have had a chance to talk."

Melanie hurried as best she could to change into something more presentable than a T-shirt and threadbare sweatpants for the ad hoc press conference she needed to give. As she changed clothes, she considered what she might say to the reporters, people always hungry for information--the juicier the better.

"What do they usually say? We'll get to the bottom of whoever is behind these deeds?"

When she went outside, the patrol car was just arriving. After being helped into the back seat, she noticed a strong odor.

"That's not me that smells like that, right?" she asked the officer as he pulled out into traffic.

"No, Ma'am. I had to take in a couple of drunk drivers early this morning, and one didn't quite make it out of the car, if you know what I mean."

"How nice." She tried opening the windows in back, but being a vehicle that transported suspects and criminals, the switches and door handle didn't work. She immediately felt claustrophobic. "Can you put the windows down, please? In my condition, I'm not far from doing the same thing most days."

The breeze that blew in from the front window helped, but not much.

"Holding a press conference at the beach, Ma'am?" he asked.

"That's right. Somehow, I need to reassure the public that our beaches and the ocean are safe, and without sounding like I'm giving a canned speech. Any suggestions?"

"Not much of a speechmaker, Ma'am. But you always sound like you know what you're talking about on TV. That's why my wife and I voted for you."

"Thanks." She wanted to say something about giving their votes more consideration next time, but let it go. As it was, she hadn't won the recent election, but the incumbent winner went to jail for corruption. As second place finisher, Melanie was stuck with the job. Getting out her phone, she called Lailanie to cancel her noon appointment.

"Everything's okay?" the hairstylist asked. "You're not going to the hospital, are you?"

"No, it's mayor business. If you have a TV there, turn it on to the local news. You'll see your tax dollars at work."

Just about then, they arrived at the beach, where Nakatani was fending off a throng of reporters and two TV crews. Arriving right behind her was Commander Hernandez, MPD chief.

"Mayor Kato, Mayor Kato! Do you have a statement for the press?" one of the reporters shouted.

Melanie was barely out of the car before having half a dozen microphones thrust in her face. "Let me talk with the lead detective and the precinct commander for a few minutes and we'll come back to you, okay?"

The reporters left the trio alone when officers called them away.

Nakatani started. "Mayor, for future purposes, don't ever let reporters make decisions."

"What decision?" she asked.

"You asked them if it was okay that we talk first before giving them a statement."

"It's just a figure of speech."

Hernandez took over. "Nak's right. Every little thing you say to them is scrutinized before being broadcast or printed in the newspaper. Believe me, they'll turn your words around backwards and inside out, just to make what you say more interesting."

"Or incriminating," Nakatani said.

"Okay, fine. Dumb newbie mayor has learned her lesson. What's going on with this dead body?"

"Yes, what's the deal with this one, Nak?" Hernandez asked.

"About the same as the first one from a few days ago. Surfer with a leash but not much of a board. The coroner is looking him over on the beach where he was found. I have a CSI crew here, getting photos, collecting whatever evidence they can from a public beach at high tide."

"What were his injuries?" Melanie asked, her medical mind kicking in.

"Basically the same as the Winston kid. Severe chest injuries. But there's something new with this one, something I didn't know when we talked a while ago, Mayor."

"What's that?"

"A shark took a bite out of this one."

Melanie got out her phone and sent a text to Josh, asking where they were and to stay out of the water. "Which means he'd been floating outside the reef for a while. Sharks rarely come close to shore on this part of the island. It might even have been the mechanism of injury that caused his death, but I'm not telling that to the press. Every time there's a shark bite within a thousand miles of Hawaii, hotel room reservations plummet."

"If there is a shark patrolling these waters, we're compelled to tell the public, Mayor, for their safety," Hernandez said.

She sighed, knowing he was right. "I know. But let's wait until we know for sure. What was bit off the body?"

"Apparently, his head," Nakatani said.

Melanie swallowed some nausea, the flavor of her morning oatmeal.

The coroner joined them, snapping off his exam gloves. "That's a mess."

"We heard something about a possible shark bite?" Nakatani asked.

"That was no shark. If it had been, it would've come back for more. An arm, a leg, whatever. They don't leave easy meals behind. No, it's too clean of an injury. Incisive rather than a tearing bite a shark would make. I think it was from a large boat propeller."

"So, definitely not a shark?" Melanie asked.

Dr. Benson nodded his head toward the beach. "Let's go have a look and I'll explain why I think that."

The CSI techs had the body covered with a tarp. When two of them lifted one end, they were careful to shield the body from reporters and their cameras. Melanie had seen shark bite victims and beheaded bodies during her time as a doctor, but this hit her differently. The body was deformed the way Kenny Winston had been, and with the head missing, made it look even worse. She clamped her teeth against more nausea that was rising.

"See the skin edge here?" Benson said, pointing to where the neck had been. "This has been incised, not bitten through. Not carefully by a knife, mind you, but chopped roughly the way a cleaver or propeller might do. Given enough time, I might even be able to tell you the quality of the propeller, if it was new or old, had any rust on it, or damaged edges. No, this definitely was not a shark bite."

"Why not a cleaver?" Nakatani asked.

"Think about it. If you were going to use a cleaver like a guillotine to behead someone, you'd go straight through the middle of his neck, right? Not this guy. This is an oblique injury, going through at an angle, taking a part of the trapezius muscle from one side.

Melanie couldn't help but look at the exposed anatomy, her imagination running wild. "There's no sign of the…"

"Head?"

"Yes," she muttered.

"Not that we've noticed," Benson said. He pointed to someone in scuba gear in the water. "We have someone checking the water, but that could've drifted in a different direction, or just sank."

"Shark probably found it before it got too far," Nakatani said. "Made a meal of it anyway."

Melanie's mind whirled for a second. Steadying herself didn't help. In fact, it made her nausea worse.

"Pardon me."

She stepped over to the privacy of shade beneath a tree and let loose of her breakfast. Once that was done, she felt a hand on her back and a handkerchief being given to her. After she wiped her mouth, Nakatani handed her a bottle of water.

"Thanks," she said, after spitting out the rinse water. "Kind of embarrassing."

"No worries. You don't have to do this news conference, Melanie."

"I want to. It was just the sight of that guy. And seriously, you guys need to clean your patrol cars a little better."

Detective Nakatani took Melanie home after their news briefing, making a stop for something to drink at a fast food place on the way. Melanie was sure to find a place in the shade, with plenty of breeze blowing through.

"One iced tea, extra sugar, no lemon," he said, setting a large cup in front of her.

She took out the straw and removed the lid to drink. "I think the news conference went okay. I didn't make too much of a fool of myself."

"It went fine. They got an update about the earlier investigation, and what we know about this one. Not much more we can tell them. I do think it was a good idea not to tell them about the guy's head."

Melanie set down her cup after taking several sips. "Let's not bring that up again, okay?"

"I wanted to talk to you for a while about the investigation into the missing artifacts."

"You said Winston's fingerprints were on all the cases of the missing things, right?"

"Full prints on the case at the library, and we found partials at the museum that would be good enough for court evidence."

"It's so strange he showed up dead right after the thefts."

Nakatani shifted uneasily. "There are some other peculiarities popping up in that investigation."

She wondered where he was going with it. "Oh?"

"As of last night, everything has been bought in an online auction, and by the same buyer, a Japanese woman in the LA area that goes by the online name of Aiko Murata. Does that sound familiar to you?"

Melanie ignored her tea, worried it might come up again. This time it was nerves instead of nausea. "There are a lot of people with Japanese names in Los Angeles, Detective."

"When we turned the auction sales into an official investigation, we were able to force the auction house into telling us the address of where the things were shipped. Guess where that was?"

"To this Murata person, I would guess."

"Not exactly. Since this is now an FBI investigation."

"Oh, those guys," Melanie hissed.

"Yes, I heard from Hernandez you and they don't get along so well. But when the feds checked out the shipping address, they discovered a man named Carl Masters had signed for them. But instead of using his name, he signed Aiko Murata's name. The really interesting thing about this Masters fellow is that he's a retired Secret Service agent."

"That is interesting. Did they arrest him, or the woman? What was her name again?"

"Murata," Nakatani said slowly. Melanie felt like he was drilling holes into her with his stare. "They didn't arrest her either. Can you guess the location of the address?"

The jig was up. She knew she'd been caught in her scheme. "1173 Old Hacienda Lane?"

"Also known as the Jack Melendez Presidential Library, formerly his private home, and that of Doctor June Kato, and a child named Melanie Kato, albeit thirty-some years ago. The only reason the FBI agents backed off was because of the location."

Melanie tried putting on an innocent expression but knew it looked more like nausea right then. "Seems more than coincidental, doesn't it?"

"It's even more coincidental that the mother of the man whose prints were found on the museum cases is staying with you as a houseguest."

"I'm still not sure how that happened, and I can't quite seem to find a polite way of getting rid of her. As it is right now, my daughter would be pissed at me if I made Mrs. Winston leave."

"I'm willing to give it the benefit of the doubt for the next twenty-four hours, if I get some straight answers from you, right now. But I have to tell you, it looks an awful lot like internet trafficking of stolen historical artifacts, which is a serious federal offense and carries severe penalties."

"Look, I was just trying to get the stuff back to Maui. When I found it at an online auction, I had to bid. There was no way I was going to let that stuff go to some collector who would stick the stuff in a corner of his hobby room, or resell it a year from now for a profit. That's Hawaiian heritage stuff and belongs here. Or in the Bishop Museum in Honolulu. It might be safer there. The only reason it was still here on Maui was because they were used by Mauian villagers generations ago."

"You don't know anything about the theft of it?"

"All I know is what you've told me."

"Why did you have it sent to your father's library?"

"You know he was my father?"

"Everybody at the precinct knows, even if most of the public still doesn't. Why send it there and not have it sent back here?"

"I was hoping not to implicate myself. In a few weeks, I was going to have it quietly returned anonymously, no questions asked. And then beef up the display cases they were kept in."

"Why get Agent Masters involved?"

Melanie smiled at the memory. "Agent Masters was a young agent on Dad's protection detail when my mom and I were living there with Dad. He was always so stern, but for some reason took a liking to me. We'd play little games, just simple little things that I'd make up on the spur of the moment. He even went along with my practical jokes that I'd play on Mom and Dad occasionally. It wasn't until years later that I figured out he would tell them ahead of time so they could play along and act surprised. Well, he remained on Dad's detail until the very end, and was even one of his pallbearers. That's when he retired from the Service and took over managing the library. I know it sounds silly, but doing things this way, I kept my name out of it. At least until now."

"Explanation accepted, for the time being. Who the heck is Aiko Murata?" he asked.

Melanie chuckled. "My mother."

"I don't understand."

Melanie dug through her pocketbook to find a small snapshot. "This is my mom when she was working as a model. That was taken several years before I was born, when she was modeling in Japan, using that name as a professional alias."

"She's very pretty." He handed the picture back. "You got your looks from her."

"Thanks, but never in a million years could I look nearly as good as Mom. Or be as classy."

"Okay, for the record. Before last week, you never met or had any business with Kenneth Winston?"

"Absolutely none."

"Or Adelaide Winston?"

"None, except that she's living with us right now. And yes, I do realize how that must look to the police."

"You don't have the stolen objects in your home, right?"

"Not at all. Once they're returned to Maui, I'll look at them through bulletproof glass cases at the museum, just like everyone else."

"Do you have any other stolen objects in your home?"

"Seriously?" she asked. "If I had even so much as shoplifted as a kid and my mom had found out, I'd still be grounded."

"Had to ask. One more thing. Did you have anything to do with the planning of the theft of those items?"

"I could no more plan the break-in of a museum for the theft of artifacts out of locked cases than flying to the moon."

"Yes or no answer, please."

"No. I had nothing to do with the planning nor did I assist in the theft of those things. You can consider that my official statement about it. Anything else?"

He flipped his little notebook closed and put it away. "Yes. Are you getting enough rest? You don't look so good."

"Detective, I'm two meals behind after losing my breakfast at the beach a little while ago, I haven't had a full night of sleep in weeks, and have an offensive lineman packed into my uterus. Right now, he's doing jumping jacks on my bladder. Not to mention the slipped disc in my back which is grating on my last good nerve. If you wouldn't mind helping me into your car, you could give me a ride home."

***

Perched on the couch, her legs sprawled, her head back on a pillow, the muted TV showing an old western, beads of sweat running down her face and neck, Melanie tapped a finger on her belly.

"Hey, you in there. Come out."

Just as she was about to doze off, she heard the back door open, followed by the sound of small footsteps through the kitchen and into the living room.

"Momma!" Thérèse shouted as she leapt onto the couch.

"Please don't bounce the couch, Sweetie. It looks like you went to the beach?"

"La Perouse. We found a coconut."

"Well, that's a good day, then." Melanie looked at Josh and Addie as they came into the room. "Island shortage of sunscreen?"

"We put some on when we first got there," Addie said.

"We might've been out for too long," Josh added.

"You know the rules, Josh. Every two hours, even in the shade and she always has to wear a hat. Can you bring me the aloe, please?"

"It's not so bad, Momma."

"I know, but let me put it on you anyway. What else did you do with Aunt Addie?"

"Went to some little shops, got sumpin' to drink."

Addie had gone to her room and closed herself in by then.

"Were you nice to her?" Melanie whispered.

"They've become best friends," Josh said, taking the aloe back to apply to his own face. "How was your day? Get some rest?"

"Not really." Melanie sent her daughter into the kitchen for something to drink, an activity that would take a few minutes. "Another body has washed ashore, but I'm not telling Addie until we know more about it."

"What happened?" he asked.

"It looks about the same as with her son. Except this kid lost his head to a motor boat propeller."

"Of all the ways to go. Anything I can do for you?"

"I've been waiting for you to get home. I'm very close to being overdue for a trip to the bathroom."

"You can't get up?"

"I seem to be stuck here. But before you help me up, go in the sewing basket and get a straight pin."

"What for?" he asked.

"You'll see." While she waited, she listened to what Thérèse was doing in the kitchen, something that was turning into a major project from the sounds of it.

"What am I doing with this?" he asked, once he was back with the pin.

"Jab it into my right big toe."

"What? I'm not going to jab you with a pin. Do your self-destructive activities on your own time."

"Just jab my toe with it."

Sitting on the edge of the coffee table, he picked up her foot. "Where?"

"Anywhere."

He gave the top of her toe a solid jab, causing her to jerk her foot back while swearing.

"Not so hard! I said jab, not ram it in." She put that foot down and tried lifting the other. "Pick up the other foot and try it again. Not so deep this time."

"Why am I hurting my wife?"

"Just do it, you big baby."

This time, he gave her a gentler jab.

"Do it again, right at the end and a little more aggressively."

He poked her again.

She tried seeing what he was doing with her foot. "Did you do it? I can't feel anything."

Josh lifted Melanie's foot so she could see her toe. The pin was sticking out the end of it. "Satisfied?"

"Okay, never mind. Take it out. Now scrape your thumbnail along the sole of my foot, heel to toe."

He did as he was told while she watched.

"Just as I thought."

"Why'd I do all that?" he asked.

"I think that bad disc in my back has finally slipped and is pushing on a nerve root. I can't feel a dang thing in that foot."

"Should I call an ambulance?"

"No, you should help me to the bathroom, before taking me for a massage and then to the chiropractor."

Two hours later, Melanie limped from the massage room at Lailanie's salon.

"Put me down for another massage tomorrow at noon, Lai," Melanie said on her way out the door to Josh's waiting car.

"Any better?" he asked as they drove to Lahaina for her next appointment.

"Relaxed, anyway. Almost forgot I was pregnant there for a while."

"Not much longer."

"I know."

"And when the time comes, you'll cry your eyes out, and six months later, you'll be wanting another one."

"I might cry, once the cussing is done, but this is the last one for me. If you want more kids, you'll have to find a girl on the side."

"Cool. Fall term starts soon. Maybe a coed."

"Did I ever show you my expert marksman medal from being in the Air Force Special Forces?" she asked.

"Every time a new term starts at school, just to keep me in line. Where's this guy's office again?"

"Her. She's on Waine'e Street. Just let me out in front and then find a place to park in the shade. I can go in by myself."

"Forget that. I'm going with you."

"You'll get a ticket if you park in the waiting zone."

"I'm married to the mayor. How could the coppers give me a ticket?" He parked at the curb with his four-way flashers blinking and went around to get the door for her. "Just let me get you inside and then I'll move the car."

They struggled up a short set of steps. "Why in the world does a chiropractor have an office at the top of stairs?" she griped as they went up, one step at a time.

After filling out the paperwork and showing insurance cards, Melanie was led to a treatment room, something like a small gym. Not only was the place a chiropractor's office but a physical therapy rehab center as well. She was just getting positioned on a bench when something occurred to her to ask.

"You've worked with pregnant women before, right?"

"Many times," Dr. Rigley said.

"As much as I'm done with this pregnancy, please don't break my water."

"I'll be very careful about that, I promise. I know some advanced techniques for women in your condition, and I'm ordinarily quite gentle. I've had quite a few women come in on their way to the hospital, just to have their hips adjusted right before delivering their babies. They swear by it."

"Good for them. I just want to get as much done as you can without stirring up too much trouble. Maybe you can do my neck and shoulders also."

Starting with her hips, the chiropractor adjusted Melanie's joints, getting solid pops from each of them on her way up her spine.

"How do you feel?" Rigley asked once she was done with the back.

"Better. My leg feels warm like it's waking up again."

"That's the idea. Ready for your neck?"

With her head turned to one side, Melanie saw Josh come into the room, watching what was being done. There was a twist and a loud pop, which echoed in Melanie's open mouth. When Melanie groaned, Josh had the look of surprise on his face.

"Are you okay?" Rigley said, putting her head straight again.

"Fine. Wait for a sec before doing the other side."

"Maybe you shouldn't," Josh suggested.

"No, it's okay."

Melanie's head was cradled in Rigley's arms and turned in the opposite direction, getting another loud pop.

"How about your shoulders?"

"Please," Melanie mumbled.

"This is okay?" Josh asked, watching as the chiropractor got into position.

"From the sounds of it, this is way overdue," Dr. Rigley said.

"This is great," Melanie said. "I need to come back here more often."

Once her shoulders were done, Dr. Rigley brought a chair over to sit in while working on Melanie's hands. "I saw your news conference earlier. That's really a terrible shame what happened. The police don't know anything more about the two surfer deaths than what you told the reporters?"

"Not much. You know how they always say the investigation is still ongoing."

"What press conference?" Josh asked.

"You didn't see it?" Rigley asked.

"See what?"

"There was a little press thing at Pohaku Park."

"You went out?" he asked.

"Just for a few minutes."

"I thought you were going to rest today?"

"It was official county business. I can't stop being mayor just because I'm tired."

"Can't Trinh help? She's your vice mayor, right? Isn't that one of her duties, to step in when you can't do something?"

"She's watching over everything else, except these death investigations. Since I already know about those, I'm going to handle that stuff. Plus, she's at work today."

"What do you mean, death investigations?" he asked, once they were in the car headed home. "I thought that Winston kid was beat up and murdered?"

"He was definitely beat up, but the police and the coroner haven't come to the conclusion foul play was involved. That's why the investigation is still being conducted."

"What about the one today?" Josh asked.

"They don't know much about him, either. Not even his name, the last I heard."

"I still don't see why you can't turn this stuff over to Trinh?"

"On Thursday. Otherwise, I'm sitting at home in my pajamas and pace a rut in the floor to the bathroom. No more press conferences, no more crooks. No more reporters' dirty looks."

"We have to take Thérèse in for her tonsils Wednesday, remember?"

"I forgot about that. We should've had that done earlier in the summer. With her starting preschool next week, we've run out of time."

"We could put it off until winter break?"

"Forget it. Ten minutes in the OR and she's done. She'll sleep the rest of the day, be grumpy on Thursday, and be back to normal on Friday."

"You're up to it?" he asked.

"It's not like I have to do any of the work. Trinh is on duty in the OR that day and has promised to take care of her during the surgery. Who knows? Maybe Kenny's body will be released for shipment back to Arizona and Addie will be gone by then."

"I almost hate to see her go," Josh said. "She's really good with Thérèse. Better than that nanny we had a while back."

"May as well just…"

"Just what?" he asked.

"Nothing. Let's just focus on getting through this week one day at a time."

He enumerated on his fingers. "House guest, murder investigations, museum thefts, tonsils, bad back, nine months pregnant. That's some week."

She patted his thigh. "Just remember, you're the glue holding it all together."

"Whatever happened with those stolen museum antiquities? That sort of got lost in the shuffle when the Winstons entered our lives."

"That's been resolved, mostly. The missing artifacts were located and should be returned in the next few weeks. I want to find a better security system so they're safer once they're put on display. Especially the kahili."

"You don't need any more projects, Melanie."

"I was actually thinking of handing that over to you."

"I'm also not one of your lackeys. Let the museum figure out what to do with it. Who found it?"

"An investigator. It's in a secure location."

"You know more about it than that, don't you?" he asked, making the turn off the highway onto their driveway.

"Maybe."

"Which means yes, coming from you."

"It's still one of those police things that can't be discussed."

"Too many secrets with you, Melanie Kato."

"Ha! That's half the fun of being married!"

Tuesday morning turned quiet when Addie went for a walk through the grounds of the resort across the road, Josh holed up in their little office to work on the upcoming quarter curriculum for his classes at the college, and Thérèse invented a game involving dinosaurs on the living room floor. Melanie made a nest of pillows on the couch, her phone in her hand. Just as she was scrolling through her phone list for someone she could chat with that wasn't at work, the phone rang with a call from Detective Nakatani.

"Please don't tell me there's been another death," she said right off.

"Not that I know of. I was wondering if Mrs. Winston has come up with any names for her son's friends or associates?"

"I know she's been reading through her old letters to Kenny. She mentioned something about finding something interesting. I'll have her call you once she's back from her walk."

"When is that supposed to be?" he asked.

"I have no idea. She wanted to see the resort grounds and go for a walk in the little neighborhood near here. I think she was looking for some privacy to think about what's happened without being disturbed by us. She took her phone, so maybe she's calling friends at home."

"If she has any hunches at all, have her call me. There is a new development, though."

"Whatever it is, I had nothing to do with it. I have alibis and witnesses for everything. And if I don't, I can manufacture one."

"So defensive," he said chuckling.

"Not that being pregnant while being mayor isn't weird enough, these last few days of your investigations into the stolen artifacts and the deaths of the two young men have pushed the weirdness gauge to the limit."

"Well, you won't like this. More Hawaiiana has shown up in online auctions."

"More museum pieces? I thought the museum has been locked up tight since the theft, and the library doesn't have anything else to steal. Other than in people's private collections, what else is there to take from Maui? Or did they break into the Bishop Museum on Oahu?"

"Neither. We've had techs analyze the images from the internet. These weren't museum pieces, at least not yet. It looks almost as if they've just recently been collected from the environment."

"What do you mean, from the environment?" she asked.

"They're grimy, like they haven't been professionally cleaned and restored. They look like they've been dug up or recovered from an outdoor location, quickly wiped clean, and photographed for auction."

"What kinds of things?" she asked.

"Battle weapons. Clubs, spears, something that looks like it might've been a shield or heavy fabric, but it's pretty worn out. About a dozen things altogether."

"The same auction site?" she asked.

"You just leave it alone, Mayor. You don't need to do our work for us."

"Just curious. I'd like to see what it is."

"Don't buy any of it. We're working with the FBI on setting up a sting operation to get the perps behind all this."

"What I've been curious about is why couldn't investigators figure out who the sellers are if they were able to figure out who the buyer was of the batch of stuff I bought?" Melanie asked.

"Good question. We were working on that, both MPD and the Bureau, but somebody interfered by purchasing all of it before we could pin down their identities. All we got was a general location stemming from the Hawaiian Islands, but no exact IP address."

"Oh. You mean somebody interfered as in me?"

"Right. That's why it's really important for you to leave it alone, Mayor. I appreciate your efforts in bringing those things back home to where they belong, but we need to get these guys. That means having this new batch of stuff left out there for as long as we can allow, just so we can build a trail back to the seller. That's not nearly as easy as it sounds."

"Why not?" she asked. "If you can figure out the buyer's identity, ostensibly through an IP address, why not do the same with the seller?"

"Because we need to work with the auction house to get sellers' private information, and so far they've been reluctant to turn it over."

"Which means they're probably complicit in the scheme?" she asked.

"That's the assumption. If nothing else, they're very protective of their sellers, making it appear to be a black market site."

"What kind of auction history do they have? Have they been in trouble before for doing the same thing?"

"That's something else we're looking into. We're trying to determine how ethical their site is in conducting business, and trying to determine what their sellers are like. Some of these auction sites are completely legit, selling bona fide art or historical objects whose ownership has been verified. Other sites are not so ethical. They'll put up anything for auction, no questions asked. Bogus trash that was manufactured in someone's garage over the weekend, and legitimate historical

144

objects that have been passed from hand to hand but should never have entered the marketplace. We think this one might be one of those."

"The FBI can't just shut it down?" she asked.

"They probably could, with a court order. But they'd need probable cause and would need to meet a few other parameters. But as soon as we shut them down, the auction house would know they're being investigated, and they'd disappear. Keeping the site open and the auctions live keeps them from knowing they're being watched. Hopefully."

"But what if someone buys something? Wouldn't it be lost to them?" Melanie asked.

"We might still be able to get it back, by claiming it as stolen goods. But if the buyer is anonymous, or uses a fake ID like you did to run us around in circles, it might be lost forever. You have to remember, buyers can be just as unethical with the purchase of fine art and historical objects as sellers are."

"I see. Well, keep me informed," she said, starting to feel tired just from the phone call. "Anything new about the deaths?"

"I sent an officer to Gonzo's Surf Shop for a second round of questions. They let him nowhere near their rental merchandise to see if they were short a board."

"Which means they felt guilty about something, right?" she asked.

"Probably feel guilty about a lot of things, including having merchandise completely unrelated to surfing, if you know what I mean."

"Drugs?" she asked, not terribly surprised.

"At least."

"If we're lucky, maybe we can shut down a pusher."

"They're known pushers. What we'd like to do is catch them manufacturing the stuff. That would make the police department very happy. Once again, please have Mrs. Winston give me a call as soon as she gets in. And Mayor?"

"Yes?"

"Please stay away from the auction sites."

After promising she would, Melanie made another call to someone she rarely called. For this call, she moved to the floor and put her puffy feet up on the couch to help drain the fluid. As soon as she was there, she became a part of Thérèse's game.

"Bruce, this is Melanie Kato. I have a big favor to ask," she said to the man who ran the day-to-day operations of one of the businesses she inherited from her father. It was a security and intelligence company, a group that collected data and prepared intelligence packets for private companies and also for government agencies. It made millions of dollars for her and Trinh every year, something only their lawyer and few others knew about. Even Josh knew little about them, and Melanie was keeping it that way. "And it might not be entirely legal."

"Cool. What's up?"

Melanie explained about the recent thefts on Maui, and the auction sites where the stolen articles were being peddled. She gave him a list of the latest stuff that been put up for bidding.

"A site named Artifacts Empire?" Ben asked.

"How'd you know?"

"When we discovered the shipment to your father's library, we checked it out. Then we saw the recipient name of Aiko Murata, and figured you were behind it. We weren't sure what was going on, since you've never shown an interest in things like that, so we put together a little packet already."

"Does everybody know that was my mom's alias a long time ago?"

"You'll have to be sneakier than that to get past us, Melanie. We still keep a pretty tight lid on your father's affairs. Yours, too."

"I guess I should be grateful. Is there a way you can dig deeper into who the sellers are? MPD and the Bureau are already trying to figure it out, but maybe we can help them somehow without interfering?"

"First, a small department like MPD wouldn't have the resources for something like this, and honestly, the Bureau couldn't find their own heads in their own rear ends after a gassy meal."

"Thanks for that visual," she muttered.

"I'd be glad to do the work myself. It sounds interesting."

"Is there a way you can do it so nobody notices? Because I've already been warned off from interfering by the police, and I really don't want FBI agents coming around being pests."

"Your personal history with the Bureau is rather famous around here in the company. But being sneaky about it is the fun part. You know, I was just thinking about something."

"Getting Secret Service involved as a distraction?" she asked.

"Exactly. It looks like Cassandra is still on your protection detail?"

"She's the only one left on the island. I guess all my whining about being left alone by them has been listened to."

"I doubt you'll ever get rid of her. Too nice of a deal, living on Maui on the fed's dime."

"Can you also run a couple of names for me? They might be related to the thefts. The first is Kenneth Winston, AKA Kenny, of Arizona. The other is his mother, Adelaide Winston, AKA Addie, also of Arizona. The son had just moved here a few months ago, and might be involved in the original thefts from last week."

"How deep do you want me to dig?"

"As much as you can without being noticed."

"Will do. I'll send you a preliminary intel packet later today, and a more extensive one once it's prepared."

"Speaking of it being nice here, when are you coming to see us? I'd like to put a face to the person I talk to every now and then," she said.

"It's so expensive to go there."

"For the amount of money you're being paid, you can afford Maui. Where exactly in the world are you?"

"Do you really want to know?" he asked.

Melanie chuckled. "Maybe best I don't."

"How's the family?"

As if on cue, Thérèse's stack of toys fell from Melanie's belly. "Energetic and due to grow by one more on Friday."

After the call, Melanie made a prolonged visit to the bathroom before finding Thérèse in her room.

"Hey, little girl. Want someone to play with?"

"Momma, can you show me how to make these things go?"

Melanie went in and sat on the floor in the middle of nearly every toy the girl owned. Legos were scattered from one end of the room to the other, along with plastic dinosaurs and action figures from Japanese manga.

"What are you trying to do with them?"

"The dinos no can walk and *akushon manu ga tobenai*."

"One language at a time, please."

The girl gave it some thought. "*Dino wa arukenai to akushon manu ga tobenai*."

"Okay, first, the dinos aren't real, so they can't walk. You have to use your imagination for that. And I think it's the same for your Yoshi Action Man. That's the fun of playing with toys, is that you get to pretend all kinds of fun things with them."

Thérèse inspected the action figure closely as though it were broken. "He flyed before."

"Flew. Was that the noise I heard a little while ago?"

"Uh-huh. He crashed into the Lego wall."

"You can make anything fly if you throw it. But you can also break your toys if you throw them too hard."

"Didn't throw him. Watch." She put the action figure of a little man in a 1960s space suit on the palm of her hand and held it aloft. "Yoshi, go!"

Nothing happened.

"I don't think he's going to fly, Sweetie. It's not that kind of toy."

"Oh, wait. Japanese kind boy needs Japanese kind talk." The girl held the toy aloft again. "Yoshi, itte!"

The toy wiggled before it seemed to jerk forward, falling from the girl's fingertips.

"Not so good now," Thérèse said, picking up Yoshi from the floor. "Maybe Yoshi got broke."

Melanie's curiosity was struck. Maybe the girl tipped her hand and Melanie didn't notice, but something made the toy move.

"Let me try." She held it aloft the way her daughter had. "Okay, tell him again."

The girl ceremoniously waved her hand in the air and pointed a finger at the toy. "Yoshi, itte!"

Melanie held her hand as still as possible. As if following the girl's command, the toy leapt from it, traveling a foot through the air. The girl nabbed it from the floor before Melanie could.

"He can do better. Maybe he needs a nap."

Melanie closed the bedroom door for privacy. "Tay, are you using magic again?"

"Maybe."

"What's our rule about that?"

"No can use magic or there's big trouble."

"Right. What else?"

"Magic is a secret."

"A secret only you and I know about, right?"

The girl nodded.

"Does Daddy know you have magic?"

She shook her head. "Big secret."

"Good girl. Let's keep it that way."

"But Daddy's not home! Why for I no can make the magic with toys if Daddy's not home?"

Melanie chuckled over the girl's grammar, knowing she would've said the exact same thing at that age. "Because it's a special thing between you and me only, okay?"

"Our big secret?"

"Right. I want you to take a nap after putting your toys away, and without using magic. We'll have lunch when you get up."

"Peanut sammich?"

"Double peanut, if you promise not to play with magic?"

The girl nodded and got to work putting her toys in what had been Melanie's toy box many years before.

"Did I hear something about magic?" Josh asked, showing his face inside the door.

"Huh? No, we were just talking about peanut butter sandwiches for lunch. How's your curriculum coming?"

They went to the kitchen where Melanie began making sandwiches and Josh poured glasses of juice. "Just about done with my two regular classes. Same thing as last year, just different exams. I learned my lesson a couple of years ago with that."

"What's the third class again?"

"They stuck me with Survey of Tropical Animal Sciences."

"Sounds interesting."

"I could do a lot with it if they'd given me more than a week to develop the curriculum."

"Can you get the curriculum from the previous teacher?"

"She just emailed it to me today. All I have to do is learn everything this week she expects the students to know by the end of the course and I'll be ready."

She patted him on the back after putting three sandwiches on the table. "You can do it."

"What was that about magic? I know I heard you say something about magic to the kid."

"Oh, you know little girls and how they believe there's magic in everything. It's all a part of the game."

"No sisters, remember? Magic is that important to her? It seems like it's involved in a lot of her games."

Melanie was stuck for an answer on how to explain her daughter's seeming ability to move things slightly. "I think it's better she plays than for us to make her sit still. Do you have any questions about her surgery tomorrow?"

"We had our tonsils out when we were kids. I sort of remember having a sore throat for a day or two, but we got lots of popsicles. It was done around Halloween, and Mom even cheated us a few times by giving us icicles from the eaves of the house, telling us they were ghostsicles, and that was why they didn't have any flavor."

"We're not cheating Tay and we certainly aren't calling anything ghostsicles." Melanie went to the freezer. "What happened to the box of them I put in here a few days ago?"

"We sort of raided it."

"We?" Melanie asked.

"Addie, Thérèse, and me. We had one or two each."

"There's only two left. Can you please go to the store and get the jumbo-sized box? And they're reserved for Tay, not you. Which reminds me. I need to get a decent meal into her at dinner so she's not hungry and whiny tomorrow morning."

"I gonna be whiny, Momma?"

When Thérèse sat at the table, Josh left for the store with a grocery list.

"Hey, little one. I hope not. Eat your sandwich. I want to talk to you about something."

The girl was suddenly close to tears. "I sorry…"

Melanie sat in the chair next to her. "What's wrong?"

"I didn't mean to play magic."

"Nobody's mad at you, Sweetie. That's not what I want to talk about."

"Not in trouble?"

"Of course you're not in trouble. Eat your sandwich while I talk." She pushed the plate with the sandwich to in front of the girl. "Tomorrow, you go to the hospital, right?"

The girl nodded.

"You know why?"

"My turtles are dirty and make me snore a lot."

Melanie smiled at the childish explanation. "Well, yes, that's pretty much it. But there are a couple things for you to know ahead of time."

"Gonna have a sore throat."

"Right. How'd you know that?"

"Aunt Addie tol' me. She tol' me I get lotsa popsicles."

"You get as many as you want. Even if you don't want them, you have to suck on the popsicles, okay? That'll make the sore throat go away faster. And when you get home, you get to stay in bed all day and play with your dino friends. And the next day, you'll feel a whole lot better."

"Promise?"

"Yep. And the best thing is that Auntie Trinh will be your nurse tomorrow."

"You no wanna be my nurfe?"

"They don't let mommies in the operating room, but I'll be waiting right outside the door."

"You'll be there when Auntie's done taking out my turtles?"

"Yep, I promise. But there is something super-duper important for you to remember."

"What dat?"

"Well, after you go to bed tonight, you can't eat or drink anything, okay?"

"Part of the game?" the girl asked.

"Not really a game, but yes, it's a big rule that we all must follow until you're done having your turtles taken out." She watched her daughter chew the peanut butter, trying to swallow it down. She wasn't convinced the kid was trustworthy to not drink water if she went to the bathroom on her own. "You know what would be fun? Why don't you sleep with me tonight? Just me and you, and daddy can sleep in your room?"

"You mad at Daddy?"

"No, but I want you to sleep with me tonight. Just us girls, okay?"

"Daddy not gonna be scared of the ghost?"

"He doesn't know there's a ghost in your room, just like he doesn't know there's magic in there, and we're never telling him, right?"

"Right," the girl said, nodding her head once.

Josh was just coming back from the store with two bags as lunch was ending. "Right what?" he asked.

"No ghosts in my room."

"Ghosts?" Josh asked Melanie as he began putting things in the freezer.

"Nothing. Just talking about a game that we're not going to play. But guess what? You're on the couch tonight so Super Girl can sleep with me."

After dropping her plastic plate in the sink, Thérèse peddled away on her tricycle, saying something about starting a new game with a dinosaur.

"How many secrets are the two of you keeping from me?" he asked, sitting at the table with her.

"No more than the usual ones mothers and daughters keep to themselves."

"Okay, for my edification, what can go wrong with a tonsillectomy?" he asked.

"Bleeding, infection, airway obstruction, respiratory failure, death."

"That sounds like one of those hospital forms everybody has to sign. And the likelihood of those happening to our daughter?"

"Well, she's having surgery. That requires an incision, in fact, two incisions. That means there will be bleeding. But her doctor will use electrocautery to stop it. Every now and then, it starts again within a day or two of surgery, but with children, that's very rare."

"And if it does?"

"If it's a lot, she goes back to the OR and has a few jolts of cautery to make it stop."

"You don't seem concerned about that," he said.

"Not concerned? I'm panic-stricken! Believe me, I know what can go wrong, and that's my little girl going in there tomorrow morning. How can I not be worried?"

"Should I worry too?"

"One of us needs to remain levelheaded, if only to keep the other under control."

"Still…" he started.

"I take care of the county and you take care of me. That's the deal we made and I'm not letting you weasel your way out of it."

"What about those other things? What about infection, or the obstruction thing?"

"By virtue of taking them out, we're preventing further infections. The obstruction comes if they happen to drop the tonsil before taking it out of her mouth. But she'll have a tube in her throat along with a sponge packed in there, so it can't go far, and there will be a large clamp on it anyway."

"What about the death part?" he asked.

Melanie blotted a tear with a napkin. "Not gonna die."

"It's a simple thing to do, right? Does anybody ever die from a tonsillectomy?"

"A very small percentage, minute. With modern anesthetics, it's even lower than it was decades ago, when they used to do it in people's homes."

"But how could somebody die?"

"Do we have to talk about this?" she asked, blotting again.

"I need to know."

"Okay, the bleeding could potentially be serious if they incise too deeply. You know the carotid arteries in the neck? Those have branches that are right behind where the tonsils are. If a surgeon gets into those, the patient could bleed to death before they gain control of it. The vessels are too big to cauterize, and too difficult to repair. It rarely happens, as in nearly never, but it is a potential complication."

Josh set aside the last portion of his sandwich. "And she really needs this operation?"

"The benefits greatly outweigh the risks."

"As said by a surgeon."

"She'll get rid of the sore throats and most of the snoring will stop. It would have to be done eventually, and she's at the optimal age for it. By the time she starts preschool on Monday morning, she'll be completely recovered and will have forgotten all about it."

"If she's alive," he said drolly.

She backhanded his arm. "Don't say that. I'm upset about it enough already, without you adding more. I have a lot on my plate this week."

"You've already transferred most of your mayor duties to Trinh. Once we get Thérèse home tomorrow, all that's left is Friday."

Melanie rubbed her face. "Yeah, Friday can't get here soon enough."

"To relieve your stress, maybe we could go in the bedroom and, you know."

"Oh yeah, like I'm feeling real sexy these days."

He flirted with her by touching her cheek. "Come on. Just because we couldn't figure out the logistics a few days ago doesn't mean we can't try again."

"Logistics?" she said. "It's sex, not an invasion, which at this point in time is about the same thing."

"I've been giving it a lot of thought. Where we went wrong before was…"

She put her hand up. "Don't want to hear about the details." After struggling out of her chair, she took him by the hand.

"I win for once?" he asked.

"No, but I will let you rub my feet and ankles."

Once she was positioned on the floor with her feet up on the couch, he sat between her legs and began to rub. "This is great. Are you enjoying this as much as me?" he asked.

"You have no idea how good that feels."

"Good enough to put you in the mood?"

"Not yet, but keep rubbing."

He started on the other foot and ankle.

"Maybe you should go check on the kid and close her door?" she said after a few minutes.

Josh almost leapt from the couch. "I'll meet you in the bedroom."

"I don't think I can get up. It'll have to be right here."

He stopped in his tracks. "Here?"

"Not the first time we've done it on the living room floor."

"She's asleep," he said when he came back.

Melanie was already positioned on her side, the only comfortable position she could still manage. "Better get the blanket off the couch."

Ten minutes later, she giggled while he fumbled at unbuttoning her waistband.

"Are you able to suck in your tummy?" he asked, still working frantically.

"Ha! I wish!"

With one last tug at the button, it came undone and she was able to wiggle out of her shorts with Josh's help.

"Don't bounce me around. We can't risk breaking my water."

"I know what I'm doing."

Melanie laid her head back and giggled again. "Yeah, you're a real expert."

The small lap blanket slipped off, exposing them. She reached for it but couldn't quite get it.

"Never mind the blanket," he whispered, kissing her neck.

"I'm just glad we don't have a mirrored ceiling."

She closed her eyes and tried her best to pretend she wasn't pregnant. Just as she was allowing her mind to drift into a fantasy, the back screen door to the kitchen clattered open and closed.

"Addie," Josh whispered.

Footsteps softly padded across the kitchen's linoleum floor.

Melanie swore. "Get the blanket over us," she whispered, trying to grab it again.

It was Josh's turn to laugh. He was just getting the small blanket over them when Addie came into the living room.

"Oh! Sorry! I'll go for another walk."

Her footsteps hurried this time, the back door quickly slamming closed when she left.

Melanie pulled up her shorts while trying to sit up. "So embarrassing."

"It would be if it wasn't so funny," he said.

"This was your stupid idea. Help me up!"

He pulled her up to a standing position. "Sorry. At least you got your feet rubbed."

"Is that what it's called these days?" She wrapped the blanket around her waist for the trip to the bedroom. "Just go get Addie and bring her home. And try to figure out an excuse she might believe."

Not even getting her shorts buttoned, Melanie waddled down the hall to their bedroom and closed herself in.

***

Once a proper amount of time passed, Melanie went looking for Addie. "Sorry about earlier. We generally…we're not…there was something of an urge, and since you were out and Tay was sleeping, we let down our guard."

"Melanie, I never noticed a thing. You took advantage of a day off. Who am I to pass judgment over what married people do in their own home?"

"Well, just feel like you can come and go as much as you want." Melanie poured glasses of juice for them and sat at the kitchen table with Addie. "Did you find anything in your letters to Kenny? Detective Nakatani called and was curious."

"Every time I start to read, I tear up. I did find a few names, though." She went to her room and came back with a slip of paper. "He mentioned Gonzo's shop in some of his later letters. Maybe they were the ones he was doing odd jobs for?"

"He was still a beginner surfer, not expert enough to work at a surf shop. Those shops don't make much money, one of the reasons they close as soon as their initial lease is up." Melanie wasn't going to mention the shop owner was a known pusher. "Did he say anything in particular about them?"

"Only that that was where he learned to surf and he was making friends with a few of them."

"That's a good lead the police should hear about." Her phone always within arm's reach, she called Detective Nakatani. Getting no answer, she ignored leaving a message. "You know what? Let's go check out Gonzo's."

"Just the two of us?" Addie asked.

"Josh is working on his curriculum and Tay will resume playing with Mister Cleveland once she wakes up. It's a nice day. No reason for us to be cooped up inside."

"Mister Crumpet," Addie said, adjusting the driver's seat of Melanie's pickup truck.

"I wonder why I can't remember his name?"

"She certainly is fond of that one. And the action figure."

"Oh, yes. Yoshi, the Action Man. She practices Japanese while playing with him, Spanish while playing with Fiesta Fernanda, Hebrew with Bathtime Bathsheba, and plays with Ka-choo Kailani when practicing Hawaiian. After tomorrow, it'll be Tonsil Turtle, or some such thing."

Addie proved to be a slower driver than Melanie. "I hear you're still looking for a nanny?"

"We had a good one but lost her several months ago. Then we got another, but she didn't last long once she discovered our busy schedules of people coming and going at all hours of the day and night. Then we decided on hiring a live-in nanny. She'd move into the room you're in, turning that part of the house into her suite. The room across would turn into the baby's room in a few months. Honestly, I don't know what people expect anymore. Free room and board and decent pay while living across the street from one of Maui's nicest beaches just isn't good enough for some people. We've even advertised on the mainland, offering a bonus and pay relocation costs. No one." Melanie took a breath. "Sorry about going on like that."

"I think we both have a lot of things to get out of our systems," Addie said. "Is there a place we can sit and chat undisturbed?"

"I know the exact right place." She pointed to a small parking lot just before they got to Lahaina. "But first, Gonzo's."

As they walked into the surf shop, Melanie had no idea of what to ask. In her condition, it was obvious she wasn't looking for a surf lesson. Instead, she pretended to be shopping for surf garments, and was glad when Addie went along with the charade.

"Can I help you?" a man asked. He was big as though he got plenty of exercise, and his hair was cut military style. He'd just come in from the back room, which led to where the rental equipment was located.

"Yeah, my hubby is taking up surfing and his birthday is coming up. Any ideas on a gift he might actually like?"

"Rash guard, leash, maybe a new board. How about a series of lessons?"

"He already knows how to surf."

"Maybe some advanced lessons in bigger surf?"

"How much are boards?" she asked.

He took Melanie to a long rack of boards along one wall. They had a full array, from short guns used in heavy surf, to long and wide tankers used in easy conditions. They also offered kite surfing equipment and wakeboards, something

Melanie had never liked much. "We have new boards, along with used ones that are here on consignment. Take my word for it, the new ones are way better."

Since he didn't seem to recognize her as mayor, she let the game unfold. She looked at the price tags on a few, about what she would expect in any shop. She had to pretend to be surprised anyway. "Kinda expensive. Anything cheaper?"

"The consignment junk is over here."

Those prices weren't much cheaper. "What about last year's rental stuff? Do you have anything like that?"

"Maybe your husband should come in and pick out what he wants?" the man said.

"Except that I'm the one with the checkbook. Is Gonzo around? I heard he's the one to see about making deals here."

"Where'd you hear that, the maternity ward?"

"At the beach."

"Well, it sounds as though someone is pulling your leg. There is no one named Gonzo, not at this shop. It's just a catchy name." He began to walk away.

"Wait. Maybe some lessons are a good idea. How much are those?"

He gave her a price list from a rack. "We'd want to see his skill level before taking him out to heavy surf. A rental board is included in those prices. No discount if the customer brings their own."

"So, you have a lot of rental boards?" Melanie asked, pretending to read the sheet.

"We have enough."

"I see. You must be the boss here, since you know so much."

"Lady, you got your price list. If you want to buy something, get out your checkbook and start writing.

Otherwise, I have better things to do than talk to some guy's pregnant wife."

She noticed then that Addie had left the shop, leaving her alone with the man. "Are all of your rental boards accounted for?" she chanced asking.

He stopped and turned back to her. "Sure has been a lot of interest in our rental boards these last few days. Who are you, anyway?"

"Just a customer."

"You're sure you're not with the cops?"

She turned to face him straight on, letting her belly close the gap between them. "Do I look like a cop to you?"

He began nodding his head, letting a grin form. "Now I know who you are. You're that lady mayor we got stuck with a while back. Well, I'll tell you something. You and the cops can keep out of my shop. Got it?"

"Just trying to figure out how a couple of kids died recently, that's all. They were using rental boards from this shop when they died."

"Look, lady. I don't care how many times the cops count my boards. Let them come in and search the place for dead bodies. I got nothing to hide."

"It seems to me you'd be a little more willing to cooperate if you had nothing to hide."

He went nose to nose with her, the oldest intimidation trick in the book. It had never worked before and it wasn't scaring Melanie off then. "Get outta my shop, understand? And tell the police that the next time they come back to bring a search warrant with them. And a few of their pals, too, because I'm not so easy to deal with as a pregnant lady."

"No, you're much more of a whiny bitch than I am."

"Look..." He began ramming his finger into her chest, exactly what she expected, and definitely the wrong thing to do right then. It just happened to be right over her twenty-year-old Special Forces tattoo.

Reaching up, she got a hold of his finger and bent it backward, not stopping until she saw anguish and pain on his face. Getting him bent over backward, she looked close at him. "Special message from the mayor's office: if I ever hear about you touching a woman like that again, I'm gonna do something about it. And I can guarantee it'll be a lot more painful than this. Okay?"

He called her a name, certainly not the first time she'd heard it. Giving his finger an extra twist, she pushed him back.

Normally a quick getaway was in order in situations like that, and she waddled as fast as she could for the door. Thankfully, Addie was waiting in the truck with the engine running.

"Sorry about the scene back there, Addie," Melanie said, buckling her seatbelt. "Good thing you stepped out when you did, otherwise you would've heard the mayor say a few things that weren't so mayoral."

"I hope you don't feel like I abandoned you. When I heard the argument start, I thought you might want to leave in a hurry."

Melanie laughed. "As in a quick getaway?"

"Did you learn anything from him?"

"Maybe a little. He was awfully protective about his rental boards. He shut up in a hurry when I asked how many he had."

Addie handed over a small stack of business cards. "While you were talking to him, I got one each of all their business cards. Not sure if it'll help any. Maybe we can look them up on the internet?"

"Better yet, if you don't mind, we could look through your letters to Kenny to see if we can match any names."

"If you help me, we could do that this evening," Addie said. "I don't mind at all if you read what I wrote to him, if it helps getting to the bottom of what happened to him."

Melanie's phone rang. "Uh-oh. It's from Detective Nakatani."

"You think he heard about what happened?"

"He seems to know everything that happens on Maui five minutes before it happens." She answered the call. "Detective, what can I do for you?" she asked with extra courtesy injected into her voice.

"Been shopping for surfboards today, Mayor Kato?"

"I can explain."

"I'm sure you can explain how our pregnant mayor beat up a small business owner. Mister Gallagher is seriously considering pressing battery charges."

"Then I will too, if ramming his finger in my breast is considered battery. Once he did that, the gloves came off. All I did was defend myself, and my baby. In the eyes of the police, who has greater priority? Pregnant women or surf shop punks?"

"I see your point. Why exactly did you go there?" he asked.

"I had a hunch and wanted to play it out. All I did was ask a few questions."

"What was your husband doing when you were asking your questions?"

"He didn't take me there, Mrs. Winston did. But she's not involved at all. In fact, she spent most of the time outside waiting for me."

"You know we've already talked to them, and have, or maybe I should say had, plans to interrogate each of them one at a time in the station."

Melanie's tic started, which she rubbed with a knuckle. "Sorry."

"I hate to ask, but did you learn anything?"

"He was incredibly touchy when I asked about the rental surfboards, especially about how many he had. That's when he recognized me and tried tossing me out. But Mrs. Winston had the good sense to get their business cards, which we're planning on spending the evening comparing to names in her letters to Kenny. Maybe we can make some associations between what Kenny might've mentioned to her and Gonzo's shop, other than renting a surfboard."

"Well, I hope you can find something. But Mayor, I must tell you I'm getting a little tired of the interference from City Hall in this investigation."

"I figured you'd get around to giving me another lecture. The good news is that I'll be at the hospital most of tomorrow while my daughter has minor surgery, and you know about Friday."

"And Thursday?" he asked.

"I'll do my best to leave the rest of Maui alone while staying home with my daughter."

"I'll take that as a promise. I'll also head off Gallagher's attempts at having you cited for battery by reminding him he touched you first."

"And a little too personally. Pregnant or not, I won't give him a second chance at that."

***

After dinner, Melanie and Addie spread out the letters to Kenny on the living room floor and organized them chronologically. Then they organized the business cards from Gonzo's shop between them. Thérèse quietly played a counting game only a few feet away, which soon turned into singing.

"Okay, we have a Jimbo, Curt, Ozzie, Franklin, and Flex," Melanie said. "We should look for any variation of those names, like Jim, James, Jimmy, Curtis, and so on." Melanie looked up at her companion, trying to judge her mood from the look on her face. She seemed all in with their little project. "For this evening, maybe we should just scan your letters for names rather than read them through?"

"And keep a list of all names and places? And businesses?" Addie offered.

"Good idea." Looking at the first letter, Melanie was immediately struck by how personal it was, almost like reading someone's diary while they were in the room with her. "You have lovely handwriting, Addie. Nobody writes in cursive anymore."

"Old habit drummed into me as a schoolgirl. You suppose Flex was that charmer we met today at the shop?"

"Seemed like an apt name for him. Ozzie sure sounds familiar."

"Should I ask what happened in the shop after I walked out?" Addie asked, setting one letter aside and taking another.

"Maybe best you don't. Just some posturing."

"From what I saw looking in the rearview mirror through the front window, you had the guy pretty well in hand."

"Just something I learned a long time ago, about what to do when someone thumps you in the chest."

"Josh said you and Trinh were in the military together. Is it something you learned then?" Addie asked.

"More like from my mother. She was quite skilled in things like that, and taught me how to manage difficult situations."

"What an interesting family you have."

Melanie laughed. "You don't know the half of it."

"I have a mention of Curtis here, a surf buddy," Addie said, reading one of her letters.

"Must be the same guy. Put his name on the list and set that letter aside."

"Momma?" Thérèse asked.

"Yes?"

"I get my turtles out tomorrow?"

"Tomorrow morning."

"If I put them in the ocean, will they get like big kind honu?"

"Different kind of turtle, Sweetie. People can't make honu."

"Even if we try really hard?"

"Nope. Sorry."

"Momma?"

Melanie tried her best not to sigh. "Yes?"

"What do people make?"

"Other people. Baby people."

"You no got honu in you, right?"

"I sure hope not. Can you do me a favor and tell me the Hebrew alphabet? Daddy said you had trouble with that the other day."

"Alif, bet…"

Melanie and Addie went back to scanning letters for names, jotting notes every now and then. Once the girl was done with the alphabet game, she wandered off to her room to play.

"I'll be glad when she starts preschool. Hopefully, they'll tire her out and she'll want to go to bed earlier than she does now."

"Is preschool expensive here?" Addie asked, taking a break from reading her own letters.

"The one we finally got her into is kind of snooty and expensive, but they have the hours we need and aren't far away. We really didn't want her in school so soon, but with our schedules and not having a nanny lined up yet, we didn't have much choice."

Addie went back to reading. "Well, whatever happens, I'm sure it will work out for the best."

Kay Hadashi

A Wave of Murder
Chapter Eleven

When Wednesday morning came around, Melanie was sure to tail after Thérèse everywhere she went before going to the hospital. Addie went to the hospital in the morning with the rest of them. Leaving the car behind, the group went in together.

When Thérèse took Addie's hand for the walk into the building, Melanie and Josh trailed along behind.

Once they got to pre-op, the girl was checked in and Melanie and Josh were interviewed by an anesthesiologist that Melanie often worked with. The girl was given a set of hospital pajamas, and Melanie took her to a bathroom to change her clothes.

"I saw you holding Aunt Addie's hand a little while ago. Just like old friends, huh?"

"I guess so. I never had an old friend before, except you and Daddy."

"Don't forget Trinh."

"Oh, yeah, her."

"Did you ask if it was okay to hold her hand?" Melanie asked.

"She seemed like she wanted to, so we did."

"Well, it was very nice. You remember your promise, right?"

"Yes, Momma."

"What is it?"

"Be nice to people at the hospital."

"Right." Melanie got the girl's pajamas straightened out. "What else?"

"No magic?"

"Right. No playing with stuff with your magic. In fact, no touching of anything. And do everything Auntie Trinh says, okay?"

"I promise."

When Trinh came to get Thérèse, the girl looked at her blankly.

"Don't you recognize me?"

"You're wearing funny clothes."

"Fancy costume, huh?" Trinh asked the girl she helped deliver three years before. She picked her up for the trip to the OR. "This is where your momma works. She dresses like this, also."

Melanie gave Thérèse one last kiss before watching her best friend take her daughter away. The conversation continued as they went to a set of double doors.

"Momma works here?"

"This is where she comes every day."

Melanie watched intently as the doors swung closed.

"You okay?" Josh asked after a few minutes.

Melanie had been scrolling through images on her phone, making a new file for the pictures she'd taken that morning. She looked at the last one, a photo of Trinh holding Thérèse just before they left the pre-op waiting area. "I'm fine."

"You don't look fine."

"I'm fine, okay?"

She went back to scrolling, moving pictures around, making a simple scrapbook, anything to get her mind off what was happening on the other side of the walls that separated her from her daughter.

"Crap."

"What?" he asked.

"Just deleted something."

"Just leave it for later."

"I need something to do."

"It's been twenty minutes. Tell me what's going on in there."

"They have monitors on her, the IV started, and she's probably just gone to sleep."

"What happens next?" he asked.

"Well, if it's anything like what I saw when I was a resident, Trinh has her covered with blankets and Doctor Isakson is using a retractor to prop her mouth open."

"Then what?"

She sighed. "Then he'll use a curved scalpel to remove the first tonsil, followed by using the cautery to stop the bleeding. Once that's done, he'll do the other side."

"How long does that take?"

"About as long as it takes for me to explain it to you."

"Then what?"

"The tech will give the turtles to Trinh to send to pathology."

"Turtles?"

"Haven't you been paying attention? That's what Tay has been calling them. Then they'll irrigate the tonsil beds to check for any bleeding. If there is, he'll touch it up with the cautery or maybe put in a stitch. They'll do one last rinse, suck all that out, remove the gauze sponge, and wake her up. Move her onto a stretcher, cover her with more blankets and take her to the recovery room. Once she pitches a fit, they'll haul us in there pretending we can control her better than they can. When she drinks some water and the wailing simmers down to simple whining, we can take her home."

Melanie went back to her phone, staring at it blankly.

"She'll be fine, Melanie," Addie said, setting aside her magazine.

"I know. It's just hard to wait." Melanie forced a smile at the new family friend. "You don't have to wait here. There's a resort right across the way. The grounds are lovely for strolling and they have a small café that's not too expensive."

"I don't mind waiting. Maybe I should go take a look at the babies in the maternity ward?"

"Third floor," Josh said, as the woman left them. "You think she's latching onto us because she's lonely?"

"She doesn't have anything else to do until the police and the coroner release her son's body for travel back home. I don't mind her."

"You don't think it's a little peculiar she made friends with us so fast?" he asked.

"She saw us in the throes of passion and hasn't said anything about it. For that, I'm cutting her a whole lot of slack."

"Except the passion wasn't quite thrown yet."

"One way or another, she got an eyeful." Melanie put away the phone. "It's been forty-five minutes. I wonder what's taking so long?"

"Just relax. You're thinking of all the things that can go wrong."

"I just have this creepy feeling."

"That's called pregnancy," he said.

"While we wait, why don't you start your nanny search again? We're running out of time."

"What was wrong with the gal that came by last week?"

"Other than having a police record, nothing."

"She explained all that," Josh said. "She got caught shoplifting as a teenager. So what?"

"You really want a klepto in the house when we're not there? And how is she supposed to take the kids around if she has no car?"

"She could just stay home with them."

"Tay needs to go to preschool and get picked up again. You want her to use a bicycle for that?"

"What about the one before her? She seemed okay," Josh said.

"She's never been a nanny, and not even a big sister. She's about as suited to being a child care worker as she is a brain surgeon."

When he began searching websites on his phone for a nanny, her phone rang with a call from Detective Nakatani.

"Not today." She answered the phone. "Detective, didn't I tell you I was taking today off? Maybe you should too."

"Are you telling me to give it a rest?"

"I could be less polite about it."

"I'm sure you could. Say, I just tried contacting your vice mayor, Ms. Park, but she said she was busy, and to call you. Anything from your little investigation last night?"

Thinking he would eventually call her that day, Melanie dug the list of names and places from her bag. "We found a few names that matched, and a couple of places. First the places. Mostly it was at his apartment, and the couple of guys that used to meet him there. One was named Curtis, and the other Ozzie, both of which match business cards for surf instructors at Gonzo's."

"I have the last name for Curtis as West and looked into his background. He's clean. But Ozzie doesn't seem to have a last name, not according to his business card."

"I don't know why that name is so familiar," Melanie said. "Trying to extrapolate what we could from her letters about the Ozzie person, it sounded like he was one of the odd job workers. Now that I know Gonzo's is known more for its drug trade than surfboards, I bet anything odd jobs means pushing drugs. Otherwise, this Ozzie guy used to come by Kenny's

apartment occasionally, talk about surfing, drink some beer…"
The tic in Melanie's eye was kicking in again, which she
rubbed with a knuckle. "Wait a minute. Try finding someone
named Ozzie Simpson, my age or maybe a year older. Maui
resident since about the age of fourteen, graduate of West Maui
High School. I remember a kid in high school with that name.
He might've dropped out of school to do the surfer dude
thing."

"Why? What's so special about him?"

"At least a juvey record, maybe adult for impaired driving.
Anything zany. The name Ozzie is unusual, and I associate
beer with it for some reason." Melanie gave Nakatani a few
more names that they found in Addie's letters to her son, ones
that she learned had been his friends, or at least associates.
"Anything from your end?"

"I have info about this latest death."

Melanie took her phone out to the hallway but positioned
herself so she could see in at where Josh was waiting. "What is
it?"

"Thomas Bechler, twenty-four, single, Maui resident for
about two years. Guess where he lived?"

"Not in the mood for guessing games."

"Kihei, and in the same building as the Winston kid."

"And that means?" she asked.

"It's a lead. I'm going to try and find out if they knew each
other. Since they both died in similar ways, and only a few
days apart, they must've crossed paths with the same people
that killed them."

Melanie checked her list of names again. "We didn't
discover his name last night in the letters."

"That would've helped tie things together a little tighter.
Right now, all we have are leads taking us in several directions,
and mostly to dead ends. Working odd jobs or pushing drugs

means he could've met a hundred other people, just in the last few months."

"Okay, but why were they killed? Who runs down surfers that have strayed too far from shore? Surfers are a dime a dozen on Maui. Nobody even notices them except other surfers."

"You might be on to something, Doc. But don't think of them as surfers, but as pushers."

"But what's the difference? How do we actually know either of them had anything to do with the theft of those artifacts?" she asked. "You found the prints from the Winston kid on the cases. So what? Maybe he visited there that day and the janitor didn't clean as thoroughly as usual that night. I just can't believe a kid like him, with a mother as nice as his, would push drugs or get involved with breaking and entering and stealing valuable museum pieces."

"Stranger things have happened, Mayor."

"Yeah, maybe." Melanie saw Trinh come out to talk with Josh, smiling and nodding her head. "Hey, I gotta go. Call me when you learn something."

She hurried back in as best she could.

"She's okay?"

"She's great! She was so cute. Laid there stiff as a board. Mel, I don't know what you told her, but she obeyed. Give the recovery room nurses a few minutes before going to see her."

"They came out okay?" Melanie asked, when Dr. Isakson came out to see her.

"Oh yeah, perfectly dry. No problem. Push the cold fluids and popsicles today, and let her have something easy to swallow for dinner. Tomorrow, she can eat whatever she wants."

Melanie got a little light-headed and Josh helped her to sit before she fell. Isakson called some nurses over, who got her onto a stretcher. They got her to a pre-op bay and attached a blood pressure cuff.

"Melanie? What's wrong?" Josh asked.

"I don't know. I just feel like crap."

"Your blood pressure is too high," one of the nurses said.

"I just need to go see my daughter."

By then, the nurses had the full array of monitors on Melanie. "You can't go anywhere right now, Doctor Kato."

"I just need to see her!"

Josh took her hand. "Hey, just relax. Trinh said she's fine."

Melanie tried pulling the wire EKG leads from her chest. "I want to see my daughter!"

While Josh talked her down, the nurses had a quick powwow.

"Okay, if you promise to stay on the stretcher, we'll take you in to where she is, okay?"

"Just do it."

Josh pushed while one of the nurses steered the stretcher. A moment later, the two stretchers were nudged up against each other. Melanie reached over and took her dozing daughter's hand in hers. Just as tears burst from her eyes, Trinh showed up.

"Hey, what's going on? They said you had some sort of episode?"

"It was nothing. I just got dizzy."

Trinh immediately checked Melanie's ankles for swelling and the vital sign monitors. "Did your water break? Are you having contractions?"

"No. I'm fine, okay?"

"Don't take an attitude with me, Mel. You're supposed to be home relaxing, not here at the hospital."

"How can I not be here when my daughter had surgery? You'd do the same thing, Trinh."

"You're too busy. Thérèse could've waited for a few weeks for her surgery. And don't give me any stuff about starting preschool next week. That could've waited for a while, also. You need to stop trying to be supermother and relax before you blow a gasket. This is the second time you've ended up on a stretcher. That's got to stop."

"Don't you have another patient to see?" Melanie asked.

"Yes, but not until after I call your OB."

"I'm not having contractions!"

"You're not exactly Zen-like right now, Mel."

Once Trinh had made the call, she left Melanie to hold Thérèse's hand from across the gap between their stretchers. Five minutes later, Dr. Chapman showed up with a fetal heart monitor.

"Maybe we should just proceed today before you have a stroke," Chapman said, after setting up the strap around Melanie's waist and watching the readout. "How did her surgery go?"

"Fine, apparently."

"But you got so uptight that you had a fainting spell?"

"I didn't faint."

"Your blood pressure is too high and your heart rate is doing the Indy 500. If I medicate you for hypertension, I put the baby at risk. If I don't medicate you, I put you at risk. Somehow, you need to find a way of relaxing for the next two days."

"You said you could induce me today?"

"Two problems with that. First, you need to take your daughter home. Second, I don't like to induce when there's a crisis, unless it's life threatening. We're sticking with Friday, and you're promising me to relax. In fact, I'm putting you on bed rest until you come back on Friday. Josh will stand guard until then, and it's not negotiable. In fact, I'm making it an order, Sergeant Kato."

Melanie tried not to smirk at the woman who had been her gynecologist since her days in the Air Force, also in the military back then. "Yes, Ma'am."

"Should I find a home care nurse to stay with you until then?" Chapman asked when taking off the monitor belt.

"Josh can help me. Plus, Trinh is right next door, and I have a houseguest that might be helpful."

"Who's going to take care of Thérèse when you come to the hospital?"

Melanie clutched at her daughter's hand again. "We're planning on bringing her along. She'd be mad if she couldn't."

Two hours later, Josh got Melanie into his SUV and then got Thérèse buckled into the child seat for the quick ride home. The girl barely fussed, sleeping the whole time.

"I wasn't expecting to have two patients today," he said as he drove.

"Just put her in bed with me. You can bring both of us popsicles."

"What happened?"

"I just got a little dizzy and the nurses made a big deal out of it."

"Trinh said your BP was high again. I'm not sure who I'm supposed to worry about more, you or the kid."

"Unfortunately for you, you'll be helping both of us to the potty, which will be as soon as we get home."

Once Melanie was situated in her bed with Thérèse next to her, and they'd both had popsicles and cold water to drink, the girl dozed off again.

"Can I get my phone?" she asked Josh.

"To call who?"

"There's someone I need to call."

"It was right after you talked to Nakatani when you had your episode."

"It's not Nakatani and I didn't have an episode. And believe me, it'll aggravate me even more if I don't make my call."

After getting her phone and having Josh close the door, she made her call. "Bruce, I have another name for you to run down. Thomas Bechler, twenty-four, from the mainland. He washed ashore the other day, in similar circumstances as the Winston victim. Did you find anything on him or the mother?"

"Not much more than what the MPD already had on him, which is nothing recent. Clean slate while there on Maui. One of the worst credit histories I've ever seen. Two overdue library books. Owns some old junk pickup that he bought cheap." He gave Melanie the make and model, along with the license plate.

"Any indication he had a legitimate job?"

"No tax information has been filed as though he did."

"That explains his credit history," Melanie said. "He told his mother he had jobs working as a waiter and working on a farm. But he was also doing odd jobs with his buddies, most likely selling drugs. That's what I'm trying to figure out, who the buddies were. I think the only way to get to the bottom of what's going on is to stick those guys in an interrogation room. What about the mother?"

"His birth certificate confirms she's his natural mother. Widowed, fifty-eight years old, lived in Phoenix all her life. No arrests, no traffic citations, not even parking tickets. Good credit record, not perfect. Member of the PTA when her son was young. Doesn't work but is an official member of several charities. Drives blind people on their errands, does personal shopping for shut-ins, serves meals at a homeless shelter once a week. Votes in every election, files her taxes properly through a CPA. Model citizen."

"How'd her husband die?"

"Car accident about ten years ago, alone in the car. Apparently, one of those dead instantly things."

"Just like her son," Melanie said quietly. "There's almost nothing to make either one of them interesting, except that the son had some trouble as a teenager and was a college dropout. How the heck did he get mixed up with crooks, and then killed for it?"

"Want me to keep looking?" Bruce asked.

"Yeah. Actually, I have another name. Check on Ozzie Simpson, maybe Oswald, longtime resident of Maui, about a year older than me. Prior trouble might have something to do with alcohol. See if you can find some sort of angle, anything that might link the Winston kid with this Ozzie person, other than surfing. I have Mother of the Year mourning the death of her son, and I can't figure out why he died. There must be something."

"Something what?" Josh asked, bringing a tray of food and drinks in.

"Nothing, Just one of my secrets," she said, setting the phone aside. "What's all this?"

"Dinosaur-flavored popsicle for her, peanut butter sandwich for you."

"Better not call it Dino flavor. Maybe cosmic space dust."

They woke up Thérèse and had lunch in bed together, before the girl went back to sleep, her arms around her mother's belly.

When Melanie's phone rang on Thursday morning, it woke both her and Thérèse from their second naps of the day. It was a call from Bruce at her father's intelligence company.

"Who dat, Momma?" the girl asked with a raspy voice.

"Someone from work. Go ask Daddy for popsicles, okay?"

"What flabor?"

"Purple moon dirt."

The girl shinnied down from the bed and trotted from the room. That gave Melanie time to answer the call in private.

"First of all, why aren't you having the police do all this background work?" Bruce asked.

"We have this new detective on the island and he's all about process and procedure. Honestly, I think he's holding as many secrets from me as I am from him in asking you to do all this. Find anything good?"

"The Bechler kid was a real piece of work. Juvey record, priors in three states, a warrant for arrest in Honolulu. Nothing violent, all misdemeanor stuff or Class D felony charges that had been dropped. My cat has a better credit rating than him. When it comes to social media, he makes himself look like a Casanova."

"I'm sure the police know all that. Is there anything more subjective that tells us about who he really was on a personal level?"

"Credit card receipts indicate he was something of a clubber. In the few weeks he'd been there on Maui, he'd hit every nightclub a dozen times. Lived in a Kihei condo, late model sedan, clothes, spas, jewelry. But no job."

"Not having a job means he was doing something dishonest to earn money, right? Or did he have a sugar momma?"

"Melanie, you're finally understanding how the criminal mind works. On the surface, he committed petty crimes, like so many people do. It was get some money, have a party, get more money. Lather, rinse, repeat. But scratch the surface a little, and you find a dysfunctional dude with no concern for other people at all. Putting it through a profiling program, it seems he had some serious psychological problems in dealing with other people beyond an initial meeting."

"Which is why he's dead? Someone murdered him solely because he irritated them?" Melanie asked.

"More like the rest of the world irritated him. You said the circumstances of his death were very similar to those of the Winston kid, right?"

"Devastating head and chest injuries most likely from a boat, suffered while out surfing, then drifted ashore with the next incoming tide. Their surfboards were from the same rental shop, and they both lived in Kihei, living an adult nightlife lifestyle. But so far, they can't be linked to actually knowing each other. Nor does the second one seem to have anything to do with the recent appearance of Hawaiian artifacts on auction sites. Any word on that stuff?" she asked.

Thérèse returned to the bed, handing over a popsicle, hers already half-eaten.

"There have been bids, but not nearly as high was what you paid. We've been able to identify the bidders. Mostly just collectors looking for bargains, nothing too sinister about them, even if they were using a dishonest system to get the stuff. But we can't quite trace the seller. They have some sort of elaborate firewall that reroutes our attempts at obtaining a true IP location. That's not the only problem."

Melanie took the grape-flavored treat from her mouth. "Oh?"

"We've been trying to locate the source of these most recent items. There have been no police reports for thefts of anything like them, and we can't match these things with the inventory of Hawaii museums. Nobody seems to know anything about the stuff, except that it appears authentic."

"You said a close examination of the images posted online indicates the things are dirty, or at least haven't been cleaned professionally, right?"

"Just as though they were recently found, and the finder didn't want to invest in the effort or money for proper preservation. Are there places on Maui where people can go relic hunting for Hawaiian artifacts?"

"Ostensibly, yes. What's already in museums was in private ownership before it was donated. But almost all those kinds of things--spears, battle clubs, bows and arrows--either were buried with the warrior who used it, or were destroyed, usually in a ceremonial fire. After cremation, the ali'i were hidden in caves with their feather cloaks over their bones, and their kahili standards were either passed on to the next ali'i or burned. There really isn't much left from the ancient Hawaiian days. That's why the stuff is so collectible, and so valuable. These things can't be replicated because the birds that made the feathers are extinct, much of the forests that provided the wood for the arrows and clubs are gone, and the obsidian used for the best of the spear and arrowheads is nearly gone and what remains is protected."

"Where could these things be found?" Bruce asked.

She handed over her melting popsicle to Thérèse to finish. "Somebody might've found a cave, or a series of caves where the island ali'i or ancient warriors were entombed. The Hawaiian elite were often cremated, or their bodies deboned. The bones would be wrapped in tapa cloth and then hidden in caves and lava tubes by the kahuna, who kept the location secret. Sometimes their most prized possessions were put there with them. Maybe somebody stumbled across one of these caves and has been pilfering it?"

"Which would be a Class C felony. Everybody knows there is a huge black market for historical items, and Hawaiiana is not exempt. Egypt, China, India, and tribal regions of North America have all been extensively looted."

"Tribal regions as in where?" she asked.

"Mostly the Southwest states, and the inland areas of the central coast of California. Most of the stuff goes into private collections, which is probably what's happening with your stuff from Maui."

She remembered what Nakatani had told her the day before, about a joint task force between Maui police and the FBI, setting up a sting to catch the people responsible, and to stay out of it. Once again, it was hard being obedient. "Unless I buy it and have it returned," she said.

"It depends on how important it is to you that those things are returned, and if you're willing to be considered complicit in the crime."

"I didn't steal the stuff."

"But you bought the first lot that was put up for auction. Even if you pled ignorance as to its origin, ignorance is no defense. Any collector would know how old these things are and how difficult it is to find something available. They'd certainly know enough to realize that they were dealing with the black market."

"So, I've already committed a felony?" she asked.

"When you bought the original group from the auction, yes. And then you tried to hide it by using a false identity, even having it sent to a location other than yourself."

"Well, going to prison for a while is one way of getting out of being mayor," she said, more to herself.

"You said that MPD detective already knows it was you who made the purchase, but hasn't pressed any charges?" he asked.

"Yes, but he made it sound like he was being reluctant about it. He also made it sound like he didn't share that info with the FBI."

"Let me dig for a while more, no pun intended. I might be able to sidetrack what the Bureau is doing and lead them off in a different direction than to you."

"That would be great. I really don't want to go to prison."

"I learned a few things about that Ozzie Simpson character, and you're not going to like it."

"I suppose he's as innocent as a newborn lamb?" she asked.

"Just the opposite." Bruce listed the offenses and the jail time the man had done. "The thing is, your name is associated with his."

"Mine? Why?"

"Do you remember an incident of riding in a car when you were sixteen years old, pulled over when the driver was weaving in traffic on the highway near a place called Olowalu?"

"Ah, crap. I knew that would come back to haunt me someday. That was Ozzie, some flunky dropout that hung out at the beach all the time. I think he gave me a ride home one day, I don't remember why. After spilling beer on me, he began to swerve in his lane, and then got pulled over for it. Since he was eighteen but still too young to have beer, he was arrested. But the police believed me and gave me a ride home. Boy, I really caught it from my mom that time. And it went on for a week, if I remember correctly. But I thought that since I was a juvenile then, my name would be redacted from the official court records?"

"It was. You were listed as MK in court records. But digging a little, I was able to find a digital photocopy of the original citation and report by the arresting officer, who had the girl's name incorrectly listed as Melinda Kato. It didn't take much to put two and two together."

"Great. Now my name is linked to some dope potentially involved in a murder investigation."

"I think I have a way of fixing that," Bruce said.

"Is it legal?"

"Not even close."

"Then why did you tell me?" she griped.

Bruce chuckled. "Tell you what? Don't worry about it. Let me dig a little more into this Ozzie fellow's life and see what I can come up with. I might be able to find credit or debit purchases made at stores that Winston patronized, at the same time and date. You said Ozzie was a surf instructor. Maybe he was the one who gave Winston the lessons? That would link them together. And if I were able to put them together doing the same things at nearly the same time and same places on the nights of the thefts, and of his death, that would implicate the kid too much, even for the Bureau to ignore."

"Well, if it's after ten o'clock tonight, call Nakatani directly with whatever you find. I have stuff to do tomorrow, and it won't involve murders, feather kahili, or even surfboards."

"What about that other thing?" he asked.

"The illegal thing that would make me seem more angelic than I already am? I'll leave that to you and your wily ways. Just don't ever tell me about it."

Once she got well wishes from Bruce, someone considered a friend even though she'd never met him in person, she ended the call but kept the phone in her hand.

Thérèse was just finishing both frozen treats at the end of the call. Her lips were tinged orange and purple.

"Hey, little one. How's your throat?"

"It's okay."

"Let me see inside."

The girl opened up wide and Melanie used the light from her phone to look inside. As a thoracic and vascular surgeon, she was no expert on throats, but it looked okay to her.

"Does swallowing hurt?"

"A little."

"You need to eat some real food. Maybe after a nap we can get Daddy to make us some lunch?"

"Peanut sammich?"

"That might be too sticky for your throat. Maybe you guys can look for something to eat in the pea patch outside? But first, it's naptime."

"Nother nap already?"

"I'm afraid so. You have to get that throat nice and strong for when you go to preschool on Monday, and I need to get rest for tomorrow."

"I really gotta go?" the girl asked.

"You don't want to? There will be other kids there to play with." Thérèse wasn't buying it, so Melanie pulled out an old trick her mother used on her many years before. "I'll tell you a secret. I've heard preschool is a lot of fun."

"I got you and Daddy to play with. And Aunt Addie."

"Well, Daddy goes back to school on Monday, and I go back to work in a few weeks. And Aunt Addie has to go home pretty soon. You know we can't stay home forever."

"Why for she gotta go home?"

"Because she lives somewhere else, remember?"

"She on vation?" the girl asked.

"On vacation? Not really." Maybe it was time for the truth. "You see, her son used to live here, but he died. Addie came here to take him home."

Thérèse seemed to give the idea a lot of thought.

"He's dead guy now?"

"Yes, but there are nicer ways of saying it than that. That's why we have to be nice to Addie, and why we're letting her stay with us for a few days. One of these days, she'll have to go home."

"That's why she's sad sometimes?"

"Sure is. And when she's in her room, we need to leave her alone, okay?"

After prying an agreement from her daughter, Melanie waited until she was asleep to make her next call to Cassandra, her Secret Service protection, someone who supposedly shadowed her activities on the island.

"Tomorrow at noon, right?" Cassandra asked.

"Almost exactly twenty-four hours from right now. It wouldn't break my heart if contractions started and the kid came flying out five minutes from now, but yes, noon tomorrow. That's when my OB starts the induction. I have to be there an hour early."

"I should pick you up at eleven?"

"We can get there on our own."

"Just this once, let me make a show of it. I need to put the Escalade to good use. Why not take the mayor to the hospital to have her baby?"

"Okay, fine. Josh is too distracted lately to drive in a straight line. He'd probably get lost taking me there."

"Thérèse and Adelaide going with you?"

"You know about Addie?" Melanie asked.

"Of course. She checks out as okay. That's the only reason I've let her stay with you."

"How did you know her name?"

"From fingerprints on a water bottle she discarded."

"So sneaky. But I called about something else." Melanie explained about the case of the stolen artifacts and how Addie's dead son might be implicated. "Can you do me a favor and check into the son's background a little? And also about the history of the original artifacts? It would help the police in their investigation."

Cassandra promised to look into it using a federal government server, and would bring a report to the house later that evening.

Josh came in to change his clothes.

"Going to the airport to pick up your mother?" she asked.

"Her flight is due to land in about an hour."

"Bringing her back here?"

"Where else would I take her?" he asked, tossing his shirt into the hamper.

"I have a little list of places, if you'd like to see it?"

"I'm sure you do. Throwing my mother off the top of the Iao Needle is not an option. Not for a few days, anyway. Would it hurt you to call her Mom?"

"Yes. I'm sticking with Dottie when she's in the room, and when I start calling her Dorothy, it's time to take her for a walk. Or at least get her out of my reach."

"Other than being a little overbearing at times, there's nothing wrong with my mother."

"A little overbearing? She was going behind my back while I was at work to change how things were done here in my house, Josh. She's brought meat into the house, and tried getting Thérèse baptized at church behind my back while I was at work, even after I told her not to. Now, I don't mind if she wants to help change diapers and bathe the baby, but we make decisions about us, not her. Otherwise, she can use that round-trip ticket to go home again. Or to a place on my list."

"She said something about getting a one-way ticket this time."

"What?" she said loud enough to stir Thérèse from sleep.

"Somehow, she heard we hadn't found a nanny yet and is selecting herself for that role."

"And I'm deselecting her. She can be here for a few weeks, or until we hire someone, then she's out. If she wants to stay on Maui, she needs to find some other place to live than our house. And yes, I'm perfectly willing to tell her that myself."

"As you always say, be nice to her," Josh said, as he finished dressing.

Melanie sighed. She knew he was right, that his mother only wanted to be helpful. "I'll be nice as long as she doesn't start directing things at the hospital tomorrow."

"I will personally duct-tape her to a chair in the maternity waiting room. What about Addie? Did she say anything about going home soon? Once Mom moves in, we'll have a full house."

"That's up to the police, when they release her son's body from evidence." It was dawning on Melanie right then how she could use one woman against the other as wedges to get both of them out of the house permanently. "Once the baby starts to cry at night, I'm sure she'll find another place to stay."

"Speaking of Addie," he said quietly, sitting right next to Melanie. "I found her outside a little while ago burning some stuff. You know what that's all about?"

"What stuff?"

"Papers. I asked her what she was doing, what all that was, and she just muttered something about bad memories of Kenny."

"Was it next to the house where she might burn the place down?" Melanie asked.

"No, just in that old barbecue near the pea patch. It was just a couple minutes before she was done."

"Maybe it was…" Melanie wondered if their houseguest was burning some of the letters she'd written to her son, that the memories they brought were too difficult to deal with.

Interrupting her thoughts was a knock at the back door.

"Who could that be?" Melanie asked.

Josh kissed Melanie and Thérèse goodbye and went to see who was there. Melanie tried listening, but couldn't hear the other voice well enough to figure out who it was. When she heard the back screen door slap shut and Josh's SUV start up, followed by clattering sounds in the kitchen, she knew she wasn't alone.

Melanie picked up her phone, ready to hit the panic button that sent a message to Cassandra. Footsteps came through the house. "Hello?" she called out.

"Just me. Okay if I come in?"

Melanie relaxed again. "Hi, Lai. Yeah, come on in, if you dare. The place is a mess and I'm even worse."

"It's not so bad. I brought flowers for you and popsicles for Thérèse."

"Oh, good, more popsicles." After telling her friend Lailanie where to find a vase, she waited for her to come back. "Not busy at the salon today?"

"I told them I was going on a long lunch break. They'll survive. How's her throat?"

"She's fine. Whenever she wakes up, I make her eat a popsicle and nap again. She'll be good as new tomorrow."

"What about the expectant mother?" Lailanie asked.

"She's a wreck. I haven't bathed since yesterday, I'm living on popsicles and peanut butter, and I just insulted Josh's mother, and she's not even in the room."

"Yeah, mothers-in-law. Can't live with them, and can't live without them. But we sure find ways of trying to get rid of them, huh?"

Melanie laughed. "Got that right. Did you come for a reason?"

"Just checking on you. Duane wants to know if we can come to the hospital tomorrow?"

"To join the growing entourage? I don't know why you'd want to."

"Just old service buddies supporting each other. You buy stuff from his hardware store and fixed his hernia. He said the least he can do is be there for you when you bring another little warrior into the world."

Thérèse stirred awake and peeked out at their guest.

"Auntie Lai, are you here to fix Momma's hair?"

"No, but she needs it, huh? Are you ready for a popsicle?"

The girl winced. "'Nother one?"

"Maybe it's time for a sandwich. I bet we could talk Auntie into making us one," Melanie said. Once she got help up from bed, she went to the bathroom while the other two went to the kitchen. Instead of joining them right away, she took a shower and put on fresh clothes. "What did she make you?"

"Mater and mayor sammich."

Melanie looked at Lailanie for an explanation.

"Tomato and mayonnaise on wheat bread. I wasn't sure what to make, but that seemed like it should be easy to chew and swallow." Lailanie picked up her purse, ready to leave. "Is there anything else I can do?"

"Other than A-B-D-U-C-T-I-N-G my M-I-L, no. Thanks, though."

"You'll bring the baby in next week?" Lailanie asked. "Everybody at the salon chipped in and we bought something for Sophia."

"As soon as I have a few hours, I promise."

Finding two cups of yogurt in the fridge, she sat down at the table with Thérèse. No sooner was she settled, her phone rang.

"Now what?"

"No be cross, Momma. Jus' a phone call."

"You're right, little one." The call was from Trinh. "How's work?"

"Kinda boring without you here."

"My life is that good for gossip?"

"The entire OR is talking about tomorrow. There's even a wagering pool on the time of birth. Hey, how's Thérèse?"

"Eating a sandwich, followed by a popsicle, and then another nap."

"I gotta take 'nother nap?" the girl asked.

Melanie nodded at her.

"And you?"

"Good for another hour, and then Dottie gets here."

Trinh began laughing. "Tomorrow evening, there's going to be six of you over on your side of the house!"

"One big happy family. But I have the idea once the baby starts to fuss in the middle of the night, some of the older ones will vacate in a hurry for quiet, air-conditioned resort rooms."

"Dottie hung in there for the duration when Thérèse was a baby."

"First grandkid. She's had another since then. The excitement has worn off. Anyway, she enjoyed being a part of the show back then."

"What about Addie?" Trinh asked.

"People keep asking that. She's a big question mark. On the one hand, I don't mind being generous to someone in her circumstance. But there's a limit, you know?"

"You're way more generous than I would be, Mel. But maybe you're right. As soon as the baby starts to wail, she'll make a beeline for the airport."

"What're you doing for dinner?" Melanie asked.

"Oh, no you don't. You're not bringing me into the fray on the same day Dottie gets here. Once she sees Addie shacked up in your house, there's gonna be some jealousy stuff going on, which will only lead to a turf war. Leave me out of your soap opera, thank you very much. Anyway, Harmon is taking me out."

"Well, at least you're getting something, if nobody else in the house is."

"I wish. I've put the brakes on all that until he decides what he really wants. This engagement ring being swapped back and forth is getting tiresome."

"The current status must still be off?" Melanie asked.

"Right. And each time he asks me to wear it again, I make him offer bigger promises."

"Yes, well, we both have our little soap operas. You'll be there tomorrow, right?"

"At work? Of course."

"No, in the delivery room."

"I'm planning on not working in a room doing cases tomorrow, just so I can sneak out to be with you. Josh knows to give me a call when the time comes."

After apprising Trinh of the latest developments with the police investigations, very much like a morning report on rounds at the hospital, she turned over official mayoral duties to her.

"I'll try not to screw up Maui too much, Mel."

Melanie laughed. "Any more than I already have."

Just as she was getting the dishes washed and the kitchen tidied, Melanie got another call.

"Tomorrow, right?" Detective Nakatani asked.

"I keep saying unless I can have it sooner, but I've run out of time. What's up, Detective?"

"There's a new vic."

Melanie stopped what she was doing. "Another surfer?"

"This one washed ashore at the Maui to Lanai ferry dock in Lahaina. Passengers were boarding, watching as it slowly floated closer. Imagine the looks on their faces when it finally got close enough to recognize what it was."

"Which ferry?" she asked.

"Nine o'clock this morning."

"Which of course is the busiest one." Melanie didn't know what to do. Some public relations was necessary, to let not just the public know but tourists that everything was fine on Maui, nothing to worry about. But it wasn't fine and there was plenty to worry about. In one week's time, three young men, recent arrivals from the mainland, had died, quite possibly murdered, and near one of Maui's most popular tourist areas. It was something the mayor would need to give a reassuring pep talk about. She was in need of her own pep talk right then, though. "Look, I can't deal with that right now. I've already handed over the reins of the island to Trinh. I'm in no condition to go to the morgue, view a body, and then put everyone's mind at ease with an inspiring speech. And I know Trinh will still be at work for a few more hours, after which, she'll be busy for the rest of the evening."

It was something of a lie, that Trinh would be busy. It was only a date with Harm.

"I'll take care of it. At this point, there isn't much to say."

"Nothing new on the first two?"

"No, but we're getting a lot of action on the auction sites."

"Speaking of auctions, whatever happened to Detective Kalemakani?" she asked. "I thought he was investigating those crimes, while you investigate the deaths?"

"Who?"

"I thought he said his name was Kalemakani when he called me the one time."

"I don't know everyone at the precinct station yet," Nakatani said. "Otherwise, I seem to be stuck with both investigations."

"Maybe now that you have a third death, you'll find something that links them all together," Melanie offered.

"Well, even though they're from the same state, the first two never seemed to cross paths until they got here. Neither had jobs or went to school at the same places. In fact, neither went to college at all. Just sort of drifted in and out of jobs."

"Wait. You said Kenny Winston didn't go to college?" Melanie asked.

"That's right. Why?"

"I distinctly remember his mother saying something about him going to college for a couple of years but not doing well. She was even hoping he'd get back in when he eventually went home to Arizona."

"I'll dig a little more, but nothing came up on our searches these last few days."

"I got the impression he was going to a community college in Phoenix right before he came here." From the corner of her eye, Melanie saw the head of someone go by outside the kitchen window, quickly followed by another. "Hold on just a sec."

She went out to the back porch and caught sight of two men just as they were trotting down the driveway.

"Hey! This is private property! You need to ask permission if you want access to the trails!"

One of the men waved his hand apologetically as they picked up speed in hurrying away.

"Melanie, what's going on?" he asked.

"Oh, just a couple of trespassers. Somehow, the trails up into the mountains behind my house have gotten into a tourist brochure. In the last few weeks, we've seen someone at least twice a week, and those are just the ones we see."

"Want me to come take a look?"

"They'll be long gone by the time you get here."

"Is there anything up there?" he asked.

"Just old trails that wind around in circles. One supposedly goes all the way over the pali into the Iao Valley. Otherwise, it's mostly open areas with old sugar cane here and there in the lower areas, and native forest in the higher elevations. Josh and I had our first date on one of those trails."

"You don't have anything worth stealing on your property?"

"Vegetables in the pea patch, and just old tools in the shed. I doubt they're car prowlers. They're always wet, as though they've just come down out of the forest."

"Have you recognized them as being the same ones as earlier times?" he asked.

"None of us have ever seen them a second time. Josh has seen them, Trinh, her kids, and now me. These guys looked like tourists with knapsacks on their backs. If it was later in the school year, I'd guess they were students out collecting vegetation samples for a science class, but kids from the college know to ask permission first. No, I'm sure they were just tourists following a trail that has been included in some island activity website."

"Have Josh take a look around out there to see if anything is missing from your property. And it might be a good idea to put up a few No Trespassing signs."

Seeing Josh driving up the driveway from the road below, she grabbed the broom from the corner and swept the porch, knocking several old slippers to one side.

"Speak of the devil, he's home, and he's brought his mother with him."

Nakatani chuckled. "Good luck with that. And I hope everything goes smoothly tomorrow."

Melanie slipped her phone into a pocket and put the broom away, and greeted Dottie with a smile when she emerged from the car. She called for Thérèse to join her on the back porch to welcome them.

"Melanie! You're so big!"

That stung.

"Thanks, Dorothy. Welcome back to Maui."

"And look at this little munchkin! You've grown so much!" Dottie said when she got to the porch. She began tickling Thérèse, which made the girl shriek.

"Mom! She just had her tonsils out yesterday, remember? Let's not make her scream too much, okay?" Josh followed along behind with the woman's luggage. By the time he got to the porch, Dottie was already in the house with Thérèse, getting a tour. He leaned in close to Melanie to whisper, "Already calling her Dorothy?"

"She called me fat."

"You are kind of big."

"It's called pregnant," she hissed. "What's her excuse?"

"Mom's not heavy," he said, going into the house.

Melanie waited until he was out of earshot, before muttering, "I meant inside her head."

She found the others at the guest rooms, one of which Addie was still using. Several years before when Melanie finished her surgical training and returned to Maui, Trinh came with her. They put on an addition of two bedrooms and a bathroom built onto one side of the house where Trinh and her kids lived for a while before building their own addition onto another side of the house. Since then, it had become the nanny's room and guest room, with Melanie planning to turn both rooms into the 'nanny suite', where the next nanny would live while caring for the toddler. By some accident, Addie was shown to that room by Thérèse when she first showed up.

"Who's in the room I normally use?" Dottie asked, looking inside the door.

"We have another houseguest," Josh said. "Just take the other room. It's the same."

"That's the nursery," Melanie said. "She can use my grandparents' old room."

It was a room rarely used except for overflow storage of clothing, and more recently, the box of stuff Dottie had sent.

Josh carried her bags in after Dottie and Melanie went in.

"Well, I can get it painted," Dottie said.

Melanie didn't say a word, only walked out. Halfway down the hall, the dam burst. "Josh!"

He came into their bedroom a moment later.

"The door."

He closed it.

She put up her finger to keep him quiet. "She is not painting. Nor will she buy us new clothes, dress my daughter in frilly dresses, plant roses in the pea patch, raise goats in the backyard, or have a fireplace installed. She is here as a guest, not as a decorator, farmer, esthetician, rancher, or social worker. Is that clear?"

Once she heard Josh end his lecture to his mother on what wouldn't happen on her visit, Melanie went back to see her mother-in-law. She sat in the corner of the room while Dottie put her things away in drawers and the closet, still making it look like she was moving in permanently. She talked almost nonstop about Wyoming, and Josh's family there. "But look at you! Tomorrow's the big day, right?"

"Tomorrow at noon."

"What's my role? What am I doing?"

There it was. She was already trying to take over. Dottie had been instrumental in assisting with Thérèse's birth when Melanie delivered in a spa during a hurricane, unable to make it to the hospital. Now, Melanie needed to relegate the woman's role to sitting in the waiting room with everyone else, and without hurting the woman's feelings. "Mostly, keeping Thérèse under control out in the waiting room while Josh is in the delivery room with me."

"But…"

"Josh is my coach and I need only one of them. Not that I need one. A bigger job is staying with Thérèse and keeping her out of trouble. Anyway, it might take a while. My OB is something of a control freak, and I'm leaving everything to her to manage."

"If there's anything else I can help with, let me know."

Melanie tried to get out of her chair but couldn't. "There isn't. Unless you want to get dinner started. We're getting tired of Josh's cooking."

"How long has he been cooking?"

"For most of the summer."

"And you're as big as you are? That's a surprise," Dottie said. She began remaking the bed.

"Why?"

"Oh, if he went camping, he could cook pancakes in a basket over a campfire. In a real kitchen, he's inept."

"Well, hopefully we're not having a basket of pancakes for dinner."

Dottie left the room, leaving Melanie behind to try and get out of the chair on her own. She heard Josh ask his mother where she was, but didn't hear an answer. A moment later, he came into the room.

"I'm stuck," she said.

"Mom said something about you craving pancakes for dinner?"

"Have you ever seen me eat a pancake?"

He got hold of her hands and pulled. "Just that time when we went camping on the beach this summer."

"Did I finish it?"

"I seem to recall you making an announcement you'd never eat one again."

As she left the room with one hand on her back, one leg waddled while the other limped. "And I'm sticking with that."

"Hey, I thought I saw a couple of guys running down the driveway. Who were they?" he asked.

"Who knows? Probably a couple of tourists that went wandering through the hills for a while. I saw a couple of them earlier."

"They seemed in a bigger hurry than just going back to the hotel."

"Go out and check the carport and shed, make sure they didn't make off with anything. I think there are a couple of my grandfather's old No Trespassing signs in the shed you can put up."

She looked in on Thérèse and found a game of some sort had started between her and her grandmother, dealing with dinosaurs charging each other. Figuring the naps were done for the day, she went to her room to change clothes. Grabbing a bottle of lotion, she set that back and took another, an expensive brand she normally reserved for passionate nights with Josh. Today, she just wanted it for the pleasant scent. She was spreading that over her belly when he came in.

He stopped and looked. "Isn't that…"

"Nope. Today, it's anti-bitch lotion."

"Your skin itches?" he asked.

"No, you heard me right." She gave him the bottle. "Feet and legs, please. And save some for your mother."

"Now what did she do?"

"She called me fat again. Whatever happened to calling pregnant women glowing, or beautiful, or stunning? I'd settle for radiant."

"Do I have to talk to her again?" he asked. "Please don't make me talk to her again. Not so soon."

Melanie watched as he applied lotion to her legs. "Do I act that way when we visit her home? I'm polite to her and the rest of the family when we go there every Christmas, right?"

"Mostly."

"Why mostly?" she asked.

"You have a peculiar expression on your face at the dinner table."

"Yes, watching as dead animals are consumed has that effect on a vegetarian."

"Finished." He gave back the lotion. "There's good news. The tropical storm that was headed here has veered off and weakened."

"As they usually do. Lightning doesn't strike in the same place twice."

He stood. "Time to find the signs."

Half an hour later, Melanie went outside to find Josh, still working in the shed.

"What in the world are you doing? I said look for a couple of signs, not take everything out."

"I got carried away. I found a spider's nest and a few other creepy-crawly things."

"Well, have fun with your project. I'm going for a walk."

"Want me to go with you?" he asked.

"The next several years of my life are going to be consumed with childcare, PTA meetings, swim meets, flute recitals, surgery, and mayoral duties, not to mention visiting relatives. I'd like one last moment of peace, quiet, and solitude before it starts."

She started waddling down the gravel driveway toward the large resort across the road.

"Can you get across the road okay?"

"I've been crossing that road all my life. I think I can manage it one more time."

After waiting for a long gap between cars, she crossed as quickly as she could. She had one place in mind, and took a circular route to get to it, following the footpath through the grounds to get there. The thing about the tropics is there were always flowers in bloom, catching Melanie's attention as she strolled. She took note of which would grow well at home, thinking up a new landscaping theme for around the house. Once she was settled on the bench that faced out at the ocean, she took off her hat and waved air at her face. It wasn't long before she heard a familiar voice.

"Hi Honey. Been a while since you've been to the bench."

"Hi Mom. Thérèse keeps me busy, and work is more hectic than ever."

"How are she and Josh?"

"They're great. He's absentminded this time, a nervous wreck for some reason. Tay's taking it all in stride."

"You're a lot bigger than last time."

"Eight pounds bigger, which is all fat. It would be nice if people quit bringing it up."

"Get back to swimming as soon as you can, or go for runs with Trinh," her mother said.

"You've seen her running?"

"Of course. I run with her sometimes. She doesn't realize it, of course, but it's nice to have a running partner."

"That would totally freak her out if you materialized or appeared, whatever it is you do."

"I've considered it." Her mother laughed. "You really think she'd mind?"

"You'd scare the dickens out of her. Even if she recognized you, she wouldn't stop running until she found a priest." Melanie stretched out her legs, pounding her fist into the thigh of one. "It'll be a while before I run anywhere with this gimpy leg."

She and her mother chatted about the pregnancy for a while. Even though her mother had died twenty years before, her spirit still came for visits at the bench, something of a Kato family meeting place. Melanie had scattered her mother's ashes in that place late one rainy night, making it unique to her for very special reasons. As for the visitations, no one else knew. As far as Melanie was concerned, she welcomed them.

"You can't form, or whatever it is you do, so I can see you?"

"Not this time, Honey."

"What about tomorrow?" Melanie asked.

"I wouldn't miss it for anything. Your dad might even be around."

"It would be nice to have him there. How is he? Do you get to see him much?"

"He's fine. You know us. We always were going in opposite directions."

Melanie chuckled, but only half-heartedly. "Yeah, but on the rare occasion you guys were moving the same way, nobody was more passionate than the two of you." Melanie leaned forward and pressed a fist into her lower back.

"What's wrong?"

"Bad disc at L-4. It presses on a nerve root every now and then."

"How bad is it?"

"Come on, Mom. You haven't been a neurosurgeon in a long time. There's nothing you could do about it, the way you are."

"Just answer my question."

"I get leg and foot pain and numbness, and have a foot drop."

"That's bad. Do you know what it's from?"

"Probably left over from a hard landing in a helicopter while I was in the service. It might be stretching the sciatic repair I had a long time ago. It bothered me some when I was carrying Thérèse, but it's a lot worse this time around."

"Lean forward," her mother said.

"What? Why?"

"Just do as you're told."

Melanie leaned forward as best she could despite the size of her belly. After a moment, she felt hands on her back, groping each vertebra one at a time. "Is this your pain here?"

"Ow! Yeah."

"What about your plantar reflex on the side of your foot drop?"

"Well…"

"Well what? Answer me, Mel."

"Positive Babinski sign."

Melanie heard her mother sigh with disappointment.

"You need surgery. You should at least be worked up with X-rays and a scan. Have you been to someone?"

"Just the chiropractor and a massage the other day. That helped a lot."

"It usually does. But if it's coming back this quickly, you need that disc taken out. Who's good at West Maui these days?"

"There's a new guy that came highly regarded. I'd have to wait until I'm done breastfeeding Sofia, though."

"Are you sure it's another girl?" her mother asked.

"Can Kato women have anything else? At least it's not twins."

"Pretty name."

"Mom, there's something else happening on the island right now."

"The murders of those three young men?"

"Oh, you know about them. They've really been murdered?" Melanie asked. "The police are still trying to figure out what happened. Do you know? Is there anything you can tell me that might help the police find their killers?"

"I might've said too much already. Even though they're dead, it's a mortal task to solve a crime."

"The thing is, they might be mixed up with the theft of valuable Hawaiian treasures. We just can't seem to figure out how to connect everything. The police need leads, or at least a few more clues. So far, they seem to be going all over the island, even searching the internet for something that might help in their investigations."

"Sometimes you need to narrow your search. Make it more defined rather than so broad. Start closer to home."

"That doesn't tell me much, Mom."

"It tells you a lot. Otherwise, all I can say is things are not always as they seem with the people in your investigation."

"Great. Another one of your puzzles to figure out."

"You'll need to figure it out if you want to solve the crimes."

They sat quietly for a moment.

"Dottie got here today," Melanie said quietly.

"Which is why you're here at the bench already."

"I wish I could swap her for Addie. Mom, how can two women be so different? One just lost her only son, but continues to be gracious to everyone she meets. But the other is demanding, stubborn, and unwilling to listen to anything Josh and I tell her."

"You're not always so easy to get along with, Mel. And don't try using pregnancy as an excuse. I know better than that."

"I know."

"You and Josh picked each other to be husband and wife. He has to deal with your family just like you do his."

"My family? You guys are dead. What's to deal with there?" Melanie complained.

"Except that your mother was a prominent neurosurgeon and successful restaurateur, and your father was President of the United States. He has to somehow live up to those standards. Plus, your only sibling lives right next door, also your best friend, and is someone you're jealous of."

"I guess I'm turning into an overbearing wife."

"No, you're not. At least I hope you're not. I wish we could talk more, but I have to go."

"So soon? We can't just sit for a while? The sun should be going down soon."

"I'm trying to save some of my energy for tomorrow, Honey. I'll see you then."

"Promise?"

Instead of an answer, she felt the gentle touch of her mother's hand on her cheek.

Sitting for a while longer, Melanie watched as the sun got low in the sky. When she heard footsteps behind her, she figured it was Josh, coming to take her home.

He sat next to her. "I thought I'd find you here."

"Did Addie get home?" she asked.

"Yes. They've met."

"What's the carnage?"

"They'll live. I think they're tougher than what we give them credit for." They sat quietly for a while. "Nice sunset."

"Yep. Best one ever."

"You say that every time we watch one."

She took his hand to hold. "And they're all the best ones ever."

Melanie stayed in bed for as long as she could Friday morning, listening to the others in the kitchen. Thérèse played master of ceremonies, while Josh acted as referee between the match of wits that had developed between Dottie and Addie. When a glass broke and some replacement words for strong language were used, it was time to get up.

"Momma!"

"Morning," she said to the group, going straight to the teakettle. "How's your throat, little one?" Thérèse opened her mouth wide, Melanie using the kitchen flashlight to look inside. "Anything hurt in there?"

"No more."

"I told you it would be easy, huh?" Melanie rubbed a smudge of jam off her daughter's cheek before tossing the flashlight in the tool drawer.

"How are you, Melanie?" Dottie asked. "Any contractions?"

"Not till noon."

"Three more hours," Josh said. He began rubbing her neck from behind as she sat sipping her tea.

"Excited?" his mother asked.

"Thrilled, panicky, overwhelmed. Just like last time. But what makes me so nervous is how smoothly things are going this time. Last time was a mess, but today, all we have to do is drive in and get started," Josh said.

"Easy for you to say. I'm the pregnant lady who has to push an elephant out her basement door."

"Gonna make a elephant?" Thérèse asked.

"Just an expression," Addie said quickly.

"After this one, you'll be an old pro, Melanie," Dottie said. "With the next one, you'll know what to do every step of the way."

Melanie gave her mother-in-law a stern look. "Pardon me?"

Josh bolted for the kitchen door, maybe realizing something was brewing.

"Where are you going?"

"I should shower."

"You've had all morning to do that, and to get Thérèse ready to go out."

"I...well..."

Melanie got up from the chair on her own and left her mug behind. "I'm taking a shower, and if anyone runs the hot water while I'm in there, heads will roll."

Cassandra showed up while Melanie was in the shower, pretending to be a family friend rather than a Secret Service agent. After getting Thérèse washed and changed into clean clothes, Melanie traded places with Josh at the kitchen table, still taking sips of her tea. Once they were left alone, the agent handed over a report that Melanie began to scan.

"Not much of interest about the names you gave me," Cassandra whispered. "I presume Addie is one of them?"

Melanie nodded. "It's the son I'm more concerned about."

"Does this have something to do with the recent deaths?"

"Her son, this guy..." She tapped her finger on the report she was reading. "...was the first."

Hearing footsteps coming down the hall, Melanie shoved the intelligence report into a drawer.

"Time to go, Melanie," Josh said, leading Thérèse along in front of him.

"We're all going in the Escalade?" Cassandra asked.

"Mom's going to drive my SUV. Apparently, Addie wants to go also," Josh said.

"Whatever," Melanie said, going to the back door, an overnight bag in one hand and holding Thérèse's hand with the other. She took her place in the back seat of Cassandra's Escalade with Thérèse while Josh rode in the front for the short trip to the hospital.

"I'd think you'd be a little more cheerful, Melanie," Josh said from the front seat.

"I'm okay. It's just that my back is bothering me a little more than usual this morning."

"Won't the epidural help that?"

"For a few hours, anyway. I think the next time I have time off, I'll have surgery on my back. That means our usual Christmas trip to Wyoming is cancelled this year."

"I doubt anyone is heartbroken about that," he said.

"Including your mom."

"I sensed some tension in the house today," Cassandra said.

"Two boarders too many," Melanie muttered.

Just as they were going in the maternity entrance, Dottie and Addie parked and got out, still bickering over what sounded like nothing.

Melanie turned toward them. "Can the two of you give it a rest, please?"

Going through the lobby, Melanie saw the local newspaper. Enough of the front page showed that she could see what looked like 'Mayor' as part of the headline. She picked it up.

"Mayor Too Tough On Crime? What the heck is that supposed to mean?"

Josh took the newspaper away and tossed it down. "Not mayor today, Melanie."

Once she registered, a wheelchair was brought for Melanie by a nurse.

"Where you go, Momma? Gonna make baby now?"

211

"Not yet, Sweetie. They're just going to get me ready. It'll be an hour or so before anything happens. But we'll see each other before then. You be a good girl and mind your daddy. In fact, why don't you take him and Grandmother to the cafeteria for something to eat? And Addie can go with you."

"And Caffander, too?"

"I think she wants to stay here for a while."

With that, Melanie was whisked away to a delivery room.

"Melanie Kato, no known allergies, due to be induced at noon today by Doctor Chapman. Is that correct?" the nurse confirmed while Melanie changed into a hospital gown.

"That's the plan."

Just as Melanie was settling into her bed that would eventually be altered into the delivery bed, Dr. Chapman showed up.

"Well, look who decided to have her baby in the hospital this time."

"Ha ha."

"Everything is okay?" Dr. Chapman asked while applying the fetal heart monitor.

"With the baby? Perfect. Having some spasms in one leg, but the epidural should take care of that. But this is only a sideshow to the rest of the circus. The main event is out in the cafeteria fighting over hash browns by now."

"Since I have you as a captive audience, let me ask how you like being mayor?" Dr. Chapman asked.

"It's everything I always thought it would be, and more."

"I always thought your mother would've been a good mayor," the nurse said, saying she wanted to be called Nurse Ito. She was small, Japanese descent like so many people in the islands, and well into her senior citizen years.

"Did you know my mother?"

"I was just out of nurses training when she started working here at the hospital. I was working in the OR back then. No longer. Too busy there. All I want these days is to see the new babies as they come into the world."

The nurse started an IV in Melanie's wrist, Melanie watching closely. "Seems like it would be more fun, on good days."

"This place was so small back then, just the one building."

"Did you work with my mother very often?" Melanie asked.

"We all took turns until she demanded they make a special team for her. Big cases she did back then."

"They'd still be big cases now, from what I've heard."

Nurse Ito officiously went about her tasks. "Once they had her here, they were able to attract so many other highly qualified doctors from the mainland and Honolulu. She didn't take to hospital administrators, though."

"Sort of a Kato family trait, to question authority."

"For what she did for this hospital in those early years, and how she built that little restaurant into the nice place it became, she had every right to."

"Well, I wish she could be here today," Melanie said.

Chapman finished her exam. "Everything is on track. Your vitals are okay, not great. The baby is in position, head down. Once Doctor Everingham is here, you can get your epidural, and then I'll start the induction. As soon as the Oxytocin goes in, we'll watch for the first contractions, and then I'll rupture your water. It'll be only a few minutes after that when you'll be a mother all over again. Is Josh ready to be coach?"

"He's pretty nervous. He might need some prompting from you guys to keep him on track."

"He'll be fine."

Nurse Ito went out to get Josh changed into hospital scrubs. When she came back in, she had a full report on the waiting room.

"You sure have a lot of people waiting, Melanie."

"Who's out there?"

"Your husband, daughter, mother-in-law, a lady named Addie, another named Cassandra, a policeman named Nakatani, and a couple named Duane and Lailanie. There are also three reporters waiting."

"Waiting for what?"

"To get all the details of our mayor's new arrival!"

Trinh came in, wearing her usual surgical garb for work. "Wow, Mel. You have quite the entourage out there. It's like the gallery in those golf matches I see on TV."

"Well, just prop open the door and let them watch me tee one up."

Trinh laughed. "Maybe a little later. Looks like you still have a few things to do, so I'll get a bite to eat."

"Are you in a room in the OR today?"

"No, the manager assigned me to float between rooms today. She's letting me hang around here for the rest of my shift. I'm supposed to report back to the troops waiting in the OR for any and all news from the front," Trinh said on her way to the door. "I'll be back."

Dr. Everingham showed up, an anesthesiologist Melanie often worked with in the OR. He went through his cursory exam before having her sit up on the side of the bed, his epidural kit on a table next to him.

"Okay," he said, feeling her back. "Okay."

When he found the sorest spot along her spine, she twitched.

"What's wrong?"

"I have a bad disc at L-4. Maybe one disc above and below, also."

"I'll have to go one level above, if that's okay with you?"

"Whatever works," she said, trying to arch her back out toward him. When she winced with pain, Chapman stepped over.

"What's wrong?"

"Just my back. My leg has gone to sleep again but I'm still getting spasms in it."

"Is it on the same side as your old injury?" Chapman asked.

"Yeah," Melanie said, trying to rub life back into her thigh. "I knew that would come back to haunt me."

"What happened?" Everingham asked, as he continued to gently grope Melanie's back for a new site to insert the epidural.

"I was shot in the rear end a long time ago. I needed several surgeries to get my sciatic nerve on that same side back together, along with some reconstructive work on the muscles. I've also been in a couple of hard landings in helicopters, which aren't so good for the back." She winced again. "What are you doing?"

"I haven't even started," Everingham said.

"Whatever you're doing is making it worse."

"Okay, that's it," the anesthesiologist said, taking his kit away. "No epidural."

"What? Why not?"

"If you already have spinal nerve root problems, I don't want to exacerbate them by doing an epidural that might not even work."

"I have to do this natural?"

"You did last time," Dr. Chapman said. "But you know he's right. It would be too much risk to your spine. There's no reason to think the induction and delivery won't go smoothly."

"Want to ask one of my partners to come for a second opinion?" Everingham asked. "Or do a pudendal block?"

"Never mind. Let's get this show on the road," Melanie said, just as a natural contraction hit.

Dr. Chapman got her things ready and Nurse Ito stood by while the Oxytocin was injected into Melanie's IV. Contractions were already hitting in full force, even as the labor induction drug was going in, and her water broke on its own. The nurse got the stirrups in position and put the head of the bed back a little.

"You better get Josh in here, because this is happening pretty dang fast," Melanie said while panting through more contractions.

Nurse Ito hurried out to fetch Josh, already dressed in hospital garb. Trinh was just coming back from lunch then.

"Big ol' herd of nurses waiting out there," Trinh said, coming in. "From the ICU, ER, OR. Even ladies from the cafeteria are out there."

"Good for them," Melanie said, panting through heavy contractions.

"How's everything in here?" Josh asked when he took his position at her shoulder.

"Not a good time for discussion, Josh. Just hold my hand, okay?"

"Really good time to push right now, Melanie," Chapman said from where she was waiting.

Pushing as hard as she could, Melanie swore.

"Okay, the next time you feel a contraction hit, put some of that temper into pushing."

Melanie swore again, this time directly at her OB.

"Not the first time I've been called that. You need to push with all your might."

"I'm trying to. But my leg, it's so painful. I can't take it being up in stirrups like that."

"Come on, Melanie. You can do this," Trinh said.

Nurse Ito joined Chapman, watching for the baby. "Push, Melanie! Just push with everything, right now!"

"You can do this, Melanie," Josh said. He was right next to her, wiping sweat from her face. "Baby Sofia is almost here."

"Push, Melanie, push!"

"It's time now, Melanie," Trinh said. "One last push."

She bore down, fighting the burning pain in her back and leg.

"Okay, that's it! Here's baby!"

Melanie heard a whimper, followed by crying. She lifted her head to look down below. Dr. Chapman was just lifting the baby to set on Melanie's chest, the cord still attached.

"Just one little unexpected complication, Melanie."

"Oh no. What?"

"Sophia might not be a good name for a son."

"Son?" When Melanie looked, the baby was already peeing a tiny stream. She put her hand on him. "A son! Josh! We have a son."

Nurse Ito quickly took the baby away as soon as the cord was cut. Trinh joined her to wash the baby.

"We got a boy after all, Melanie," Josh whispered to her, still wiping sweat, and now tears from her face.

"Yeah, a boy. Tay was right all along."

"Apgars are nine and ten, Doctor," Nurse Ito said, while she swaddled the baby. "Weight is good and he'll be tall like his grandfather."

"Great. Let's get Melanie's legs down from the stirrups."

"I forgot they were up. You're sure Everingham didn't do the epidural anyway?"

"Not at all."

Dr. Chapman gave Melanie's belly a quick rub and then examined her legs and feet. "Do you feel me pinching you?"

"No." Melanie had the baby back by now, but looked at what Chapman was doing. "I don't feel anything in my left leg at all."

"Trinh, can you see if there's a neurosurgeon available? Or even one of the ER docs," Chapman said.

"On it," Trinh said, already holding the phone to her ear.

"What's going on?" Josh asked.

"My legs are numb," Melanie told him.

"They're supposed to be. You had that epidural thing."

"I didn't. We decided against it."

"Carlson is on his way," Trinh said hanging up the phone. Dr. Carlson was a neurosurgeon at the hospital, somebody responsible for diagnosis and treatment of brain and spine problems.

Without waiting for anyone to tell her, Melanie began feeding the baby while the small delivery room exploded with activity. Dr. Chapman watched over vital signs and massaged Melanie's belly, while Nurse Ito stood near the bed, watching over the baby.

"Trinh, can you get Tay for me and bring her in?"

A moment after Trinh left the room, Thérèse burst through the door looking as if on a mission. "Where's Sophia?"

"Hey, little one. You were right about Sophia being a boy. We need to think of another name."

While the girl gave it some thought, the room door opened and several nurses came in followed by Lailanie and Duane, making the room crowded. Dottie was at the front of the pack, swooning over the baby, and congratulating mother and father. Addie remained at the back, smiling, but with wet eyes.

"Okay, before we go any further, the name on the birth certificate?" asked Nurse Ito.

Melanie looked at Josh for an answer, who seemed close to passing out with all the noise and confusion. When she saw Addie at the back of the room, still trying to compose herself, she knew there was only one name.

"Kenny."

"Kenny?" Josh asked.

Melanie nodded her head in the direction of Addie, who was now in a full-blown cry, but smiling through it.

"Okay, Kenneth," said Nurse Ito, writing the name on a name band.

"No, just Kenny. No one will ever call him Kenneth, and Kenny is so much friendlier."

"Middle name?"

"Jack."

"Kenny Jack Kato-Strong," said Nurse Ito, finishing her writing.

"Sorry, but it should be Kenny Jack Strong-Kato. Since he's a boy, he should have his father's name first."

As Nurse Ito filled out name bands to put on the baby, Melanie, and Josh, Dr. Carlson came into the room. "Sorry, I must have the wrong room."

Trinh pulled him back in. "No, believe it or not, this is the right place."

Everyone was shooed out by Nurse Ito, except Trinh and Josh. While Melanie fed the baby from her other breast, Dr. Chapman filled Carlson in on what the problem was with Melanie's back. He did a quick neurologic exam, mostly on her legs.

"Yes, well, I know this is a huge moment. You just want to spend time with your baby, but I think we should get some scans of your back, at the very least, X-rays."

"What do you think the problem is?" Melanie asked.

"I think you're right about there being a disc extrusion, but it goes beyond that. There's so much pressure on that nerve root right now, it's at risk of permanent failure. If my suspicions are right, I should operate as soon as possible to decompress and relieve the pressure."

"Today?"

"As soon as the scans are done. As you know, if you lose that nerve root, your ability to walk will be lost. This isn't simply a slipped disc, but more like an injury suffered in a car accident and a fractured vertebra."

Josh pressed his cheek against Melanie's as she began to cry.

"I just want to be with my son."

"Mel, you need to think of the future," Trinh said. "Just get the scans and have the surgery, if you need it. Kenny will still be here later."

"Okay." Melanie tossed aside the box of tissues she was given. "But I want to hold Kenny again. Josh, you're staying with Kenny. Trinh, send all those people home and then you're coming with me."

When Nurse Ito bent over to take Kenny from Melanie, she smiled and leaned in close to whisper. "You can trust Doctor Carlson."

Melanie looked at the smiling face of the nurse, settling on her eyes. There was something familiar about them, something motherly, eyes she'd looked into every day of her life before leaving home.

***

After an emergency scan of her back, Dr. Carlson came back with the films and the results. Melanie couldn't read his expression.

"There's good news, and there's bad news. The good is that your nerve root looks intact. The bad is that you're significantly overdue for surgery. And like I said earlier, if I don't do it today, right now, you're at serious risk of permanent and irreversible damage."

After getting a primer on what he was going to do, and reading the consent he gave her to sign, the exact same surgical consent she gave to hundreds of patients each year, she signed. She was quickly into the OR where Dr. Everingham was waiting to be her anesthesiologist. He quickly gave her the first syringe of medication, following that with putting the gas mask on her face.

Carlson took Melanie's hand when her world began to spin.

"Trinh is here to be your nurse, and I'll get that disc out," the surgeon said. His voice had changed from a masculine baritone to a soft and familiar one.

Melanie's mind swirled from the meds washing through it. "Mom?"

"Yeah, Honey. You're going to be fine. This might take me a little while, but you'll be as good as new when we're done."

Melanie barely heard the last of her mother's words before her mind tumbled off to sleep.

***

Once she was asleep and positioned on her belly, sterile surgical drapes were attached to her back covering most of her body, and the team got started.

"I didn't get a complete story of how she hurt her back originally?" Dr. Carlson said.

Trinh took over the explanation. "When we were in the Air Force together, she was a medic in Search and Rescue. They often flew missions in helicopters, and they didn't always go well. Like she always says, helicopters are flying shoeboxes, but the wings are the propellers, and those don't always stay on."

"She said something about being in a hard landing?"

"Probably more than one, for as much as they flew. A hard landing in a helicopter is anything but. Any time a helicopter lands bottom side down, it's called a landing, no matter how much damage is done. What the rest of us might call a crash, the military calls a hard landing. The only time they call it a crash is if some other part of the helicopter hits before the bottom. That's how she has explained it to me."

"She was the real deal, then?" he asked.

"She was as studly as any of the men. She had to be, just to cope with all the brutality and stress of Special Forces. But you'd never know that now, especially when Thérèse came along. Melanie's taken after her mother."

"How so?" Carlson asked.

"She's at peace with the world, and all she wants is peace in the world. When the rest of us feel like slapping some jerk for whatever reason, that's the farthest thing from Melanie's mind. Just like her mother." Trinh chuckled. "I wouldn't try to force her into a corner when she's pissed, though."

***

It was winter on the Korean Peninsula when Staff Sergeant Melanie Kato, Search and Rescue medic, stood in the open door of the rescue helicopter. They were flying low, barely over the treetops, on a night mission to rescue the crew of another helicopter that had gone down in the Demilitarized Zone that separated North and South Korea. They hadn't known until airborne that the downed bird was in fact a small spy helo used by the CIA for surveillance. For late-night so-called 'dark ops', they would ordinarily have a second support helicopter go with them, probably an Apache attack helo, since their only weapons were two outboard .50 caliber machine guns used only in self-defense situations, and their rifles. This time, they only had another SAR helo in high orbit, carrying their officer in command of the operation. Logistics aside, all

222

Melanie wanted was a clear area to land somewhere near the downed craft and no combatants to deal with. Clinging to a strap, she stood in the door, watching the landscape below.

The crew chief held up three fingers. "Three minutes to gear drop!" he shouted over the heavy drone of the twin turbine engines and rotors.

She nodded and gave him a thumbs-up. Their helicopter would drop to a low hover and they would push out crates of her medical gear and jump out before the helo would lift up and bank away, waiting to be called back again. She had two bins that needed to be shoved out the door, followed by her leaping in the dark, hoping she would land on her feet without breaking a leg or arm. The worst thing that could happen to a rescue team was to lose their medic.

It was complete dark as the helo began its vertical descent. She could see the area around the downed craft below them, a cornfield now fallow with patches of snow in ruts, a few small fires still smoldering in the wrecked cockpit of the small Cayuse. When the descent light turned on, it illuminated a small patch of the ground directly below. At thirty feet up, the crew chief began hollering, swinging his arm in a circle.

"Go, go, go! Get your shit off my bird!"

She shoved her two bins overboard, watching as they hit solid ground.

Her earbud crackled to life with a message from their captain, who was in the other helicopter that was in high orbit.

"Swede and Clocker out first," Captain Collins called over their radio comms. "Set up a wide perimeter. Poi Dog, you go out right after Zito. Just get the Cayuse crew onto litters and back in the Bad Karma. Don't screw around wasting time. Over."

"Roger that," Melanie said into her mouthpiece.

It was the same message as always, don't screw around on the ground, and do most of her treatment on the deck of the Bad Karma, their rescue helicopter, on the way back to base.

"Clocker, set enough munitions to blow the Cayuse. Light it up once you're off the ground."

"Roger that," he said into his mike.

"I'm giving you ten on the hard deck before you're up and away, Poi Dog. Out."

Melanie didn't get the chance to respond. The rest of the SAR crew began crowding the doorways on either side of the helicopter, waiting for their signal to disembark. She kept her hands on the backs of her teammates, watching the sky around them. If one helo could be shot down, there was every reason to think it could happen again.

They were still ten feet up, winter ice crystals from the ground swirling through the air. In two more feet, they would be told to leap.

Interrupting the crew chief was a yellow streak through the air.

"Rocket! Incoming rocket!"

"RPG!"

An alarm sounded with a *wheep wheep wheep* blare. As the helicopter lifted and banked, the team scrambled for the safety of the interior, reaching for anything they could grab.

"Brace! Brace!"

More alarms.

Melanie reached for a strap but missed it.

The rocket hit the tail end of the fuselage but didn't detonate, just tumbling through the air. The evasive maneuvers of the pilot had averted disaster, but the helicopter was barely under control. Still trying to grab anything, she got a hold of the flight suit of the crew chief, but didn't have enough fabric in her hand. When the craft continued to spin out of control, she tumbled backward.

Another alarm blared, but Melanie barely heard it. Instead, she was dropping through the air, and she wasn't sure how far she was going to fall before she hit. Her training kicked in, and she tmaneuvered onto her side as she fell.

When she hit, it was with her rump first. The jolt sent a flash of pain up through her spine into her ribs. She'd also hit her head.

She wasn't sure if she was waking from being unconscious for a moment because it was so dark. Even through the pain, she unhooked her rifle, rolled onto her belly, and took up a defensive position. All that kept her conscious was the stabbing pain in her back.

She listened to the chatter of calls between the pilot of the Bad Karma and that of the command helo in a high hover. The situation was barely under control, while the Bad Karma continued to spin.

"Rescue medic! Rescue medic! Come in, Poi Dog!" her CO called.

Melanie heard the thumps of her teammates hitting the ground nearby. Duane started calling her op name. "Dog! You okay? Where are you, Dog?"

"I'm okay, Zito. Twenty feet to your three o'clock." She reached for her mike button. "Poi Dog on the deck, kicking dirt. Out."

Once her team had a defensive perimeter set up, Melanie went to the burnt-out shell of what had been the Cayuse helicopter. She found the remains of the pilots, the only crew on board.

"Op command, this is Poi Dog. The mission is recovery, not rescue. Repeat, two dead squirrels, over."

"Roger that, Dog. Bag them up, call your bird back, and get out. Clocker, set your charges. Command, out." Their CO came back on. "Be advised, we have two bogies closing fast, twenty minutes out. You need to be up and away in ten."

"Roger that," she said into her mike. Working in near pitch-black, Melanie called for the Bad Karma to return to her location, and to maintain a low hover while her crew got the bodies of the two CIA operatives loaded for the trip home. She had a long bag open and rolled a burned body into it. "Zito, does Collins not realize we could work faster if he didn't interrupt us all the time with pointless calls?"

"He's an officer." Zito kept his rifle level while he scanned the terrain around them. He was her 'six' on missions, the one responsible for watching her back while she did her work as a medic. He was also from Maui, and they had formed an easy friendship during training. "He has to do something to earn his paycheck."

She opened another body bag. "Gettin' tired of this stuff. Ever think about what you're gonna do once you're back home?"

"Get married," he said.

"To a girl?"

"To the prettiest one on Maui."

"Brah, that's me."

"Not when you're messin' with dead guys. I thought you were going to some big, fancy doctor school?"

"Like I can afford med school with what the government pays us."

"You save every penny you earn."

"And six years of military wages will just about cover one year of med school tuition, maybe two if I'm homeless and don't eat."

Their headsets crackled to life with a message from their CO. "Cut the chatter and get off the deck."

"Roger that," Melanie said, zipping closed the second body bag. She and Zito dragged them from the burnt craft to an open landing zone and signaled for the Bad Karma to descend. "Clocker, we're clear. Are your charges set?"

"Wired and armed. Det set for five minutes. We need to hustle."

Melanie heard the whining of an animal in the dark. "Anybody else hear that?"

The team scanned the area.

"Probably a dog sniffing around for a home-cooked meal," Zito said.

Melanie heard it rummaging through the wreckage. "Can't leave the dog to get blown up."

"What is it with you and animals?" Swede asked. "It's a stray. Who cares?"

"Not gonna let it die like that." Melanie found a couple of stones and threw them at the dog to scare it away from the wrecked helo that was due to be blown to bits in less than four minutes. "Hey! Get out of there!"

"Knock it off, Kato!" their CO said over the radio. "Forget the damn dog!"

The Bad Karma was just setting down, ice crystals flying about madly in the rotor wash. They loaded the two crates of gear first, followed by the bodies. Melanie and Zito were the two last to climb in, the bird slowly lifting as they were being pulled in.

Melanie looked down, trying to see the hungry dog. She shone her flashlight in the wreckage and saw movement.

"Anybody got an MRE?"

The crew chief tossed her one from a compartment. "What's that for? Dead bodies make you hungry?"

She tore into the package and found the foil pouch of wieners and beans. Tearing that open, she flashed her light at the dog again. "Hey! Dinnertime! Come and get it!"

She waved the flashlight at the pouch and tossed it out the door, aiming the beam to where it fell. As the Bad Karma banked away, she saw the dog trot away from the wreckage, sniffing the ground as it went.

"Poi Dog, you took a bad fall back there," Swede said. "You okay?"

She buckled into her place on the narrow bench, keeping watch over her two dead bodies. They belonged to her, at least until they got back to base and signed them over to the hospital morgue. "I'm okay. A trip to the base chiropractor will get me right again."

"Maybe you should go to the base hospital to get checked out?" Swede said over the noise of the churning rotors and drone of the engines turning them.

She looked at her crew one at a time. "No one says a word that I fell out of the helo, got it? Not a word, or I will personally make each of you miserable for a very long time. This story never gets told. Understand?"

Zito chuckled and patted her on the shoulder. "And she will, too!"

***

Melanie felt tapping on her chest, followed by a vigorous shake to her shoulder.

"Mel, time to wake up."

Instinctively, Melanie reached up and grabbed what it was that disturbed her sleep. Such blissful sleep.

Trinh pried her hand from Melanie's string grip. "Hey, it's me, Trinh. It's time to wake up. Your surgery is done, Mel. Time to wake up."

Melanie opened her eyes to see her best friend looking down at her. "Surgery?"

"Your back, remember? It went great. Doctor Carlson got your disc squared away, which was worse than what the scans showed. But with physical therapy, you'll be okay. Your legs are going to be fine, Mel. Did you hear me? You're going to be fine."

She tried focusing her eyes. "What about the dog?"

"What dog?"

"The one at the Cayuse. Did it get blown up?" Melanie asked, still trying to get her mouth working properly.

"Yes, the dog was okay," someone said.

There was more shaking to her shoulder, followed by Trinh's voice. "Melanie, time to wake up."

When Melanie opened her eyes, the world was still a little blurry from the anesthesia. "Where's the baby?"

"Ha! First thing a mother would say," Trinh said. "Are you having any pain?"

"I want my baby. I want Kenny."

Melanie got so many calls in the hospital the next day from friends wanting to come by and see the baby, she had to make appointments for them all. By noon, she was exhausted and turned off the phone. Kenny was asleep in his bassinet next to her bed. When Trinh came by, she told her to close the door.

"Get my clothes," she said. "I need to get out of here."

"You're not going anywhere until both Chapman and Carlson say you can. I just looked at your chart and they both recommend you staying until tomorrow."

"Just get me my clothes."

"I'm not helping you leave early."

"Afraid you might get in trouble?" Melanie asked.

"Afraid I might lose my job."

"If you do, I'll hire you as my nanny."

"Oh, now wouldn't that be special. You could boss me around every day, telling me I'm not holding the bottle the right way, the diaper is too loose, the diaper is too tight, I use too much powder. Forget it, Mel. But why haven't you guys hired a new nanny? You've had all summer."

"Qualified nannies aren't exactly standing in line to work for us. If we lived in LA, or even Honolulu, yes. But not here. They're either looking for jobs to pay for their beach bum lifestyle, or are twenty-year-olds with no experience with kids."

"What about that gal a few weeks ago? She even had a weekend sleepover."

"She left when she discovered how small the house is. People think we all live in giant air-conditioned mansions on Maui. Surprise! More like humble little sweatboxes that have seen better days."

"Well, you have three weeks before you're bringing Kenny to work with you."

"What if I retired and became a stay-at-home mom?" Melanie offered after a moment.

"Oh no, you don't. You put in too much work to get to where you are today. I watched how much time you spent studying, how long your days were. I'm not letting you walk away from what you've built."

"Mom retired early."

"She retired from medicine when she was a decade older than you, mainly because she had a shake in one hand, and then promptly opened that restaurant. That took as much of her time as working at the hospital. Anyway, you can't survive on Josh's salary from the college."

"I have money in the bank. It's just sitting there doing nothing."

"Which is being saved for Thérèse and now Kenny. You never go near it because of them."

"We could live off the interest it earns for us, easy."

"Mel, I'm not letting you walk away from your career, so get over that idea. You have three weeks to find somebody and move her into your house. Focus on that. How's your back?"

"I could use a pain pill."

"Not as long as you're breastfeeding Kenny."

As though he recognized his name, the baby began to fuss.

"That's his 'I'm hungry' whine. Bring him to me."

Once Kenny was feeding, Trinh pulled up a chair next to the bed. "You didn't wake up so good yesterday."

"I was having the craziest dream."

"Mel, nobody ever wants to hear about someone else's dream. And your internal life is too weird to hear about."

"This one seemed to have a meaning, almost like I was having a premonition."

"Okay, what was it?"

"Well, at first, I could hear you guys talking about me, like I wasn't completely asleep yet. Then all of a sudden, I was back in Korea on a mission. Something went wrong with the landing, and I flew out the door."

"You have those dreams all the time," Trinh said. "You take bits and pieces of things that really happened and then paste them together into a bizarre dream. They don't mean anything, except that you're just trying to work through all that stuff. Seriously, you need to see a therapist if you want to quit having those dreams."

Melanie moved Kenny to the other breast. "That wasn't all, though. That dream turned into something even weirder. It was like I went back in time to old Hawaii. There was some big battle raging here on Maui, just up the slope from our house. Then I, or someone took an arrow in her back, but she kept fighting until she died. Then she was buried in a cave up on the pali, a spear and the arrows that killed her put there with her."

"How do you know it was near us?" Trinh asked.

"I recognized so much of it. But it was so odd."

"What was odd? All you did was change the place from Korea to Maui, and you became a Hawaiian warrior. You said in the dream you got shot in the back with an arrow, right? Well, that was probably right when Carlson was working on your spine. And you turned the bullet you were really shot with once into an arrow."

"But in the dream, I died. Or at least the Hawaiian warrior did. Then all of a sudden, I was back in Korea again, Collins yelling at me on comms about not wasting time."

"I don't know, Mel. It's your nutty dream, not mine."

"Hand me my phone," Melanie asked.

"Who are you calling? You're supposed to be getting rest."

"No one. I just want to look at pictures."

Trinh handed it over. Once it was turned on, Melanie went to saved images that she found at the online auction site.

"These are them!"

"They're what?" Trinh asked, trying to see the screen.

"The artifacts that were put up for auction bids were the same things as in my dream. The spear, the arrows, the red kahili. It's all the same."

"Of course they're the same. You simply put those things into your dream."

"I never told you the end of the dream. I was back in the Bad Karma, heading back to base, with two bodies recovered from the wreckage."

"Only two? We have three dead bodies in the morgue. And where does the helicopter come into play?"

"I don't know. But in the dream, the two bodies were Hawaiian warriors. In real life, they were white CIA operatives." Melanie rubbed her face for a moment. "Then I was feeding a dog, or something stupid like that. It was really odd."

"I'm not a therapist or a dream interpreter, Mel. I have no idea what that might mean."

"All I know is that in some weird way, it makes sense."

"Anything weird makes sense to you, Melanie Kato," Trinh said, standing. "Lunch break is over. Back to work."

"Hey, before you go, did you see yesterday's headlines?" Melanie asked.

Trinh rolled her eyes. "Something about the mayor being too hard on island crime. The reporter said you beat up some guy at a surf shop in Lahaina. Nobody's going to believe that, Mel. Just forget about it."

"Maybe there's a little bit of truth to it."

"What happened?"

Melanie told the story of the salesman at Gonzo's thumping her in the chest, and her putting him on his knees.

Trinh laughed. "Just what Maui needs, a cranky mayor who was in Special Forces!"

After Trinh was gone, Melanie called Detective Nakatani.

"Hey! Congratulations to Maui's newest mother! I heard there was a surprise?"

"Boy instead of a girl. So much for the accuracy of ultrasounds."

"No, I mean you needed surgery?"

"How'd you know that?" she asked.

"It's in the newspaper. They said you needed to be rushed into emergency surgery to save your life. Something about bleeding to death, or whatever."

"I wasn't dying. How'd they find out?" she asked.

"There were three reporters waiting with all the rest of us to hear about you and the baby. Once you went to emergency surgery, someone came out to talk with us."

"Which doctor?" she asked.

"Well, it wasn't a doctor."

Melanie had a sinking feeling. "Don't tell me…"

"Your mother-in-law held something of a press conference about your condition and the planned surgery. I have to admit, she did a decent job of it. Very dramatic."

The tic came back to Melanie's eye. "I'll deal with her later. I have a question. On those latest artifacts, the dirty ones that look as though they've just been collected, is there any indication at all of where they came from? Did the other detective figure out anything like that?"

"That Honolulu detective went home. We couldn't afford him for another week, so you have me to figure that out, along with the perps behind the deaths of those three men. We've sat each of Gonzo's surf instructors in an interrogation room, and one or two might give up something if we press them a little harder a second time."

"Not officially classified as murders yet?"

"It would probably be wrongful death or manslaughter when the time comes. Why are you asking?"

She gave him a short version of her dream. "There are so many trails up into the hills and over the pali that someone could've discovered something up there, and has been bringing it down with them, selling it off at auction."

"And I suppose you have a troop of experienced trackers and climbers to go check out every inch of two hundred square miles?"

"No."

"That's what it would take."

"Unless we find someone who knows something. I just wish Josh had been able to follow those guys the other day. I bet you anything they have something to do with the stolen artifacts. Or more," she said.

"We do have a lead on the decapitation injury."

"Somebody saw something and came forward?"

"No. Somebody found the head."

"Where?"

"A recreational scuba diver found it stuck in coral in the reef near Lahaina. Apparently, it had been stuck there for a while, from the way the reef fish had been nibbling at it. Kinda hollow inside."

Melanie's stomach turned. "Thanks for sharing that."

"At least he's altogether again."

"To change the subject to something a little less gruesome, has the coroner come up with anything about the propeller marks on the guy's body? He said that first day he might be able to figure out what type of propeller did the damage."

"Yeah. I got a couple of uniforms checking out the marinas again, looking for a specific size and style of outboard propeller. It's been pretty slow going, though. Not everyone likes the cops sniffing around their boats. On the other hand, we've made two arrests of drug mules using boats to move the stuff."

"That's something, anyway."

Now that Kenny was done feeding and sound asleep, Melanie felt like napping also. Setting her phone aside, she snuggled in for a snooze.

***

When she woke again, Melanie wasn't alone. But it wasn't Josh or Dottie there, or even Trinh on another visit, but Addie.

"Addie, I'm so sorry I've been so difficult lately. It's just that…"

"It's just that you've been waiting to have your baby, and your back was hurting you so much, you needed surgery. After the week you'd just had, I can understand completely why you were so upset. When your mother-in-law got here, that seemed to push you over an edge."

"Please don't say anything to Josh or Dottie, but she really has a way of getting under my skin."

Addie chuckled. "I get the idea she has that effect on quite a few people."

"Did you just come from home? Are the others okay?"

"They're fine. Thérèse sure is a little trooper. She's making some decorations for the nursery."

"I can't wait to see. The two of you sure get along well. Tay doesn't always take to people right away."

"She's a special little girl. I'll miss her when I go."

"Have you decided to leave soon? You really are welcome to stay. I'd almost prefer you over, well, you-know-who."

"I made a flight for tomorrow," Addie said. "The police still don't know how long it will be before they release my son. I guess I'll have to trust a mortician to ship him for me when the time comes."

"I'd be glad to manage that for you, Addie. I doubt it'll be much longer."

Kenny woke and began to fuss.

"That's his 'diaper needs changing' whine," Addie said.

"I'll call the nurse."

"No, I can change him."

Melanie watched from her bed as the woman gently cleaned Kenny and changed his diaper.

"Funny how we never forget how to do something like this," she said, giving the infant a tickle. "I guess we do it so many times, it becomes ingrained in the memory of our hands."

She picked the baby up and held him close to her chest, patting his back to burp him.

"Addie, when you go home, what will you do?"

"Oh, go back to my clubs and charity things, I suppose. My friends will look at me with pity on their faces, and it won't be long before I feel lonely again."

"Why don't you stay here? You could be our nanny. You and Thérèse get along so well, and you certainly know what to do with a baby."

"Me? A nanny? I think those years have passed me by. I just don't have the energy."

"We'd pay you well, and you'd have a place to live. I know that room isn't very big, but with the other room turning into Kenny's nursery in a few months, it seems like it would be a good arrangement."

"You honestly want me to be your nanny?"

"It would only be five days a week, when Josh and I are at work. You could even take half days off on Wednesdays when he gets home from work early. You wouldn't have to start for two weeks. That would give you enough time to go home and settle whatever affairs you have there. We'd even buy you a car to take the kids around in. What do you say?"

"Can I think about it?"

"Of course. But you know I'm going to have Thérèse work on you."

It wasn't hard at all for Melanie to stay in bed when the others went to church on Sunday morning. After all, Kenny was there with her, beginning his first full day at home.

"So, what's the deal? Are you going to be a mind reader? Because we already have someone in the family who sees ghosts and another that knows magic. What's your shtick going to be?" she asked her son as he consumed another meal.

Like it always did, her phone rang. Once again, it was from Detective Nakatani.

"Please tell me another body hasn't washed ashore."

"Not that I'm aware of. Were you expecting one?" he asked.

"One on someone else's island would've been interesting to read about in the newspaper. Two is definitely too many. But three is just absurd. And they all happen to be on my island. The families must be looking for them. Have they been contacted?" she asked.

"We're still looking for the family of the second. It might turn out that he has no one interested in knowing he's dead. The third is still unidentified. We are making progress on the investigation, though."

"How?"

"First, the bad news. We haven't been able to identify the seller yet. They're proving to be a lot trickier than what we first expected. But we have been able to identify many of the bidders, and there have been a lot of them."

"Can't really do anything about them until they buy the stuff, right? Is bidding breaking the law of black market trafficking?"

"That's a gray area in the law. Money actually has to change hands, or accounts in the case of the internet. But by identifying them, getting personal backgrounds and knowing what else they've bought through online auctions, we've been able to digitally triangulate those purchases to common sellers."

"That narrows the field of potential places to look for whoever is stealing the stuff, right?" she asked.

"Exactly. It also helps pinpoint with a high degree of accuracy who our sellers are. We've come up with three possibilities, with two here in Hawaii, and one on Maui."

"This trafficking of historical artifacts from Maui has been going on for a while?" she asked.

"Probably since the missionary days, when things were sent back to European museums to fill displays with Polynesian crafts. But Native American Indian objects of unknown origin have been coming up for both live and online auctions for almost a year. Nearly everything has been in the same condition as these latest artifacts, of not being cleaned or preserved professionally."

"Now it's started here on Maui. It sounds like we never would've known about it if they hadn't stolen from the museum."

"Which has been our conclusion. We've been able to talk with an expert in Hawaiian culture and history from the university on Oahu, someone familiar with recent excavations in Hawaii, and who has done university and Office of Hawaiian Affairs-sanctioned digs. He said some of the richest areas on Maui for finding old things is on the south slope of the West Maui mountains."

"Which is just behind my house," she said. "Do you suppose the trespassers we've seen have something to do with the relics that're for sale? Maybe somehow they found a cache of the stuff and raided it, and are now secretly selling it off piece by piece?"

"Let's not turn these jokers into Indiana Jones, Mayor. But, yes, that's something we've been mulling over. How often did you say you've seen trespassers? When did they start?"

"A couple times a week, I guess, and just in the last few weeks."

"Which fits our time frame for the items turning up for auction. I bet if you guys could pin down the exact dates you saw them, it would closely correspond with the starts of new items for auction."

Melanie moved Kenny over to her other breast. "And all this time we thought they were harmless hikers, just being pains in the butt by walking through our property. We never would've guessed they were tomb raiders. That's all they are, after all, tomb raiders. Most of those things were old weapons, and warriors were often buried in caves or lava tubes with their weapons, or with the weapon that killed them." She stopped for a moment, something bothering her. The idea seemed so familiar, as though she'd recently talked about it or had seen the same thing in a movie. "Is there anything else?"

"Now that you've mentioned it, something that just went on auction yesterday is a bone with an arrow tip in it, along with two other similar arrows and a spear tip. It's being auctioned as a group. That goes with what you were saying about a warrior being buried with the weapons that killed him, right? An arrow tip stuck in a bone?"

Another stroke of déjà vu hit her. "Uh, yeah. Could be. What bone?"

"A spine bone. I'll send you a picture of what's online."

Melanie waited for a moment. When the image showed up, it was a police image, a blow-up of what was online. Sure enough, it was a stone arrow tip stuck deep in a vertebra, something that likely would've caused a lethal injury.

"Yeah, that would do it."

"Mayor, while we're on the topic of things being in a gray area legally, maybe you could do me a favor?"

"I can consider it."

"Is Mrs. Winston still staying with you?"

"She's gone to church with the others. For some reason, we've become rather religious in this household lately, and I'm beginning to think it has something to do with getting away from the cranky lady who owns the place. Why?"

"Did she happen to take her phone with her?" he asked.

"I don't know why she would. I haven't heard it ring yet, and she barely knows how the thing works."

"Maybe you could do me a favor and take a look at the history in it?"

After putting Kenny in his bassinet, she put on a robe. "Got nothing else better to do. May as well go on a caper. I can call it physical therapy." She went to Addie's room. Finding the door hanging open, it almost seemed like an invitation to go in. The phone was on the nightstand, turned on. She tapped a few times until she learned how to use it. "What do you want to know? The numbers she calls, or the numbers that call her?"

"The most common ones in either direction."

"Okay, this is odd. Almost every call she's made since she's been here has been to the same number, and that has a Hawaii prefix. A few others have been to me and a couple to Josh, but none to the mainland." She gave him the number. "The other weird thing is that her personal number is a Hawaii prefix, not mainland."

"Maybe she got a local SIM card when she got here?" he asked.

Melanie kept scrolling. "No. The calls that have gone back and forth are months old, long before she ever got here a couple of weeks ago. She's been using this phone a lot more than she lets on."

"I hate to make you dig, but are there any saved texts?" he asked.

"You know, this is how Trinh and I discovered her husband was cheating on her, by looking in his phone when he wasn't around. Somehow, I get the idea there could be just as much trouble this time, but for me." She put the phone back where she found it without looking for text messages. Just as she was getting back to bed, there was the clatter of the back screen door opening, followed by the sounds of small feet running through the kitchen. "Detective, my family just got home and I'm about to be invaded. Just keep me informed on whatever you learn, okay?"

"Momma!" Thérèse announced, just before she bashed into the side of the bed, misjudging where she was. Getting up off the floor again, she climbed up onto the bed. "How's Kenny?"

"Maybe a little quieter, Sweetie. Kenny's just going back to sleep."

"Oh, yeah. Sorry, Kenny."

"How was church?"

"No for go church."

"Oh?"

"Went on a big drive. Sawed lotsa ocean."

"Really? What color was it?" Melanie asked.

"Blue. The mad parts were white. Did you know there's ocean all the way around us?"

"Sure did. That's why Maui is called an island."

Josh came in. "We decided to take a lap around the island. Addie wanted to see a little more before going home later."

Melanie heard Addie's door close, sparking some worry about the phone, that Melanie's snooping might be discovered. "How's she doing?"

"Pretty cheerful today. Probably excited about finally leaving for home. Did you guys have a talk about something?"

Melanie sent Thérèse to her room to change clothes. Once she was gone, she said to Josh, "I forgot to tell you. I asked her to be our nanny."

"Addie?"

"Think about it. She's perfect. She knows our routine. She and Tay get along great, which is half the battle with any nanny. Doesn't seem to mind eating vegetarian. And acts as though she likes Maui. So, I offered her the job."

"Except for one big thing. She lives in Arizona. I think she said once she's lived there her entire life. You really think she wants to move to a place where her son recently died? Plus, she has a flight to catch pretty soon."

"I don't know. She seemed interested yesterday when I offered it to her."

"Let's not get too excited about that. I have a gal coming by tomorrow for you to interview, and another on Tuesday. Hopefully, you'll find someone satisfactory."

"Where's your mother?" Melanie asked.

"We dropped her at church. She said she'd get a ride home from Trinh."

"Sounds great, except this is Trinh's weekend to work. You know she goes to church only every other week, and not always that often. When she gets off work on Sundays, she takes the kids to a movie and goes grocery shopping. You know that."

"Mom's stranded in Kihei?"

"Worse places to be stranded than Kihei. Your mother is resilient. She'll figure out something."

"She's resilient in a Wyoming ranch kitchen, not in the tropics. She'll melt out there, Melanie. Or fry like a slice of bacon."

"I'm not the one who dropped her off and left her behind, Josh."

Addie came to their door, her travel suitcase at her side. "Okay if I come in?"

Melanie pulled the sheet up. "Sure."

Addie carefully sat on the edge of the bed near the baby. "How's Kenny?"

"Couldn't be better. Thanks again for letting us use your son's name."

"I'm so glad you did. Somehow, it seemed fitting. How's your back?"

"Kinda achey, but I have feeling in my legs and that's what counts."

"Which reminds me," Josh said. "As soon I get home from the airport, you have physical therapy to do, and don't try and weasel your way out of it."

Stroking her fingertips over Kenny's forehead one last time, Addie stood. "Well, if you don't mind, we should be on our way."

"Addie, I'm terribly sorry about what's happened. I wish there was some way of helping you."

"You already have, Melanie. Much more than you'll ever know."

Melanie felt genuinely sad when she heard Addie say goodbye to Thérèse, and wondered if the girl really understood she would never see her again. When Josh's car started up and drove off, she looked at Kenny, still dozing. "Maybe I should just stay home with you. Watch you grow up. Be there when you walk for the first time. Teach you how to use chopsticks. Hear you speak your first words. Would you like that?"

Thérèse came back in and climbed up again. "Time for our nap, Momma?"

"Time for mine. You can play in your room if you want."

"Better in here. When's Daddy going to the hospital?"

"Why do you want him to go?" Melanie asked.

"I been there. You been there, and Kenny got borned there. Time for Daddy now."

"Well, let's hope he doesn't have to go to the hospital, little one." Melanie stroked the hair from her daughter's eyes. "Can't call you little one anymore, can I? You're a big sister now."

"Maybe big one?" the girl asked, yawning.

"Not for a few more years. I'll have to think of something."

Melanie never did get to sleep, and Thérèse was just waking up from her nap when Josh got home. He had brought his mother with him, who had been walking along the road in Kihei. She immediately went for a shower and to put her feet up.

"Before I get started with my physical therapy, can you change the dressing on my back?"

"What do I do?" he asked, after she turned over onto her belly.

"Not much to it. Just pull off the old one and describe what you see."

Thérèse sat close, watching intently. "Momma, you have a big owey on your back."

"I know, Sweetie. I got that in the hospital, remember? Josh, is it red?"

"No, everything is okay. Just normal looking skin. What do I do with it?"

"Put another gauze pad on there and stick it down with tape. By tomorrow, we should be able to use a large Band-Aid."

"Momma, is that how Kenny got borned? He came out of there?"

"No, that's how the doctor fixed my back so I could feel my legs again."

"How Kenny get outta your tummy?"

"Well, that's very complicated. After you go to school for a few years, I'll explain it, okay?"

"Can I go play dinos?"

Melanie was relieved there weren't any more questions about the birds and bees. "Sure can."

Once the girl was gone, Melanie went to the living room to start her physical therapy, Josh helping her.

"Addie had a decent send off?"

"She seemed sad to go, but said she would be happy to get home."

"You reminded her I'd send Kenny's body home once the police release it?"

"Yes. And please don't assign me assistant vice mayor tasks anymore. That's hard to do, tell a woman her son would be shipped home in a box as soon as possible."

"I got a call from Detective Nakatani this morning. He has a lead on who the culprits might be." She explained how they were in the process of finding potential links between previous buyers and current sellers, and how the seller might be a Maui resident, and that the stolen items never leave the island until they are shipped to a buyer. "We both agree that they might be using the trails up into the hills behind the house as an access point to finding and stealing from ancient Hawaiian graves. Just like the hikers we've seen a few times."

"Now we have to watch out for people and make citizen's arrests?"

"No, but it sounds like the police might set up some sort of sting operation. A pattern has emerged, how two days after something is sold, something new shows up at auction. We figure on that day between is when they go up into the hills to get something new, bring it down, give it a cursory cleaning, and put it online."

"Clever scheme. They don't have to have stolen stuff sitting around their home looking like incriminating evidence. But it sounds like they went to the well a few times too many." He helped her turn over to do a new set of exercises. "But Melanie, you need to leave it alone. You have Kenny to take care of, and your back to get strong again."

"I'm not chasing down any perps. I'll be glad when I can walk from one end of the house to the other without having to take a rest halfway."

"You're sure it'll be okay for me to go to work tomorrow?"

"You can't miss the first day of the new school year, buddy. You have to show off new baby pictures to all the other professors, and make a Baby Kenny PowerPoint to wow your students. Anyway, Trinh will be watching over us like a hawk. The schedule is Trinh takes Tay to preschool and you'll pick her up on your way home from work. We have everything covered for this week."

"Poor kid," Josh said. "First day of school and her own parents won't be taking her."

"She'll live. Her aunt has known her all her life, knows her as well as we do. May as well just turn her over to Trinh to raise. Do a better job than I ever could."

"By the way…" Josh started to say.

"No, you may not marry Trinh if I die. I don't care how lonely you get or what excuses you dream up about the kids needing a mother, you may not marry Trinh."

"I was just going to ask what you want for dinner?"

***

On Monday morning, Melanie had the house to herself and Kenny after Josh had gone to work, and Thérèse was at preschool. Even Trinh had stayed away, going into town for the day. After her first shower in days, she put the baby in his bassinet and did her physical therapy exercises. Going to the kitchen to reheat some morning coffee, she opened the window blind that looked out at the little parking area for their cars. Her pickup truck was there near the carport, and her trusty old surfboard on a rack built onto the side of the shed, seemingly mocking her.

She took a sip of her coffee and went back to the window.

"As soon as my back is strong again, you and me have a date," she said to the surfboard.

When she heard the sound of a car engine at the lower end of the long driveway, she figured it was the first of two young women coming to interview for the nanny job. Waiting for her to come to the door, she reviewed the application materials and reference letters. When no one came, she went out to the porch.

Instead of a small sedan, something she'd expect a young woman to drive on Maui, it was a four-wheel drive pickup truck stopped partway down, its engine still idling. Trying to figure out if it looked familiar, she waved.

The engine revved once and stayed at a higher RPM, but no one got out. Surprising her, a man ran past her, wet and muddy from the knees down, an old knapsack on his back.

"Hey! You can't come on this property!"

Unable to make chase, Melanie could only watch as he kept going and tossed the knapsack into the back of the truck. Even before he got the door closed, the truck revved up and sped off down her driveway, kicking up gravel and dust as it left.

Melanie grabbed her phone and dialed Nakatani's personal number to report what just happened.

"Did you get the license plate?"

"HRD, but not the numbers. It got away before I could get a second look. It was full-size, red, and four-wheel drive."

"Ordinary truck for this island, but that's a Honolulu plate. Should be easy to spot. You said the guy tossed a knapsack into the back of the truck? Any idea what might've been inside? Nothing was sticking out? Did it seem heavy?"

"Couldn't really tell. Just an old green knapsack, like book bags kids would use, but old and worn out. The guy was dirty, like he'd been hiking through the fields and up into the mountains."

"Well, that's proves our theory about the timing. That batch of stuff that had been on auction, the one with the arrow tip in the bone, was purchased last night. I was just trying to arrange for a couple of officers to stake out the trails up there. Maybe have one somewhere near the trailhead, and another further up. Looks like I'm too late."

"Find that pickup truck and you have your guys, Detective."

"I need probable cause to search it. If an officer can see the knapsack without searching, that would be good enough. But if they've already taken the stuff out and hidden the sack, we're out of luck."

"But you have a witness that saw someone come from the trail that goes up into the mountains, and an ID on the truck," she said.

"I have a property owner who witnessed a trespass, who has not informed me of anything being stolen from said property, and a partial on the plate, and not even the make or model of vehicle. That's how legal defense would frame it, and the ADA wouldn't be able to bring charges without better evidence."

"Come on. You know me better than that. So does the ADA. I'm the mayor, for crying out loud. Don't I get bonus points for that?"

"Not really. You're also a woman only three days past giving birth and having surgery. The defense lawyer would have a field day with that. You're a hysterical housewife at home alone with the baby, and panicked when you saw a day hiker get picked up by his friend. Your meds are playing tricks on your mind, the anesthesia hasn't fully worn off yet, whatever."

"I'm not taking any pain meds because I'm breastfeeding Kenny, and the anesthesia was completely out of my system yesterday morning. And Detective, I hate to press the point, but I was in Special Forces for several years and currently work as a cardiothoracic surgeon. How does someone turn that into a panicky housewife?"

"The defense could also paint a picture of the mayor trying to find a scapegoat for the crimes, just to make herself look good. In fact, you'd look heroic, solving the crime on your own, just a few days after giving birth and having emergency surgery. How many extra votes would you get in the next election because of that?"

"What? The next election isn't for another three years, and who said I'm signing up for this nonsense again?"

"I know, I know. Just relax. Those are the arguments any decent defense lawyer would use. Canned responses, but they work every time. If we picked those guys up with so little evidence, they'd walk in an hour."

"That's it, then?" she asked, feeling doubly demoralized that more things had been sold, and more had been stolen. They had suspects but there was nothing they could do about it.

"You can count on us stopping that vehicle if we see it. We'll cite them for everything we can. Follow them home, or in circles around the island if we have to. They live somewhere. It might not be today, but we'll get those guys in an interrogation room one way or another. But please, Mayor, stay out of the way."

"Not like I'm going far with a sore back and a new baby."

"Let me ask you one thing. Did the truck look familiar?"

"Not particularly," she said. "Like you said, there are a lot of pickups on this island."

"Did you happen to notice what other vehicles were parked in the lot at Gonzo's when you went there the other day?" he asked.

"If I remember correctly, the lot was empty. I wish I could tell you a red pickup was parked right in front, but I can't."

As the call ended, a young woman walked up the driveway to the porch where Melanie was standing. It was Anita, the first nanny applicant. The interview went quickly, and she was a solid candidate, even if she had never been a nanny before. Her only real experience with children was having a younger brother and that she had helped with his care as a baby.

"But you don't have a car?" Melanie asked. "How did you get here?"

"A friend dropped me off at the resort across the way and I walked over."

"Well, some of the duties we'd expect would be to run errands with the kids. We'd need the nanny to drop off Thérèse at preschool in the morning before doing errands. You'd have to take Kenny with you. When do you plan to get a car?"

"Oh, I don't have my license yet."

Melanie did her best not to sigh with exasperation. "Okay, well, we have other applicants to interview. We'll let you know in a few days."

"Not going to hire me, huh?"

"Afraid not. We need someone with solid driving experience. If they were your children, would you put them in a car with an inexperienced driver?"

"I guess not. Do you know of any other jobs on the island?"

"The resort across the way is always looking for housekeepers."

"Something else I don't know how to do I'm not sure they'd want to hire me any more than you do."

"Tell you what. Go over there right now, fill out an application, and put my name on it as a reference. Just tell the HR manager to call me. I'll be glad to talk to them on your behalf."

"You'd do that for me?"

"You have to start somewhere. I got my start working there a long time ago as a housekeeper. It's a great place to work, the pay is good, and they treat employees pretty well. There are worse jobs to have, such as being nanny at my house."

She walked the girl out to the porch but before she could leave, Melanie noticed some activity further up the slope. Someone was just coming through the gate that divided her property from the public access lands above.

"Anita, go in the house and stay there. I want you to call the police and have them come right away, but please stay with Kenny, okay?"

"The police? What for?"

"Tell them there's a trespasser at the mayor's house. Make sure you use the name Detective Nakatani when asking for the police." Melanie reached for the broom that leaned in the corner. "Better tell them a fight has broken out. That'll get them here faster."

Anita did as she was told, taking Melanie's phone with her to make the call.

Melanie had to hurry to limp down the steps to the ground level. Hiding behind the back of her pickup wasn't easy since she still had a hard time crouching. She was able to watch through the pickup windows as the man came down from the trailhead, walk past the pea patch, and between the house and the carport. He hurried as he passed by, getting to the stretch of driveway that led down to the main road.

Just as he went past Melanie, she swung the broom with as much force as she could, catching him in the back of the thighs, hamstringing him.

Down the man went to his hands and knees, yelping in pain. Just as Melanie thought he would, he had a knapsack on his back.

Wincing from a jolt of pain in her back, she raised the broom over her head and sent it down across his rear end, laying him out flat. The broom handle broke, one end flying away, leaving her with almost nothing to fight with.

The man stayed on the ground, still yelping, reaching for his back.

"What the hell!" he shouted, still trying to right himself and stand.

"Stay on the ground!" she shouted back.

Seeing an opportunity to keep him from running off, she set one foot on his wrist and rested her weight on it.

"Hey! That hurts!"

"Too bad."

Melanie had to keep him from running away. Not even close to being healed up from her recent back surgery, the only way she could restrain him without bending over was to stand on him. To keep him from thrashing around too much, she put her other foot on an ankle, resting the remainder of her weight on that. Now all he could do was pound at the dirt with his other fist.

"You can't do this to me! I'm calling the cops!" he cried.

"They're already on their way." As if on cue, sirens blared in the distance. "That's them now. But while we wait, what were you doing up there?"

"Nothing. Sorry I walked through your place, but it's the only way to get to those trails."

"You need to ask for permission. We have signs up with a phone number to call. What were you doing up there? What did you steal?"

"I didn't steal nothing!"

As he writhed and cursed on the ground, she gave him a second look. He was just like the young men who had washed up on shore: young, athletic, bottle blond. Typical Maui beach bum and wannabe surfer.

"You know what those guys you work for would do to you?" she asked as the sirens got louder.

"What guys? What work?"

"I know what you've been stealing, and the police do, too. Why were you stealing Hawaiian artifacts? You must've known that carried stiff penalties as a felony, and is just plain wrong."

Two police cars made the turn up the driveway, the sirens being cut off but their blue lights still flashing.

"I never stole anything."

"You expect me to believe that?"

He seemed to give his alibi some thought. "I was just out on a hike looking for stuff. Honest!"

Before she could continue her interrogation, officers leapt from their vehicles, guns in their hands.

"This the trespasser?" one asked.

"That's him," she said.

She stepped back while one of them cuffed the kid, the other keeping his gun trained on the man's back.

"Are you the homeowner?" one asked.

She took a couple more steps back, now that the man had his wrists cuffed in front of him. "Yes."

"Hey, wait a minute. Aren't you Mayor Kato?"

"That's me!"

"What'd you do to him?"

"She gave me a beating!" the kid yelled.

By then, Anita had come out and was standing with Melanie.

"Is Kenny okay?" Melanie asked.

"Never woke up."

"Is that true?" the officer asked Melanie. "You gave him a beating?"

"Gave him a couple solid whacks with a broom handle. Broke my broom, too. One piece is over there, and the other piece is under the porch."

Moving the kid's clothes around, they found the red marks across his rump and thighs. One of the cops laughed. "That's just a good old-fashioned butt whoopin'."

"Hey, aren't you going to call for an ambulance?" the kid asked.

Melanie walked over to where one officer had his hand on the guy's shoulder to keep him calm, while the other made notes in his notepad. "Dude, really? Three days ago, I gave birth and then had emergency surgery on my back. You just had your butt handed to you with a stick, and you're whining about wanting to go to the hospital?"

Detective Nakatani was just arriving then, his blue police light flashing. He was quickly filled in on what had transpired by one of the uniforms.

After a few more minutes of talking with the officer, he took Melanie by the arm and led her away.

"Look, the kid is saying he didn't steal anything, and his knapsack is empty. About all we got on him is simple trespass."

"What's he doing here, then?"

"It doesn't really matter. We'll book him for trespass and let him go. He'll come back to see the judge, pay some piddly little fine, and that'll be the end of it."

"He has to be one of them. Why have an empty knapsack if he wasn't going to steal something? He even said he went looking for stuff but couldn't find anything."

"He's denying that now," Nakatani said. "He's saying he knows nothing about relics or maps."

"Should've figured as much," Melanie muttered, glaring at the kid.

"Both you and he have said he was coming down from the mountains, and with nothing in his sack. There's no crime in going for a walk on public access lands with an empty bag, for as silly as it is."

"Come on, it fits the pattern we just talked about this morning and you know it."

"Melanie, you're lucky he isn't pushing to cite you for battery. The second time in a week, I might add."

"It's my property, and there are signs. I was defending my family. Anybody got a problem with that, take it to City Hall." She smirked. "Oh, wait. I'm City Hall."

Nakatani gave her a wink and went to where the kid was having his rights read to him.

Anita got Melanie's attention. "I should go."

"Yeah, sorry about all this."

The girl started to walk away but stopped. "You know, I'm glad you didn't hire me. This isn't what I thought being a nanny was about."

Melanie tried to laugh, but her backache had progressed to pain. She turned her attention on Nakatani again.

"What's your name?" Nakatani asked the kid, jotting notes of his own.

Melanie listened, just to know who would be getting let loose later, and to watch for his name in the police blotter section of the newspaper later.

"Kenneth."

"Kenneth what?"

"Winston. W-I-N-S-T-O-N."

That caught Melanie's attention. "Kenny?"

"Yeah. How do you know me?"

Nakatani kept Melanie back. "Your name is Kenneth Winston? Also known as Kenny? Originally from Phoenix, Arizona?"

"Yeah, so? How do you know that?"

The arresting officer handed over the driver's license that had been collected from the kid's wallet.

"Your mother has been staying here at the house all week. She just went home today," Melanie said.

"My mom? What was she doing here? How do you know my mom?"

"She came here to take your body home," she said.

"My body? I'm not dead. Are you nuts, lady?"

Nakatani got in the kid's face. "Knock it off. That's the county mayor you're talking to."

The kid's expression changed but not to respect. "What's going on? I don't understand."

"Neither do we, son. All I know is I have a body in the morgue that looks a lot like you and was positively identified by a relative. But you also answer to the same description, and have a driver's license with the same name. Can you explain that to me?"

"I don't know. Why was my mom here?"

"We'll figure it out at the station, but for now, it would be best to keep your mouth shut until the public defender sees you."

Something occurred to Melanie. "Doesn't he have to sign that report, Detective Nakatani?"

"Huh?" The detective seemed confused by the request but went along with it. "Sign the form at the bottom."

He held up a pen for the kid to take. Even with his hands cuffed, he reached up and took the pen with his left hand and scrawled along the bottom. Nakatani led him to one of the officer's cars and got him inside. After, he went to where Melanie was on the porch, now holding her crying son.

"Cute little guy."

"Stow it, Nakatani. What's the story with the kid? Is he Kenneth Winston or not?"

"We'll run his prints to find out who's who."

"And his mother just went home today. She's probably in the air by now."

"You have any pictures of her?"

"We got a few while she was here. Why?"

"I'll put her in a photo lineup with a few other pictures of women about her same age. If he can pick her out, he might be telling the truth."

She used her phone to send several pictures of Addie to Nakatani's phone.

"What was the deal with the signature?" he asked.

"He signed with his left hand."

"So?"

"That first body that was discovered had the broken rib and jaw on the right side, something a southpaw would've done to him."

"And only ten percent of the population is left-handed. You might be on to something, Mayor."

"Plus, he looks a lot like that same kid. Young, fit, bottle blond hair."

"How do you know it's from a bottle?"

"His lashes are dark, as is his arm hair. He had that done in a salon, not a home dye job. Anyway, I've had the same color once or twice."

"Maybe a lead. I'll look into it." He started for his car but turned around. "Would've been prettier of you than him."

Once the baby began to fuss even more, she took him inside for a meal, letting the police do their work.

Trinh was just coming in with Thérèse as Melanie was getting Kenny tucked into his bassinet.

"Hi Momma!"

"Hey, look at you! The big schoolgirl! I missed you so much. How'd it go? Make some new friends?"

She heard all about a boy Thérèse had spent the day with, the games they played, and her competitive side rearing its head, how she was able to spell better than him.

"We saw police cars leaving here. What's going on, Mel?" Trinh asked.

"Oh, nothing much. I saw a guy coming down from the hills and confronted him."

"You're not supposed to be going outside. You're supposed to be resting in bed and doing PT, not confronting strangers."

"I guess I forgot. Can you do me a favor? Change my dressing."

"Didn't Josh do that this morning before he went to work?"

"Yeah. I just need you to take a look at the incision."

"What'd you do?" Trinh asked. "You did something to the trespasser, didn't you?"

"I just gave him a whack with the broom."

Trinh chuckled. "What are you, an old lady now, hitting strangers with your broom?"

"Just…"

"Maybe Josh can start yelling at people to stay off the lawn!"

"Ha ha, funny," Melanie said.

"I saw the broom out there all busted up. It looked like you gave him more than a whack." Trinh lifted Melanie's shirt in back and peeled away the dressing. "The stitches are okay but maybe it's opened up slightly. Mel, you can't keep beating up guys for the rest of your life. Not right after you had surgery and gave birth to a baby."

"Momma, you make another baby today while I was at peeschool?" Thérèse asked, watching closely what Trinh was doing.

"Preschool, and no. Still just Kenny. Why don't you go say hello to him?"

"Can't be dumb about these things, Mel. What if he had a weapon?"

"I already got that lecture from Nakatani. Was I supposed to let the guy go?" Melanie asked, while Trinh put on a new bandage.

"You're supposed to follow your doctors' orders and take it easy for a while, not go cage fighting. I don't care if he was trespassing or stealing old stuff he dug up in the hills. You need to think about your family first. Who was this guy, anyway?" Trinh asked.

"Turns out, he might be Addie's son." Melanie explained about the kid having a driver's license with the Winston name on it, and the possible misidentification at the morgue. "Nakatani is making sure he's the right guy now."

"Just let the police do their jobs, Mel. You don't let other people do your surgeries, right?"

Melanie ignored her. "You know, there's something awfully peculiar about the Winstons. I had Cassandra do a background check on them, and the mother is clean, but the son has a record back home in Arizona."

"So?" Trinh asked.

"So, the son has been here on Maui for a while but the mother supposedly just got here a few days ago, right? But when I looked at her phone yesterday, she's been using a local number for several months."

"You looked in her phone? Is that legal?"

"As legal as when you and I did it with Harm's phone that time. Even more so. It was in plain sight, turned on, and in my home. She never told me I couldn't look at her phone."

"I think that would be implied, Mel."

"Look in that top drawer over there, the junk drawer."

Trinh opened the drawer. "What am I looking for?"

"Cassandra's report on the Winstons. I shoved it in there one day."

"Nothing like that in here. Just shoelaces, rubber bands, broken pencils, old cell phones."

"I could've sworn I put it in there."

Trinh checked other drawers. "What did it say?"

"Only that the mother was clean, but the son had been in trouble off and on since a teenager. Dang. I wish I knew where she's been living these last few months."

"Mel, you and I work in a hospital. For some reason, we got tangled up in being mayor and her pathetic sidekick. We know nothing about law enforcement, and right now, I'm glad about that." Trinh got a pair of sodas from the fridge for them. "Leave the investigation alone for the police to deal with, okay?"

"You know what the weird thing was? When Nakatani told me about the most recent things available for bid on those auction sites seemed so familiar, almost like I already knew they were there, but I haven't looked at those sites in several days."

"Did you just hear me say to leave it alone?"

"Just go along with me for a minute more."

Trinh sighed. "Familiar how?"

"He said one was an arrow point stuck in a vertebra, and there were other arrows and a spear tip. I could see them all very clearly, but not from the auction site images, but as though I'd seen them for real."

"When you woke up from your surgery, you were all weird about something, Mel. You were saying stuff about warriors and having something in your back. You were telling me to continue on, to attack someone. It took a little while to get your mind squared away and woken up."

"Really? Like old-time Hawaiian warriors?"

Trinh took a swig of her soda. "Honestly, I don't know what you dream about sometimes, but don't include me in them, okay?"

With that, Melanie's phone rang with a call from the detective.

"Well, Mayor, I started with asking the kid about his life back in Phoenix," Nakatani said. "He knew the address of the house he grew up in, the same place his mother still lives, and described it. When I found images of it at Google Maps, it was close enough to be considered accurate."

"He could've looked at the same images," Melanie said.

"Then I asked him the name of the hospital he was born in. He knew the name and general location in Phoenix. That's when I put his mother's image in a lineup of a dozen white women in their fifties. I did that three times, and each time he picked out Mrs. Adelaide Winston."

"Did you check his fingerprints?" she asked.

"Pending, but he has to be the right kid to know so much about Kenneth Winston."

"Yeah, it sure sounds like it. I'm glad for the mother, but I sure don't like the idea of telling her the good news after all she's been through these last couple of weeks. Especially after she's just gone home in mourning."

"I'll call her. It's a police matter anyway, not one for the mayor's office. But you might get involved later, if she decides to sue us for mental and emotional distress over all this."

"At least she gets her son back."

Half an hour later, Nakatani called Melanie back.

"Well, did she have anything to say? Was she relieved?"

"She seemed reluctant to believe me. In fact, she's coming back to see this kid in person."

"She must be halfway home. She's planning on coming back to Maui already? Just take a picture of him and send it to her."

"I offered that, but she wants to see him in person."

"Can't blame a mother for wanting to see her son after the scare she's just had," Melanie said.

"She never left the island. Her connecting flight to Phoenix wasn't until tomorrow. Apparently, she didn't want to interfere in your lives any longer and found a room in town somewhere. So, I had a uniform pick her up and bring her to the station in Wailuku."

"I'd like to be there to meet her."

"Can you travel? Your back is okay?"

"I'm fine, really. I'll have Trinh bring me in."

"Mrs. Winston should be here pretty soon."

Melanie told Trinh of the plan to go in to the police station in Wailuku and see Addie verify her son's identity, and to offer an apology for the mix-up.

"Now you want to go for a drive, and you're not supposed to sit for that long," Trinh said in a scolding tone.

It took Melanie five minutes to change her clothes, and ten more to wash the baby and change his diaper.

Using Trinh's old child carriers, the four of them rode in her large SUV into town.

"You can come in and look officious as my Vice Mayor. Bring the diaper bag, just in case."

"Yes, exactly what the Vice Mayor does," Trinh said, slamming her car door closed. "Lug around the Mayor's diaper bag."

Addie had just got there and was talking with Detective Nakatani when Melanie went in, carrying Kenny in a carrier in one hand, and holding Thérèse's hand with the other.

"You shouldn't be carrying so much weight," Addie said. "Let me hold the baby."

"Maybe we should go see your son?" Melanie offered. She handed over the baby to Trinh and told Thérèse to wait with her in the waiting area out front.

"Okay, I have him in an interrogation room. But before you go in, I want you to take a look through the window of the observation room next door to where he is, Mrs. Winston," Detective Nakatani said. He led them through the squad room to the interrogation rooms at the far end. He showed them into an observation room with a large window hidden by a set of blinds. Melanie stood next to the woman at the window, waiting for Nakatani to open the blinds. "Okay, this is one-way glass. You can see him but he can't see you."

"Do we have to go through all this?" Addie asked. She was shaking with excitement, or nerves. "He said he's my son. Just let me go to him."

"Just take a look first."

He opened the blinds. The light was bright in the interrogation room, giving them a clear view of the young man inside. He sat there picking dirt from under his nails, unaware he was being viewed.

The woman almost looked to be in a panic. "Oh my goodness."

"That's Kenny, right?" Melanie asked. It was the first time she had a good look at him since his arrest. He had the stereotypical surfer dude look, with unkempt blond hair, and an athletic physique. To her, he could've passed as a brother to the man in the morgue.

"My Kenny," Addie said, just before fainting.

When Mrs. Winston fainted, Nakatani took her from Melanie's hands and lowered her to the floor. He propped her feet up on a chair seat while Melanie waved air at her face. The woman came to right away.

"What happened?" Addie asked.

"You fainted. Can you sit in a chair?"

They got her into a chair and Melanie sat with her.

"I'm sorry for all this commotion. Please let me see my boy."

Nakatani sat with them. "Take another look. You're sure it it's him? Maybe his appearance has changed since you've seen him last."

Addie looked through the window again. "I know my son, Detective. Why are you making me wait?"

"He's being held for interrogation and possible booking."

"I don't care about that. I'd like to see my son, please."

Melanie was impressed by how reserved the woman remained, knowing she would've been pitching a fit if it were her.

"Not quite yet, if you don't mind. I'd like to interrogate this kid for a few minutes and then talk with you again," Nakatani said.

Addie looked like she wanted to protest, and Melanie wanted to also, until a uniformed officer came in with a printout of something for the detective. They had a brief chat about it before the officer left.

Nakatani took Melanie out of the observation room. "We just got the positive identification from the FBI on this kid. According to his prints, he really is Kenneth Winston, age twenty-five, of Phoenix, Arizona. That kid resembles the Arizona driver's license picture, which resembles his current

Hawaii driver's license. Maybe a few years one way or the other and some hair dye, but the resemblance is good."

"If this is the real Kenny Winston, who's the kid in the morgue?" Melanie asked.

Nakatani shuffled the sheets of paper in his hand. "He's Corey Nelson, also of Arizona, not Kenneth Winston. This is his rap sheet. Everything on here fits with the current crimes we're investigating. Theft, burglary, grand theft auto. Dye his hair blond, and he becomes a good match for the Winston kid. They could be brothers."

"That's no excuse for screwing up something like this and then telling the mother her son is dead," Melanie said. "And I don't want to hear any crap about getting county lawyers in here to straighten it out. I want to know what happened."

"It was a foul-up on a lot of people's parts. Evidently, the FBI only partially ID'd the kid in the morgue as Kenneth Winston, but didn't bother telling us that. The fingerprints that were collected weren't great, and when they finally got the final results, they somehow suppressed them, or just didn't bother sending the proper ID to us until just now when we made another request. Sorry."

"Sorry my butt. Why did it take so long to get his fingerprints straightened out?" Melanie asked.

"Who knows? Back log, red tape, bureaucracy, anything."

"What do we tell Mrs. Winston?" Melanie asked, looking at the complex set of sheets that comprised both rap sheets. To her eye, fingerprints were simply blotchy swirls.

"Any suggestions?"

"You do what you want. I'm telling her the truth," Melanie said, before going back into the observation room.

"Why are you making me wait?" Mrs. Winston demanded again.

Melanie explained about the mix-up, and tried implying it was mostly the FBI's fault.

"Mrs. Winston, do you have anything with you that your son might've touched that hasn't been cleaned?" the detective asked.

"I don't know." She opened her pocketbook. "He sent me this picture a while back, him and his friends. I put it in a little sleeve. You want his fingerprints, don't you?"

"If we can collect prints from something we know he touched, we might be able to definitively match them to either the young man in that other room, or the man in the morgue."

The woman handed over the snapshot, along with a plastic key ring her son had sent her.

"Why didn't you do that several days ago?" Melanie asked, after she followed the detective outside the room.

"We thought we had a positive ID when she ID'd him in the morgue."

"You made her look at that body, even after it had been in the water for at least a day. You saw what shape it was in, and you relied on that as a positive ID?"

"Like she just said a few minutes ago, a mother knows her son." He pushed past her to take the snapshot and key ring for fingerprinting. "She said the exact same thing in the morgue when she viewed the body. You tell me, Mayor, which time was she correct?"

"Okay, you have a point. Let's just get this figured out for the poor woman."

Melanie sat with the stunned woman for a few minutes, waiting. Nakatani returned with images of enlarged fingerprints, along with the original photo and key ring. He gave those back to Addie.

"Did it help?"

"Yes. The man in the other room is your son. His prints match what was on your snapshot and that key ring, and match the files the FBI sent us. Oddly enough, an index finger and a thumb are a close match to the body in the morgue, which might be the reason for the mix-up."

"I'd held out hope that there had been some mistake. When you called me earlier, I was so happy. I knew I'd been right all along. May I go see him now?"

An officer took the mother to the interrogation room for the reunion, while Melanie and Nakatani remained behind. They watched as mother and son hugged. To allow them privacy, the detective muted the speaker as they reconnected.

"It sounds like she's happy enough to have her son back that she won't sue us," Nakatani said.

"Couldn't blame her if she did," Melanie muttered.

She followed the detective into the interrogation room.

"Now what, Detective?" Mrs. Winston asked, still seated next to her son.

"We'll be able to release him now. He's already been booked for trespass, and I bet Mayor Kato would be willing to drop those charges, under the circumstances."

"Yes, I suppose so," Melanie said.

"What happens next?" Addie asked.

"He can go home, either to his apartment in Kihei, or with you to Arizona. Personally, I'd prefer he stay here for a while in case we have any further questions."

"Maybe I should leave that up to Kenny?" She beamed when she looked at her son's face, patting his hand. "I know Kenny wants to stay here. Maybe a mother's influence might keep him on the right track. Anyway, I was offered a job the other day. I'm interested, if it's still available to me? At least until Melanie finds a suitable replacement."

"Of course, Mrs. Winston."

Detective Nakatani said he would take Kenny home to his apartment in Kihei, while the mother would go home with Melanie and Trinh, with a planned dinner reunion between them later in the evening after Kenny got his pickup truck from the impound lot.

Melanie suffered the indignity of watching as the man was released. Leaving the station through the front door with an officer leading him out, he walked right past Melanie as she bounced baby Kenny on her hip. To her, there was still the matter of trespass.

"What about your luggage?" Trinh asked once they were in her SUV.

"That's halfway to Phoenix by now," Addie said. "Just forget about it. I'll have a friend go to the airport to pick it up and keep it for me."

"Addie, maybe you can help us with finding your replacement nanny, not that there's any hurry," Melanie said.

"Once your nanny is hired and I move out, I'm moving Kenny and me into a decent place. Maybe on this part of the island. I like it along here."

"I never did get the chance to apologize to your son for hitting him with the broom the way I did. I still don't know what he was doing up in the hills behind my house."

Addie sat quietly for a moment until the answer seemed to come to her. "I asked him about that. He said he went hiking in the mountains with some friends, but left them behind when the weather turned rainy. When they decided to stay back and wait out the bad weather, he let them keep the tent and food. That's why his knapsack was empty."

"I see," said Melanie. Since the mountains were steep and heavily vegetated, not conducive to tent camping, it was a peculiar explanation but she accepted it. There was enough that was peculiar about the Winston family without adding more to it.

Addie looked so happy, now that she knew the truth, and had her son back. "He left Phoenix to come here. Whenever I spoke to him, he sounded so happy. He has his new friends here, and his girlfriends. I'm surprised he wants to spend the evening with his old mother instead of them."

Melanie looked at Trinh and fired her a warning glare to keep quiet.

***

Once they were home, Melanie called Detective Nakatani with more questions in the privacy of her bedroom. Something just wasn't sitting right in her mind about the misidentified man.

"Mayor, if I may make a suggestion, just give it a rest. That part of the puzzle has been worked out. Now we need to adjust our focus in a different direction. It might just be that the dead bodies in the morgue are responsible for the thefts. There haven't been any further postings of items for auction online since the third body has turned up. If that trend continues, we might have to assume those three are our perps, plain and simple."

"But to know for sure, you'd have to solve their murders, right?" she asked.

"Or at least find out how they died. That's our next big piece of the puzzle to solve."

"You said all the stuff that had been up for auction has been bought?"

"By several different buyers." He cleared his throat. "You bought the first two batches. Since then, four buyers have bought the other six batches. We're still trying to link buyers to one specific seller, and see if it has something to do with any of our dead bodies. Or Kenny Winston."

"He's still a suspect?"

"Definitely on my list. He's dirty for something, I just can't quite figure out what," Nakatani said. "Stroke of brilliance on your part for hiring his mother."

"Why?" she asked.

"That kept him here. I couldn't keep him here, even if I cited him for trespass. But he couldn't very well leave if his mother is still on the island. As long as she's here, he is too. It worked perfect."

"Detective, it was less about me being brilliant and more about needing a nanny," she said.

"Mayor, whatever it was, if you happen onto a brilliant idea again, run it past me before enacting it. Please let me run my investigation using good old-fashioned police work."

"Maybe Detective Kalemakani can figure it out."

"Who?"

"Never mind," Melanie said. She willingly agreed to stay out of it and let him go. Her next chore was to write up a work contract for Addie, with an open-end date. Just as they were finalizing the details, Josh got home, bringing his mother who had spent the day in town with him.

"I just talked to Trinh outside. Why was my grandson in jail when he's only three days old?"

"He wasn't in jail." When Addie performed her first task as their nanny and took young Kenny to his bassinet, Melanie explained the situation of the newly discovered Kenny crossing over their property and Melanie subduing him until the police came. "That's why Addie is still here. The police found her before she left."

"You just had surgery and had a baby. Can't you leave law and order to the police for just a few more days?"

"I've already been scolded by Trinh and Detective Nakatani. How was your first day of school?"

"Not as exciting as your day. You've hurt Mom's feelings by insisting on hiring someone else to be our nanny. Now it turns out you've hired her arch rival on Maui."

"Maybe she should've spent the day at home with me and Kenny instead of going shopping at the mall? If she really wanted the job as granny nanny, she'd be sightseeing less and grandmothering more."

"I'll talk to her. What's for dinner, anyway?"

"Kenny will be wanting two bottles of free range milk pretty soon. Since we have a houseful again, maybe get a couple of pizzas. Your mother can even have meat on hers."

"You're letting meat come into the house?" he asked.

"Not on our side, but she's welcome to sit over at Trinh's and eat whatever she wants."

On Tuesday morning, the people left the house one or two at a time, with Josh leaving first for his job at the college in town. The plan was for Addie and Dottie to take Thérèse to preschool before making a trip to town for Addie to buy new clothes. It was Melanie's sneaky way of them getting to know each other better.

"Dottie, you know your way around the island better than Addie does. Be careful driving my truck. It's peppier than what you might think."

"We're just going to the mall," Addie said. She looked as put out as Dottie did.

"You know where to go? It's right in the middle of town. You can't miss it."

"What are you doing while we're gone, Melanie?" Dottie asked.

"Probably watch Kenny sleep. Otherwise, I'll find something."

She watched the two women drive off, pretending to be friends for some reason. With nothing else to do, she sat in a chair next to Kenny's bassinet and stroked his cheeks while watching him sleep. Pulling the sheet up over him, she checked his diaper and closed the blinds.

"Okay, little buddy. Time for your mommy to take a long and undisturbed nap. After that, you're making your public debut."

Two hours later, Melanie wore the reversed baby carrier on the front of her, Kenny wearing two layers of sunscreen and a tiny camouflage boonie hat, while she walked through the grounds of the resort. She'd stop at each tree or plant, tell him the name, take a selfie of the two of them, before strolling again. Every now and then, a vacationer would stop and ask about the baby. It finally came time to go to the bench.

She popped open an umbrella for shade and offered him a meal. While he suckled, she drank water. His eyes were barely open when he finished and he was arranged safely on the bench, but he seemed to gaze out at the ocean in front of them.

"That's where you'll learn to swim someday," she told him. "I learned there and your sister is learning there."

He fussed a little. Checking his diaper, he didn't need changing.

"You're worried about those little waves? That's the best part. Once you learn to enjoy waves splashing over you, you won't ever stay out of the water. Maybe someday you'll be a champion surfer here on Maui."

"Hey, Mel. Already making the kid an uber-achiever?"

Melanie looked over her shoulder. "Hi, Trinh. How was your run?"

"Not as easy as they used to be." After sitting, Trinh used towelettes to wipe her face and hands, before picking up Kenny. Just in a tank top and shorts, she was in a full-blown sweat from jogging. She played with the baby for a moment until he smiled. She held him close. "Wedding is on again."

"I thought I heard some celebratory activities on your side of the house last night."

"Not the first time for you to hear Harmon and me."

"The first time for Dottie and Addie. Is there a date yet?"

"Next month, unless I call it off. Hey, what was the deal with that Kenny? I never did hear how that all shook out."

"Talk about high-maintenance." Melanie explained how if she agreed to drop trespass charges against him, he wouldn't seek a lawyer to bring a suit against the county for how his mother had been treated.

"That's not so bad," Trinh said.

"A part of his mother's nanny contract is that I need to find him a job with the county."

"Easy. Put him in charge of cleaning storm drains after every rainstorm. I'll even pay his wages." Trinh chuckled when she set Kenny aside. "Now that you know he's alive, are you going to keep calling your Kenny that?"

"Josh and I were talking about that last night. We might secretly change his name, but keep calling him that as long as Addie is our nanny. Once she's been replaced, we'll call him something else."

"Just come up with a cute pet name for him. What would you call him?"

"Oh, after our grandparents, I guess."

"Jack Francis or Francis Jack?" Trinh asked.

"To keep peace in the family, Francis Jack. I'll probably stick Arthur in there, too."

"After my dad?"

"Why not? Mom's last husband. She was happiest with him. Honorary grandfather."

"Mel, you are the sappiest of them all." Trinh's sports watch alarmed. "Rest break is over. See ya."

"That is very sentimental, Honey," someone said after a moment.

"Mom! How long have you been here?"

"I've been sitting here waiting for you all day."

"Why didn't you say something earlier?"

"Because Trinh was coming. Is it okay if I hold him?"

"Of course. Please."

Melanie watched as a pair of slender arms picked up the baby, holding him close. She saw her mother for the first time in quite a while. "You look so young, Mom."

"Believe it or not, I was young once. And before you ask, no, I don't have any control over it. I guess I'm just feeling very young today, holding this little guy."

Melanie looked out at the ocean, the same way she always had as a kid growing up when they came to the bench for a long talk. "This is so weird, how you come and go, showing up and then disappearing again."

"I wish we could meet more often."

"I wish you could be my nanny. Is that at all possible?" Melanie asked.

"Sorry."

"Me too. Is Dad around?"

"Not for a while. He's quite happy about this little guy, though, and proud to be one of his namesakes."

"How could he not be? But we might switch out Kenny for Arthur."

"He'd be happy, too."

"Did Dad and Arthur ever meet?" Melanie asked after a few minutes of them sitting quietly.

"Oh, yes. Arthur was funny about it, too. He actually went to visit your father to make sure it was okay with him that he marry me. Completely behind my back."

"That's so romantic or gallant, whatever the right word. Apparently, Dad approved."

"Oh, yes. He even wanted to hold an LA reception for us at the hacienda. They still get along quite well."

"You mean now? They're both dead."

"Doesn't mean they can't be friends, Honey. They often play golf or go to church together. They saw you there a while back."

"Dad and Mister Park go to church in Kihei together? Wait, are they…"

"The two men Thérèse was asking about, the ones holding hands in church?" Melanie's mother chuckled while she set the baby back in his little nest of blankets on the bench. As soon as she let go, she began to become transparent. "I'll let you figure that out on your own."

"Wait! Mom!" Melanie looked around for anyone close enough to hear her. "Oh, come on! You can't leave me dangling like that!"

She got the baby bundled up again and headed off for a shadier place with air-conditioning. After a stop in the restaurant she owned to have a salad and iced tea, and to show off the baby to the waitresses, she went next door to the hair salon.

"Well, look who finally showed up!" Lailanie said, quickly taking the baby from Melanie. "I've been waiting and waiting for this cute little guy to come see his Aunt Lailanie."

The other stylists crowded around to ooh and ahh, at least until Lailanie sent them back to their customers. Melanie filled in the blanks of the story of why she needed the emergency surgery on her back right after giving birth, but everything was back on track now.

"I have time if you'd like me to do something, Melanie."

"Not really why I came in, but since my son has abandoned me by dozing off, you may as well."

Once the baby was in a crib with a clean diaper, Melanie was given a style magazine to look at while her hair was washed.

"Time for a makeover, lady."

"Maybe. I was thinking it might be time to go back to that funky blonde pageboy you gave me a long time ago?"

"I like the short and funky idea. Something to bring out your natural wave a little more. This year that's called deconstructed."

"Which is exactly how I feel these days," Melanie muttered, flipping through pages in the magazine. "Deconstructed."

"There's also a trend starting of going not completely blonde but just on the tips." Melanie was taken to a styling station and given some salon photographs to look at. "Okay, don't freak because those are guys in the pictures, but I really like the style and color of that for you."

Melanie shuffled through photographs of several men. She did like the style, being loose and shaggy, long in front and short in back, much too effeminate for men. But what caught her eye were the faces of the men. When she got to the last picture, she held it up. "Are these guys salon customers?"

"Yeah, that style seems to be popular in the island gay community right now. Does that make a difference?"

"Well, no, not as far as a style goes. But these guys have been your customers?"

"For the last few months. That guy in your hand started coming here about a year ago. If I remember right, he'd just moved from the mainland and was just coming out then."

Melanie shuffled through the pictures. "And these other guys?"

"They were all referred here by that first guy. I guess they were gay. I don't know why they all had to have the same hairstyle, though."

Melanie didn't pay any attention while the stylist combed her wet hair, only sorting through the pictures again. She picked out the two that were most familiar, but not Kenny Winston. "You remember these two guys' names?"

"Probably in the appointment book. Why?"

"Is it breaking any kind of privacy laws if you tell me their names?"

"Like patients at the hospital? No, but we don't really share that stuff so easily."

Melanie made eye contact with her trusted friend and long-time stylist. "Please?"

With a sigh, Lailanie got the appointment book and brought it over to where Melanie waited. She started flipping through pages. "It was about three weeks ago since the one was here. We don't get so many men as women, especially ones that make appointments. Yes, here it is. That first one is Danny Benet, pronounced the French way, he said." She flipped a few pages looking for another name. "And that other one is William—not Bill—Lockhart. They both spoke like they were from the mainland but were trying to fake local accents as though they were trying to fit in. They've been here twice each."

Melanie wasn't convinced. She got the picture of the third man with dyed blond hair that Lailanie had manufactured, the one that looked least effeminate of all of them. She tried to imagine if that face belonged to the head that had been found by a scuba diver. "And this guy?"

"Been here only the one time. Angelo Davis. I don't know why he changed his hair. He was hot to begin with, and I had a hard time believing he was gay, but he said he was sent to get the exact same thing as the others. If I was twenty years younger, I would've tried…never mind."

Even if they were the three men that had been found floating in the ocean recently, those names might not be their real names. "What's this guy's name?" she asked, holding up the last picture.

"I don't have to look for him. Kenny Winston. Regular, once a month. Real cheapskate, too. Full service client but never left a tip. Not even so much as a thank you before he bolted for the door."

Melanie got out her phone to make a call. When she felt Lailanie begin to comb again, she told her to hold off for a moment.

"Detective Nakatani, I think I have a lead for you." She explained about seeing the pictures of the three men, their circumstances, and provided their names. "Not trying to interfere. This just sort of happened."

"You're where?" he asked. "I'd like to get those pictures and compare them to the bodies in the morgue."

"Tropic Flowers in the retail area of Napili Winds Resort. It's not far from…"

"I know the place. I'll be there in a few minutes."

After Melanie ended her call, the stylist sprayed water. "Time to get started."

"Yeah, you know what? I might not have time today. I got the idea I would need to go with that detective to look at something."

"What do you want me to do?"

Melanie dug through her bag to find a magazine picture folded up. "This is a picture of my mom a bazillion years ago when she was working in Japan. Josh thinks she looks totally hot with her hair pulled back and in a little bun like that."

The stylist found the same part in Melanie's hair as in the picture. "You do realize it's a little weird that your husband thinks your mother looks hot."

"As long as he doesn't think Trinh looks hot, I'm good with it."

Just as Lailanie was putting the finishing touches on Melanie's tidy, sleek bun, Detective Nakatani showed up.

Lailanie beat Melanie to him. "Detective Nak, good to see you. You're not due until next week."

"You know him?" Melanie asked her friend.

"He's a regular. Once a month."

Melanie beamed at the detective and watched his face closely to see if his cheeks turned red. "Why, Detective, I never would've expected you to come to a girly place like this."

He seemed put out. "Those pictures?"

"Oh, yes." While Lailanie provided the names for each picture, Melanie got the baby ready to leave. Once he had what they thought were the correct spellings, he called them in to the station for background checks and rap sheets.

"You're sure cozy with him," Melanie whispered to Lailanie. "Anything I should know about?"

"I'm not guilty of anything, if that's what you're asking."

"Not of the body, but what of the mind?"

"Maybe once a month, I let my imagination go off on its own for a while. So what if I spend a solid hour on a haircut that would take ten minutes? He doesn't complain. He gets it for free."

"Get's what for free?" Melanie asked in her quietest whisper.

"In my imagination, anything he wants. But don't tell Duane that."

Melanie chuckled. "Or Josh. But I knew it would never work out between us when he saw me puke at the beach."

Sure enough, the detective wanted Melanie to go to the hospital morgue to compare dead faces with the pictures.

"The baby is five days old. I'm not taking him to the morgue," she said as they drove along. "Get Bobby Brown from the ER or Benson the pathologist to help you with that. They're already familiar with the bodies and your investigation. Can't you get digital photos and run them through a facial recognition program?"

"Not with their heads all bashed up. Maybe with the decapitated head. That one was still pretty intact."

"Okay, have fun with that. Just drop us at home, if you don't mind."

***

"You did your hair different," Josh said that evening after Thérèse was in bed and the baby was down. Addie and Dottie had retired to their respective rooms. Melanie and Josh were on the couch watching an old Hitchcock movie with the sound turned down.

"Lai did it for me. I know it's against everybody's orders to go out, but I needed to go for a walk with the baby. It's a mother's right to show off her baby."

"It's okay. You know what's best for your back."

"Lai almost did something different but we didn't have time. Are you ready for a surprise yet?"

He touched the bun, still intact, and the hair that was combed tightly back from her face. His hand slipped to her neck, and then around her shoulders, pulling her close. "It's not a surprise if I know about it."

"Well, in that case…"

Melanie's phone rang. She almost didn't answer when she saw the calling number.

She took the phone in the other room. "Detective Nakatani, I'm busy with something. Can this wait until tomorrow?"

"It won't take long. I ran those other names I got from Mrs. Esposito and all three have mainland rap sheets. None of them had been here long, and each was from Arizona. We're currently trying to find any associations between each of them, and between them and the Winston kid."

"So, for once I was able to be helpful without interfering?"

"You were, and thank you. Once I have anything else on them, I'll let you know."

"Detective, just exactly how well do you know Mrs. Esposito?"

284

"Once a month, I spend an hour with her. Why?"

"An hour doing what?"

"Nothing worth gossiping about. I'll give you a call in the morning."

Melanie watched Josh in the other room use the remote to change channels to a sports channel. She knew the moment they were about to share was now gone.

"Detective, I'll make a deal with you. If you don't call me with updates every few hours, I won't interfere with the investigation. In fact, the next time either of us hears the other's voice will be when there's an arrest, okay?"

The next morning played out the same as the day before, with Addie and Dottie taking Thérèse to preschool, leaving Melanie alone at home with the baby. Since they were going to town to look at cars for Addie to buy and use as the nanny-mobile, Melanie called the dealership to give them the okay on the expense. Once she was done with giving the baby the first of what was turning out to be several lunches a day, she put him in his bassinet.

"Okay, little buddy. I need to abandon you for a few minutes to pick some vegetables from the patch. I won't be long, I promise."

Turning on the baby monitor, she left him to his dreams and went out to the backyard pea patch, taking the monitor receiver with her. Trying to crouch the best she could without straining her back, she pulled a few carrots and onions, tossing those into her basket. Checking the tomato plants, nothing was ripe. She found one pepper, all she needed for the soup she was planning for dinner. The morning was turning out to be quiet, almost too quiet for her tastes, but in a way, she was enjoying the nothingness of the day.

Until her phone rang. It was a police department number but didn't have a name attached to it.

"This is Mayor Kato."

"Mayor, this is Keanu Kalemakani. How have you been?"

"Fine, thanks for asking. How is your part of the investigation going?"

"Quite well. But there is something you should know. Sometimes these investigations strike a little close to home, as do the perpetrators of the crimes."

"Yes, we've learned that the hard way with all these trespassers on the property. Any suggestions of what we can do to curb that a little?"

"Only to keep a close safeguard on what is most valuable to you. Often, dishonest people are much closer than you think."

The line went dead, maybe the call being dropped. Waiting for a moment for him to call back, she put the phone back in her pocket.

"Closer than what I might think? What's that supposed to mean?"

Looking at her basket of vegetables, she figured she needed more. The baby monitor had been silent, so she checked it before going back to her gardening.

"Crap. I've had the stupid thing turned off."

She switched it on and turned up the volume. Right away, there was noise.

"What's that?"

She turned it up a little more. When she distinctly heard footsteps in the house, she tossed down the monitor and took off for the back porch as fast as her back would allow.

No mother would go anywhere but to her baby in such a situation, and that's exactly where she turned to. Kenny was crying, really putting up a stink about something, easily heard from the far side of the house. Just coming out of the master bedroom where Kenny had been sleeping was a man. In his hand was a framed picture of something.

It didn't matter to her what it was he was stealing. All she knew was that the man she'd subdued and called the police to come and get only two days before had come back. Kenny Winston was just coming from the room where her baby was crying.

"Why are you here?" she screamed. "What are you doing in my house?"

"Not doing nothing to your precious little miracle."

"I knew you were dirty for something. I just can't figure out what. But this time, that trespass arrest is going to stick! And anything else I can think of to have you charged with."

He laughed. "You really are stupid, you know that?"

Hearing the baby kick up an agitated wail, she reached into her pocket for the phone. With two taps on certain buttons, she sent the emergency signal to Cassandra's phone that she needed the help of Secret Service. She didn't wait. Instead, she stomped down the hall straight for him. "You messed with the wrong mother."

He stood still, laughing. "What're you gonna do? Beat me up? You don't got your broom this time."

"You'll be lucky if that's all I do to you."

He looked surprised, but when he balled his left hand into a fist and raised it, she struck first with a stout kick to his crotch. The framed picture flew from his hand and hit the floor, the glass shattering. Dropping to his knees, he clutched at himself in a protective pose and moaned.

"Why are you in my house? What did you do to my baby?" she screamed.

"What'd you do to my baby?" he said in a mocking falsetto, standing up again.

The baby continued to wail from his bassinet.

When he threw a left hook, Melanie dodged it. Her hands balled into fists, she jabbed once before sending home a right cross. That knocked him back but not enough for her tastes. He was still on his feet. Throwing another right cross, he fell back against the wall. Still not going down, she planted one last punch to his face, dropping him to the floor.

"Melanie!" someone shouted from behind her.

She glanced to find Dottie, but Melanie barely paid attention. She went after Kenny on the floor, trying to get his arms and hands working again. Blood ran from both his nostrils.

Dottie called her name again.

"You picked on the wrong woman, you pathetic…"

Just as she was raising her fist to continue the beating, Melanie's arm was wrenched back.

"Stop, Melanie. He's had enough."

Melanie tried getting free from her mother-in-law. "He was in there with Kenny."

"You've done enough. He's learned his lesson." After pushing Melanie down the hall to get her away, Dottie went back to where the man was struggling up from the floor. She already had her phone out, dialing the police number. "I don't know who you are, but you better stay down, or I'll slap you into next week," she said to the man.

Kenny sank back to his knees, and then to a sitting position, as Dottie stood over him while speaking to the police dispatcher. By then, Cassandra was there, slapping handcuffs on him.

Watching as Dottie gave the man a verbal browbeating, Melanie held the crying baby in her arms. Trinh had come over after hearing all the noise. Twenty minutes later, with Cassandra standing guard over the man the entire time, Dottie continuing to go off on him, and Melanie pacing back and forth with the baby held close to her chest, Detective Nakatani and two police officers exchanged Cassandra's handcuffs for theirs and led Kenny out.

"Remind me to never piss you off, Melanie," Nakatani said, as the group sat in the living room a few minutes later. Dottie and Cassandra were giving witness statements to police officers. Trinh was attending to the broken skin on Melanie's knuckles while Melanie cuddled her baby. "Is he okay?"

"He's fine. Just needs to be put down. It can wait, if you don't mind a little crying."

"And your hands?"

Trinh had Band-Aids on her knuckles by then. "They're fine."

"I was actually headed here to talk with you when I got the emergency call, Mayor. I was also hoping Mrs. Winston might be here, also." He read back the statement she'd already given him about what had happened in the house. "You're absolutely certain you gave no indication that you might be welcoming him into your home?"

"None. The first I saw him, he was coming out of the master bedroom, the baby crying." Melanie kept cuddling her baby, as much to comfort herself as to comfort him. "Sure, his mother lives here with us now, but that doesn't give him permission to come in uninvited, or go near the baby. If he had knocked on the back door, I easily would've heard him. But he didn't."

"But what was it that made you mad enough to beat the crap out of him?" Trinh asked.

"Made fun of the baby."

"What? How could he do that? His mother is your nanny," Trinh griped.

"Not anymore. She doesn't know it yet, but her butt's been fired."

"What's all the broken glass on the floor?" Nakatani asked.

"He was stealing a picture and I knocked it out of his hand," Melanie said.

"Picture of what?"

"Does it matter?"

"I guess not. I wish Mrs. Winston was here. She might be able to clear up what's going on."

"She's at the airport," Dottie said, joining the others.

"What?" Nakatani asked.

"She said she needed to be dropped at the airport to look for her luggage, and that I didn't need to wait for her, that she'd give Josh a call to bring her home later."

Nakatani made a quick call, sending officers to the airport for the woman.

"That doesn't make sense, since she sent her luggage home to Phoenix yesterday," Melanie said.

"Yesterday? Why was she still here today?" Nakatani asked.

"She was set to leave yesterday, but we talked her into staying for a few more days, at least until we had a nanny hired." Melanie gave her mother-in-law a glance, but saw no reaction on her face. "He bags would've been sent on to Phoenix on the flight she was supposed to have taken. She told us it didn't matter, and made the plan to go shopping for new clothes at the mall today with Dottie."

"That's right, Officer," Dottie said.

"Detective," Nakatani said. "What was in the picture frame that broke?"

Sweeping broken glass aside, Melanie got the picture. "A portrait of my parents on their wedding day. I don't know why he wanted that. Not worth anything. Just sentimental value to me."

"Which wedding?" Trinh asked quietly, looking over Melanie's shoulders. "Oh, that one. That's a nice picture."

"Probably just trying to piss you off," Nakatani said.

"It worked. What happens to him now?"

"He's in a world of trouble, be sure of that. We've found partial prints in both the museum and in the library that match his. We've also recovered a few pieces of Hawaiiana from the auctions, which also had partials on them that match his prints."

"That's something, anyway."

"You don't know the half of it. We found four boats with propellers that match the kind and size that killed the second man, Angelo Davis, one of your dead bottle blond friends. Three of those boats checked out as not being out of their slips in more than two weeks. But the fourth was found moored in the Lahaina small boat harbor with a tarp over it, as though someone was trying to hide it. When crime scene techs collected prints and evidence, they found prints belonging to guess who? Kenny Winston. They also found fragments of red feathers that we think were tracked in on the soles of someone's shoes. We don't know quite yet, but we've sent them to the Bishop Museum in Honolulu to see if they can match those feather fragments to the feathers on the old kahili in their museum."

"It wasn't their kahili that was stolen," Melanie said. "It was the one from the Maui Museum."

"You explained it to me yourself a few days ago. There were very specific types of birds they got those red feathers from and never dyed them. To us, that would be very incriminating. We should hear back from them in a few days, but if they match, this guy and his accomplice are going to prison for a very long time."

"Does the boat tie them to the deaths of those other young men?" Melanie asked.

"It could. The crime scene techs removed the propeller and have done a cursory exam in the lab. They found some damage on one blade. If you remember, Doctor Benson said according to what he found on the wounds on the neck, there might be damage to the edge of a propeller blade."

"That's not enough to bring charges against this Winston guy?" Trinh asked. "You have his fingerprints on a boat with a damaged propeller, and a dead body with wounds made by a damaged propeller. It seems pretty incriminating to me."

"I need to lean on him to get the names of his accomplice, and see what kind of alibis they have, but yes, between the prints and feathers on the boat, it should be enough for the ADA to bring charges."

"How do you know he has an accomplice?"

"Because we found another set of fingerprints and we have a positive ID for them. We just need to find the person that has been helping Winston."

"You keep talking about an accomplice as though you know who it is," Melanie said.

"We do. I'm quite glad you've fired Mrs. Winston, because it saves us the trouble of doing it for you."

"Addie is his accomplice? What are you talking about?"

"It was her fingerprints on the boat, and her partials on the recovered artifacts. Phoenix police were able to confiscate her luggage at the airport upon their arrival. Inside were several more pieces of Hawaiiana that look authentic, according to Phoenix PD forensics. That's why I was headed here a little while ago, to take her in for questioning."

"Wait. You've known all along she and Kenny were the perpetrators?"

"Not until two days ago, when we finally started getting matches on all these fingerprints. Those pictures you received yesterday helped confirm the victims' names, and ruled them out as suspects, or at least complicit in being the ringleaders of the little gang that has been stealing historical artifacts in four states. It might turn out that they did some of the legwork of stealing things, but they weren't the ones running the operation."

"Now I really am confused," Melanie said, holding the dozing baby in her arms.

"It all came together this morning when I talked to the Phoenix PD about Mrs. Winston's luggage. They confirmed that the Winstons have been stealing historical artifacts in Arizona, Nevada, and California for years, then turning it over for a profit by using the internet as a fence, but they've never been able to catch them with the stuff, or confirm their identities from the internet auction sites. When the pressure got to be too much there and the police got too close, the Winstons moved their show here and focused on Hawaiian treasures rather than Indian."

"Same scheme, different legacy," Cassandra said.

"But she just asked me to drop her at the airport so she could get her luggage," Dottie said.

"It appears she's been lying to us every step of the way," Melanie said. "Sorry you had to get mixed up in all this, Dottie."

"So, you just need Mrs. Winston," Trinh said.

"It won't be long," Nakatani said.

"How did everybody get here so fast?" Melanie asked.

"Good thing we did," Dottie said. "You were mad and then some."

Cassandra took over. "Detective Nakatani and I spoke last night. We decided it would be a good idea if I watched your house a little more closely than usual for a while, from right across the road, just to keep tabs on Mrs. Winston's movements, and on your house. When she and Dottie went out, I remained close. We were expecting the Winston kid to show up again, but to look for artifacts in the hills, not come into the house. I had positioned myself to watch the trail, not the house."

"That's how you got here so fast."

"But I never saw him go in," Cassandra said. "I need to figure out how he did that without me seeing him."

"Well, I was just getting to like that Addie. She was fun to talk to," Dottie said.

Melanie rubbed a knuckle into the tic that started in her eye. "Loads of fun, for a murderer and thief."

***

The next day, Trinh took Melanie to the police station to give one last witness statement, albeit a long one. Dottie came with them, watching over the baby while Thérèse stuck to Melanie every step of the way.

"Nother place you work, Momma?" the girl asked while the group waited in the public area for someone to come get Melanie.

"This is where Detective Nakatani works, when he isn't at our house arresting people."

"Why everybody being nice to us?"

Melanie didn't know how to answer, that being the mayor, she was their boss.

"Police officers are very nice to honest citizens," Dottie said.

Maybe the girl understood, maybe not, but she still had more questions. "Momma, is Addie coming home soon?"

"No, Sweetie. She has to go away."

"Where she have to go?"

Melanie sat her daughter on her lap. "It's very complicated. Addie was a very bad lady and broke some important rules, and now she has to be punished."

"Rules like ghost and magic rules?" the girl whispered into Melanie's ear.

"Even bigger rules than those. Super-duper big, the biggest of all rules."

"She broke your rules?"

"She broke everybody's rules. And you know the worst thing? She broke our biggest rule at home. You remember that one?"

"Never tell the lie?" the girl asked.

"Right. She told us many, many lies, just so we'd like her."

"She cheated at the game," the girl said, quite matter-of-factly.

"Exactly. That's sad, huh?"

The girl touched Melanie's eyelids. "Momma's sad? Gonna cry?"

"Maybe later."

When Nakatani came to get Melanie, Thérèse begged to go with her.

"It's okay with me if it's okay with her," he said.

Melanie took the girl's hand as they followed the detective to a desk in the squad room. An hour later, Thérèse had drawn several pictures and Melanie completed her formal statement.

"What did you draw?" Detective Nakatani asked, looking at the drawings.

"Addie. We don't like her anymore."

Melanie would've laughed had the images not been so sad. On each sheet was a rough drawing of a face, with Xs scratched across each.

"I have her in an interrogation room, if you have anything to ask her."

"I wouldn't know what to ask. I'd just end up giving her a piece of my mind."

"If you promise not to go off like you did with her son, I'll let you have two minutes."

"The blinds closed, no cameras and all recording devices turned off?" she asked.

"You alone in a room with a Winston? I don't think so. I'd have to be there with you."

"Sweetie, you want to say goodbye to Addie?"

The girl gave it some thought before nodding her head.

He led them past desks where officers were writing reports and working on computers, hearing several of them greet her politely as Madame Mayor. Melanie picked up Thérèse when Nakatani unlocked the interrogation room door.

Addie was inside, her hands cuffed together. When Melanie went in carrying Thérèse, she hid her hands in her lap and smiled at the girl. "Hi Thérèse! Did you come to see your Aunt Addie?"

Melanie glared. "Shut your f…"

Nakatani tapped her shoulder to calm her. Before Melanie could gather her wits, the girl spoke up.

"Why you lie to Momma? You not a nice lady. Nice ladies no lie to my momma and daddy. You make my momma sad. You a mean lady. I no like you anymore."

Nakatani tapped Melanie's shoulder, letting her know their visit was done. When she looked at Addie one last time, their eyes met.

Addie sneered. "Get your little witch away from me."

Once they were outside the room, Melanie gave Thérèse's cheek a kiss. "Never mind her."

"Sorry, Momma. Maybe I say something wrong."

"No, you said the perfect thing, Sweetie. You were very brave to say those things."

Three days later, Melanie sat at the back of the courtroom during the preliminary pretrial hearing for Mrs. Adelaide Winston and her son, Kenneth Winston, listening to the evidence that was being brought against them. After the hearing, and having a strong assurance both were going to prison for a very long time, they were led out, still in their shackles and simple jail outfits.

There was a pause before the bailiff called for the next case to start, another that was just as close to Melanie's heart. Five suspects were led in and seated at the same desk as the public defender. After paperwork was handed back and forth between the public defender, the prosecutor, and the judge, the charges were read. Multiple counts of the manufacture, trafficking, and sale of drugs were heard, and with a swift slap of the gavel, the judge made his decision to hold all suspects without bail pending their trial. Melanie wasn't familiar with this particular judge, but he seemed particularly stern with the owner and employees of Gonzo's Surf Shop.

"My turn," Lailanie said, nervously shifting on the bench.

Melanie gave her hand a squeeze. "You'll be fine. Just tell the truth, smile politely, and be agreeable."

"Mrs. Esposito, you've been in my courtroom before, yes?" the judge asked, staring down at her from his dais.

"Yes, your Honor."

"This is the third time for the same offense, speeding. Seventeen miles per hour over the limit, fourteen miles over, and most recently eleven miles per hour over the speed limit, and each time along the same stretch of highway in West Maui."

"Yes, your Honor."

"Do you have anything to say about that?"

"I'm getting better, your Honor. I'm not speeding as fast lately."

"That's something to celebrate." He looked directly at her over his half-glasses. "Is there somewhere in particular you are going that you can't be late? I think it's work, right?"

"Yes, your Honor."

"Is there a reason why you can't leave home half an hour earlier? Eat breakfast earlier, get up earlier? Get your day started half an hour earlier?"

"No, your Honor."

"This is a very difficult decision for me, Mrs. Esposito. On the one hand, you are the owner of a popular small business on the island, a member of the chamber of commerce, and island better business bureau. On the other hand, you seem to have a disregard for our basic traffic laws and safety. Now that your third time has come, I really must do something about it."

"Yes, your Honor."

"Please approach the bench, Mrs. Esposito."

Lailanie stepped close to the judge and quickly began nodding her head while listening. Melanie tried hearing what was being said but gave up. The judge opened what looked like a large schedule planner and jotted a few things. After nodding one last time, Lailanie stepped back again.

"You agree to the terms of community service as already discussed, Mrs. Esposito?"

"Yes, your Honor."

When the paperwork had been signed by all concerned and the procedure ended, Lailanie left the courtroom, Melanie following after.

"It sounds like you got off with just community service," Melanie said. "You're lucky. He usually isn't so gracious."

"I'm not so sure how lucky I am," Lailanie said, entering a time and date into her personal planner in her phone.

"Why? What was the community service?" Melanie was imagining the worst, collecting litter along the road for three weeks, doing laundry for homeless people for a month, cleaning public beach restrooms on weekends.

"He has a teenage son."

"Yes, so?"

Lailanie looked as though the idea made her sick. "It seems that he's kinda shaggy and unkempt after living at the beach for a while, and I have to help clean him up by cutting his hair. In my salon. Three times."

Melanie wanted to laugh at her friend's plight of having an unpleasant man come to her girlish salon and spa. "That's not so bad. But how did the judge know you have a salon?"

"Oh, Judge Cartwright is one of my regular monthly clients. Has been for years."

Melanie couldn't keep from chuckling over the idea that the toughest judge on the island went to the same girlish spa she did. After reminding her friend to drive home slowly, Melanie met Detective Nakatani in the small courthouse cafeteria.

"See this morning's newspaper?" he asked, handing it to her.

She looked at the headline.

Maui Mayor Tough On Crime!

"Better than last time they dragged me into the news," she said, setting the paper aside.

"The Winstons' lawyer let it leak to the news how you beat up the son. Twice. But I doubt anybody wants to press charges."

Early that morning, Melanie had received a lecture from Judge Cartwright in his chamber about leaving law and order to the police and legal system, and just wanted to move on.

"Well, it sounds like the Maui Police Department got some interagency help from the feds this time, thanks to Cassandra and the Secret Service," Melanie said. "But it was you and Detective Kalemakani who cracked the case. Is it okay if I say that? Cracked the case?"

"Okay by me. But who's this Kalemakani you keep talking about?"

"That's who called me the very first time about the stolen artifacts. He said he would be helping solve the case. And then, he called me again on the day of the arrest. He said the strangest thing. Something about the culprits being very close to home. That was right when I heard noise on the baby monitor and went back into the house. Somehow, he knew the Winston kid was there."

"We don't have anybody named Kalemakani at the station, not even close to that name. The other detective assigned to the case was named Grant, but I did most of the legwork."

"Grant? How could that be?" Melanie muttered. "Whatever. Do you think the murder convictions will stick? I got lost in all the legalese mumble jumble in court."

"We have evidence that one or both of the Winstons were driving that boat when it struck and killed at least two of the men. The damage on that propeller matches the injuries of the decapitated man, and marks on the skin of the others matches the metal ridge on the hull of the boat. Along with their fingerprints all over everything, that's good enough for the judge to hold them over for trial, and should be good enough for any jury to convict."

"Okay, dumb question of the week. What were the roles of the other three men, and why were they killed?"

"That was the most fun part of the investigation. When we pressed the mother, she rolled over on her son, saying it was his idea. Then we pressed the son, and he rolled over on his own mother. Can you imagine that? They ratted each other out to save their own butts."

"I still don't get it. Saying what was whose idea?" Melanie asked.

"This whole gay lifestyle that Kenny was portraying was a hoax, just a part of a simple disguise. Even the name Kenny was a ruse. They believed no one would ever think to associate the name Kenneth with him. He simply put on a big act when he came here, something his mother knew about all along. The pretty hair, the way he dressed, how he led people to believe he was gay was simply a distraction."

"It worked. He had me and Lailanie fooled. But what about the three men they killed?"

"They worked for him and the mother. The men were the actual thieves, while the Winstons did all the planning. Once they did a couple of jobs, they were killed to keep the identity of mother and son hidden. In fact, we nabbed them just in time. They were ready to move on to Alaska to start stealing Eskimo and Inuit treasures from museums there."

"Why did those other men have blond hair, the same as Kenny? And their surfboard accidents?"

"They were supposed to look like Kenny. Just in case anybody started to figure things out or asked too many questions, Kenny would claim he was being mistaken for the other three."

"The Winstons thought a fake mistaken identity would work?"

"It worked for them in other states. All they were doing here was rehashing what had worked elsewhere, but instead of killing men by pushing them off cliffs or leaving them to die of thirst in the middle of the desert with broken legs, they ran them down with a cabin cruiser. We think one or two of the victims here might've already been dead before they were taken a few miles out to sea and put onto rental surfboards.

Then they ran them down in the water with the boat a couple of times, just to make it look like a surf accident."

"What about the day I found Kenny coming down from the mountains with an empty knapsack? What was that all about?"

"He and his mother had run out of people willing to grave rob for them, so he went up looking for stuff on his own. It seems he's not suited for the task of rooting around in dark places with creepy-crawly things living in them. His mother really had something to say about that, how that was the beginning of the end for them. When she had your mother-in-law drop her off at the airport, she was leaving her son behind to face the consequences alone."

"Some mother. And to think I almost hired her as our nanny. I wonder why she agreed to that when she knew she was leaving the island soon?"

"She's been staying with her son for the last several months since getting here. But when you dropped into her life, it was like a gift. She could keep an eye on the investigation through you, and once the police got too close, she was going to abandon ship, with or without her son."

"And I suppose those days when she went out on her own, it wasn't to mourn her son but to plan their next theft and how to get the stolen stuff off the island. She played me for a fool every step of the way."

"People like that are experts at it, and these two had a lot of experience," Nakatani said. "They had us running in circles for quite a while. Good pickup on Kenny being left-handed. That was the clincher, to focus our murder investigation on him."

"I'm still confused, but right now, I just don't care about the fate of the Winstons. Did you ever get any idea why Kenny was stealing that picture of my parents?" Melanie asked.

"Just to piss you off. To let you know he was able to get into your house and mess with your life. You'd messed with his, so he was going to do the same in return. Oddly enough, that picture of your parents led to his downfall, and his mother's."

"Glad to know my mom and dad are still good for something, even if it's just an old picture of them. When do Maui County residents get their museum pieces back?"

"Spoken like a true mayor!" he said.

"What do you mean?" she asked.

"Only a mayor that cared about the county and the people would ask that question. That's why so many people voted for you."

"Some days, I wish they hadn't," she muttered. "Do I need to call the families of the victims?"

"I've taken care of it. Since those guys also had criminal backgrounds, it might be best for you to leave it alone."

"Maybe so."

"Did you hear me, Mayor? Leave it alone."

"Roger that. Nice nab with the guys from Gonzo's."

"Thanks. Having them out of business will put a dent in the island drug trade. We're still looking for your old friend, Ozzie Simpson."

"Not my friend. No surprise he was selling drugs, though."

"He might be part of the Winston case. Turns out he had a part-time job with the county cleaning buildings, and had a set of keys to every county door in town. We figure he let the crooks into the museum and library after hours."

"But he didn't clean the set of fingerprints that were left behind?" Melanie asked. "Why leave evidence?"

"That's what we can't figure. Once we round him up, we should be able to get the last of the facts of the case. Once he comes out from wherever he's hiding and starts pushing again, we'll get him."

"I don't get it," Melanie complained. "Isn't Maui nice enough? Why do people use drugs if they already live in what most people consider paradise?"

"They don't know how to surf or golf. Ever find a nanny?" he asked.

Melanie pressed a knuckle into the tic in her eye. "My mother-in-law. Unless you're applying for the job? Minimum wage for one-hundred-twenty hours a week, free room and board, and a new car."

"As exciting as your lifestyle is, I think I'll leave the nanny business to someone more capable. I imagine you'll be coming up with a new name for the baby?"

"We already have. It turned out that the birth was never registered, and when we looked at the birth certificate, Nurse Ito had filled out the baby's name in pencil. So, when no one was looking, Josh and I fudged a little and changed it. Don't tell City Hall or there might be trouble. Wait, I'm City Hall. Never mind."

"What's his new name?" Nakatani asked.

"We were a little indecisive."

Nakatani sat back in his chair, waiting.

"We considered Juan Aito Francis Kirby Arthur Strong-Kato, one name representing each of his grandparents."

"For all one kid?"

"Yep. But we can't agree on the order."

He shook his head. "That's five names. Most families have only four grandparents."

"We're not most families, Detective."

Kay Hadashi

More from Kay Hadashi

Maile Spencer Honolulu Tour Guide Mysteries
AWOL at Ala Moana
Baffled at the Beach
Coffee in the Canal
Dead at Diamond Head
Honey of a Hurricane
Keepers of the Kingdom
Malice in the Palace
Peril at the Potluck

The June Kato Intrigue Series
Kimono Suicide
Stalking Silk
Yakuza Lover
Deadly Contact
Orchids and Ice
Broken Protocol

The Island Breeze Series
Island Breeze
Honolulu Hostage
Maui Time
Big Island Business
Adrift
Molokai Madness
Ghost of a Chance

The Melanie Kato Adventure Series
Away
Faith
Risk
Quest
Mission
Secrets
Future
Kahuna
Directive
Nano

The Maui Mystery Series
A Wave of Murder
A Hole in One Murder
A Moonlit Murder
A Spa Full of Murder
A Down to Earth Murder
A Haunted Murder
A Plan for Murder
A Misfortunate Murder
A Quest for Murder
A Game of Murder

The Honolulu Thriller Series
Interisland Flight
Kama'aina Revenge
Tropical Revenge
Waikiki Threat
Rainforest Rescue

www.kayhadashi.com

https://amazon.com/author/www.kayhadashi.com